THE ST

ELLEN FAITH

THE STORY OF US

The Story of Us

Copyright © 2014 Ellen Faith

ISBN-13: 978-1495367298
ISBN-10: 1495367290

Cover Design – Berto Deigns – Rebecca Berto

DEDICATIONS

To my mum. Thank you for always encouraging me, no matter what.

To my fiancé. For putting up with 'all the magic in my head'.

To my amazing cat, you will always be my Mr Beefy. RIP little guy.

Thank you and I love you
X

CHAPTER ONE

Bang
Bang
Bang

My eyes fly open as the mirror crashes unceremoniously to the floor and shatters. Crap. Does the seven years bad luck thing count if you only witness it breaking, or does the ownership rule kick into force?

Bang

There it is again. I throw the covers back and dart to the window. I have no idea what the hell is going on but it's the first Saturday I've had off in months and now I'm up at....glancing at my clock I snarl....7.33am. Craning my neck as best I can at the window and squishing my face up against the cold glass, I realise that there are builders stomping up my drive, attacking my house! I reach for my mobile phone and quickly call Walker.

"I thought you were going to have a lie in this morning Alex? What can I do for you?" His voice purrs at me down the phone. I am so not in the mood this morning.

"Walker, why are there workmen currently taking sledgehammers to our walls?" I grit my teeth in an effort to stay calm.

"Oh, those. Yes, I forgot to tell you didn't I? The extension begins today. Sorry about that."

I can feel my blood pressure beginning to rise; this is so typical of my fiancé. Walker Harrison, CEO of Harrison Finance, formerly one of London's most eligible bachelors and absolute twit - that's the politest way I can phrase what I'm really thinking. What's a vowel between friends?

"What the actual f-"

"Oh, have to go sweetheart, my first appointment has just arrived. Make sure you take care of the workmen won't you, there's a good girl."

Click.

I stare at the phone slack jawed. Not only did he cut me off mid-sentence, but he actually hung up on me. If he thinks he's getting any how's your father later on he is sadly mistaken. The Winnie the Pooh pyjamas will certainly be making an appearance again tonight. That's how he usually knows he's in trouble; the terribly unsexy, fleecy, childlike nightwear comes out.

Accepting the inevitable - that I don't have a hope in hell of getting back to sleep now - I decide I may as well make myself presentable.

After a quick shower, I throw on my ever faithful skinny jeans and a vest top, pulling my hair up into a high ponytail and sigh at my reflection. I've been putting that many hours in at work recently that I have bags under my eyes big enough to see me through a world cruise. I'm hoping that come next week when the appraisals come around, I'll get the promotion that's up for grabs. If I don't then I may have to seriously consider leaving.

I've worked at Mooney Advertising now for six years. six long, hard, painstakingly slow years. It's time that I got the creative directors job - after all, I practically do that job now, I just don't have the fancy title and hefty salary to match.

Walker and I decided that while I was working my way up the career ladder that we would put the wedding on hold, but as soon as I find out one way or the other next week, I'm planning that damn wedding. At least it will be something positive to focus on. I'm sick of my aunts and both sets of grandparents laying on the guilt, saying they probably won't be around much longer to see us get married if we keep going on the way we are. They want to know why after four years of being engaged, six years of being a couple, that we haven't set a date yet. I see the way they look me up and down, like they're trying to find my pointy tail or something, some reason why I haven't been rushed down the aisle yet, but nobody seems to believe that it's because I want to climb the career ladder and Walker's just lazy. Neither of us are ready for a family yet anyway – to be honest the thought terrifies me. Imagine having to look after another person, one that needs and relies on you 100%. What if I dropped it on its head or forgot to feed it? Social Services would have a field day.

Shuffling into my slippers I drag myself down the stairs greeting Mr Beefy, our Calico kitty, with a sloppy kiss, earning myself a nuzzle in return. Sometimes I think Mr Beefy is the only consistent male in my life.

"Come on hot stuff, let's get you fed." Squeezing out the sachet of pungent food turns my stomach, duck and veg in gravy at 8am is not for the faint hearted let me tell you. He seems to like it though.

Flicking the switch on the kettle I survey the contents of our American style fridge. The bright interior light dazes me for a second in my zombie like state. I nudge the tub of butter out of the way and sigh. Unless I want mustard and lettuce in a wrap for breakfast, it looks like I'm right out of luck. This was absolutely the wrong weekend to give our housekeeper some time off, what was I thinking?! Actually, I know what I was thinking. I thought that I'd get some time alone with Walker, a lazy morning in bed, a picnic in the park and maybe a film tonight; but once again we found ourselves putting work first - or Walker was anyway.

Sighing I pour my coffee and inhale the aroma. There really is nothing like the smell of coffee in a morning to bring you around and wake you up. When I was a student I survived on pretty much coffee alone, it was my saviour during the exam periods. I had to be weaned off the stuff eventually ....bad times.

As I pick up my latest copy of Elle from the marble kitchen counter, I smile. The make-up ad that I worked on should be in this issue which is a huge deal for me and should definitely cement my promotion. Maybe I'll even frame the page, I think idly as I flick through the glossy pages of handbags and shoes, after all it's my first tear sheet, or so my best friend keeps telling me – not sure it works the same as styling to be fair but her enthusiasm is heart-warming. As I coo like a proud mother over the magazine, I realise that it really is time I put all my experience and knowledge to use and got the appreciation I deserved. I've worked under John Smith now for six years as a copywriter/assistant/general dogsbody, and have done everything from pick up his dry cleaning to arranging theatre tickets for him to take his mistress to see her 'favourite ever production', Jack and the Beanstalk. Yes, really. I don't know how much longer I could

have bitten my tongue for if I'm completely
honest, so his retirement has come at a good
time. For the both of us.

Bang
Bang
Bang
Bang

Take care of the workmen indeed. I refuse to go
outside, refuse. I'm not playing servant to
builders all day. There's nothing more
intimidating than a group of workmen when
you're the only woman, even if they are working
for me.

Standing on my tiptoes at the kitchen
window, I try to get myself at a better angle to
see what's going on without landing head, or
boobs, first into the sink full of last night's
washing up. All I can see is builders bum, and
although it's a very nice bum, I'm still none the
wiser. You see, if I'm being completely truthful
with you, I don't even know what the extension
is for. I switch off a LOT when Walker starts
bleating on about how small the house is and
how we 'simply must' extend or move. I love this
house so moving is not an option. Okay, so it's
not a mansion, but it's still a four bedroom
detached and we're only two people, why would
we need anything bigger?!

A loud knock on the front door breaks me

from my thoughts. Please don't be a workman, please don't be a workman, I chant to myself quietly, hoping that it's the jolly old postman with a parcel that I'd forgotten I'd ordered from Topshop. I do love it when that happens, and it happens a lot!

I fumble around with the key, slowly open the door and am greeted by a pair of eyes that are the deepest shade of blue I have ever seen, and I recognise them immediately.

Oh boy.

"Lexi?!!"

"Luke!" I shout, and before I can think better of it, I throw myself at him nearly knocking him off balance and the both of us back down the front stairs. Pulling back I blush. "What are you doing here?

"Working!" He laughs with that same crooked smile that he had when we were 17. "What are you doing here?"

"I live here. And I meant England, what are you doing in England?" Hands stuck firmly on hips, I frown at him.

"Oh, yeah, I moved back a while ago now." He rubs the back of his neck and smiles sheepishly. "Wait a minute, you're not with that arsehole Walker are you Lex?" He stares at me open mouthed.

I grimace and hit him and as I notice his

face drop, my stomach somersaults. No man has ever made me feel the way my first love has, but that's normal right? Perfectly natural.

God I hope so or I am screwed.

"Um, well yeah." Snapping back to reality I hold up my left hand by way of explanation and as he quickly recovers himself, I see the mask come up as his face becomes emotionless.

"Well, congratulations then I guess. Anyway, I just wondered if I could use a tap please, need water." He holds up a bucket and I nod silently, stepping back to let him over the threshold. As he brushes past me my knees go weak. He smells amazing……and I really hope he didn't just hear me smell him because that would be so many kinds of awkward.

"Through here." I grunt. I'm annoyed now. Annoyed that I feel so self-conscious in my own home, annoyed that I feel the need to defend my decision to marry the man I love, annoyed that I didn't even know one of my oldest friends and first love was back in the country after 13 years, but most of all, I'm annoyed that I have raging teenage hormones making me want to leap on him right here, right now and have him take me in the hallway. Gah.

"Nice place you got here by the way. You've done good Lex." As he fills the bucket I take the chance to have a good look at him. He hasn't lost his looks at all over the years, if anything he has just got remarkably hotter.

Delicate stubble lines his jaw, just begging to be licked, and he has a golden tan from all the time he must have spent outside in France. His messy short brown hair is just long enough for me to run my fingers through, if I wanted to of course. Which I don't. Obviously.

As the bucket fills I catch the muscle in his arm tense and bulge and judging by his body, he definitely works out. I wonder what his abs are like. I bet they're like steel, lord knows that arse must be. God I really do want to run my hands through his hair.

"Hello?!" I crash back down to earth as I realise he's stood watching me, obviously waiting for an answer. I swallow hard and lick my lips, thankful that he can't mind read, though that smirk on his face tells me he must have some idea of what was running through my head.

"Sorry, what did you say?" I cough trying to hide my embarrassment. Dammit, my daydreaming will get me into so much trouble one day. Smiling and nodding at someone when you haven't been listening properly is never a good idea - trust me. I learnt this the hard way back in school when I just started laughing and agreeing with a friend who'd just told me her dog had died. Little bit awkward.

"It doesn't matter," he laughs. "Best get back to work anyway, we have a deadline to meet and if we finish late we'll be penalised. See you around though yeah?"

Nodding weakly I can't even manage a smile. Well then. Luke Garrett is back. And I need a really strong drink.

CHAPTER TWO

"NO. FREAKING. WAY!" Rosie almost spits her drink across the table when I tell her Luke's back, making me jump in my seat. I don't manage to dodge in time though and have a nice smattering of wine trailing down my arm. Wrinkling my nose in disgust I wipe it with her jacket sleeve that sits next to me. "Is he hot? I bet he's hot."

This, right here, is why I love my best friend.

Rosie, Jason, Luke and I all grew up together, all joined at the hip and our parents were convinced we would marry each other one day. Not in a weird way obviously. Ew.

That plan hit a bump in the road though when Luke's parents decided to up and leave for France. We were 17 and madly in love in that way that only teenagers can be. I often look back and wonder why Luke didn't stay here with me, after all at 17 he was more than capable of looking after himself, and his parents knew that he had plenty of others who would look out for him. But he didn't stay. He left. He left me. I cried for months, and I mean months - I was quite dramatic as a teenager you see. I still remember vividly how I felt back then, I thought my life was over the day I kissed him goodbye at the airport and I'll never forget his parting words to me - 'if it's meant to be, fate will bring us back together one day'.

What a crock.

Taking a long drink of my wine I nod. "You have no idea. God those eyes, I've never seen another pair like it." My hearts beats faster just thinking about him; surely this isn't healthy at nearly 30 years old? "You should see the muscles on him too, he's just so....wow."

"He always did look after himself though, bet his abs are like something from a movie right? Man of steel style." Signaling the waiter Rosie orders us another round of the same. Again, this is why I love her so much, we are absolutely on the same wave length and she never fails to make me laugh. We have been through thick and thin together, I even wore a peach bridesmaid dress for her, that's how good a friend I am. It still makes my heart pang a little with jealousy when I think of how she got to marry her childhood sweetheart and Jason still adores her as much as he did when we were 12. They truly were made for each other.

Kicking me under the table I wince, meeting her big brown eyes. Pursing her red lips at me she narrows her eyes and I know she's just waiting for the waiter to deposit our drinks before she gives me the same lecture she's given me every time I've brought Luke up, or every time I question whether marrying Walker is the right thing for me.

"Enough. I know what you're thinking; I can read you like a book Lex. I love Luke, you know I do, and Jason is going to be over the moon when I tell him his 'brother from another mother' is back on English soil again but, you've moved on. Hell, he's probably moved on too. I mean, for all you know he could have some gorgeous French girl and a baby waiting for him when he gets home. You can't keep thinking about the past doll, all this that you're feeling now is just lust. He's a hottie, you can't deny it, but you need be sensible about this. For now though, be a good girl, drink your wine and get absolutely hammered with me."

I stumble through the door well after 8pm and I know Walker is going to be pissed. He's always telling me how Rosie is a bad influence and that if I want to get on in life I need to find some new, respectable friends, like his lawyer sister in law, Harriet. Now, Harriet is a nice enough person, but she never wants to go shopping, counts calories like her life depends on it, and worst of all, never laughs at my jokes. I mean seriously, I'm hilarious, everybody knows that!

Okay it's possible that I'm a lot drunker than I initially thought.

"Walkerrrrrrr," I sing happily through the house. No response comes which can only mean he's either sulking - this from the man that left me on my day off to go into the office – or he's not even home yet. The most likely answer is that he's not home, I'm sure he wouldn't be able to resist giving me a lecture about how drunk I am if he was home.

Kicking off my too high heels I rub my feet, more women should design shoes, then maybe we wouldn't have to suffer for the cause. Maybe I should invest in some Charlotte Olympia's.

Climbing up the stairs on my hands and knees I groan. Why isn't he home to help me? Luke would come and help me, I think uncharitably. As I reach the top of the stairs I give in. I'm too tired to even crawl through the door directly in front of me so decide to curl up where I am, thankful that we invested in a really good carpet.

Walker will be here soon enough.

Bang
Bang
Bang

Oh. My. God. Not again. I want to die.

I bravely open one eye and realise I'm still laid out at the top of the stairs. Where's Walker? And uh-oh, is that drool on the carpet? Does drool stain?

A familiar cough comes from behind me and as I struggle to sit upright to turn around, I freeze. I don't need to see him, I can sense him.

"Good morning Sleeping Beauty! Let me guess, Rosie?"

Slowly, I turn to face Luke who looks ridiculously happy with himself, but I just don't have the energy to snarl at him. I feel so delicate.

"Yeah. What are you doing here? What time is it?" I squint at my watch but give up eventually. It's just not worth the effort.

"Again, I'm here because I'm working," he laughs. Yes, he's actually laughing at me. "And it's just after half past nine. Come here, let me help you." As he puts his arms around me I flinch and he must feel it too because I hear his breath hitch. Just a simple touch has heightened every single sense in my body. Finally standing on my own two feet, looking remarkably like Bambi, I thank him.

"Have you seen Walker?" I hold onto the wall for support, I really don't trust my legs right now.

"Yeah, he's in the kitchen I think, he let me in to use the bathroom but forgot to mention that you were sprawled out here. Lovers tiff?" He mocks, which only increases my annoyance at Walker. The idiot left me here all night, what a shitty trick.

"Screw you, Luke. Bathrooms that way." I point to the door and skulk off slowly into the bedroom.

My mouth feels like the bottom of a bird cage. An empty bird cage, because the bird that belongs in there is currently hammering away at my head. I am never drinking red wine again. Ever. Probably. Avoiding the mirrors in our bedroom, I manage to make it into the safety of our en suite before I have to face my reflection, and when I do it is not pretty. Think Morticia Addams crossed with Medusa. I can't believe Luke has seen me like this. As I slowly peel out of yesterday's clothes I scoff, who am I kidding, Luke has seen me look a lot worse in my teenage years, but aren't we supposed to grow up one day? Is Walker right? Sighing I detangle my hair from the bobby pins and let it hang down my back; it's just meeting my waist now and is finally at the length I wanted for the wedding. Not that we have set a year never mind a date, but hair can take a long time to grow sometimes, a girl has to plan ahead.

As the hot water washes over me, I'm thankful for the tranquillity and the chance to collect my thoughts. You know how some people say they do all their thinking on the toilet - gross I know - but they do, well, I do my thinking in the shower and the longer I'm in there, the madder I get with Walker. Maybe it's the humiliation of Luke mocking me, knowing that I'd been left there all night, but I am seriously pissed.

Flicking off the switch I dry myself in record time, leaving my hair to dry on its own, and throw on my velour track suit. I know Rosie would kick my arse for it, but you can't deny their comfort.

Stomping down the stairs and into the kitchen, I see Walker sat with a cup of tea and a plate of toast and my stomach growls in a very unladylike way. What I wouldn't give for a full English breakfast right now.

"Good morning darling," I say, my voice dripping with sarcasm as I walk past him. "Oh, no that's fine, I'm not hungry, and yes thank you, I slept very well."

"Oh I see we're acting like an adolescent again today, just lovely. You were like that when I got home; I wasn't waking you up from your drunken stupor." His eyes never leave the morning paper once as he addresses me, making me feel like I'm dealing with my dad. Although at least my dad had the decency to look me in the eye. There were so many mornings that I would roll home at after 3am, usually waking most of the neighbours because Rosie would insist on singing at the top of her lungs, her song of choice usually being Wannabe by the Spice Girls. The cats loved her though. To this day I wonder whether it would have annoyed people as much if she were singing a song by Cilla Black or some other retro diva.

"You left me there to be found by one of

the workmen Walker! And what time did you get home anyway?" I decide against telling him who Luke is, I can't risk him firing him, it's clear he's already been a bit of a dick to him and I don't want to give him any more excuses.

"Oh, erm around five I think, it was certainly too early for you to be laying across our landing like that." His eyes flick to mine then back down again as I frown knowing full well he wasn't home when I got home, I wasn't THAT drunk.

"Five? But-"

"Enough," he snaps, holding his hand up at me. "I'm reading Alexandra, now be a dear and let me read in peace. We'll be eating at my parents this afternoon so do make sure you tidy that hair up." And with that I'm dismissed. Huh. Maybe working our weekends is better for our relationship after all.

Sliding off of my stool I saunter into the living room, reminiscing over when I first met Walker. He hasn't always been this way, the recent stresses of work for the pair of us have put a strain on our relationship to say the least, I almost don't recognise the man I fell in love with anymore. Gone are the spontaneous weekends away, the flowers 'just because', date night every Saturday and even the little things like holding my hand. Gone. I try to work out exactly when everything changed but it's useless, the last time he was truly relaxed was when we went on holiday to Cyprus and that was two years ago. Maybe I should suggest a holiday for us, a week away somewhere, just us two so that we can reconnect again and relax. Hopefully it will bring out the old him and I'll remember why I said yes to becoming his wife in the first place because for the last few months, I've struggled to remember.

An hour later I drag myself from the sofa to start getting ready for his parents. Penelope and Edward Harrison are a force to be reckoned with. Any outsider coming into their fold have their work cut out for them, and with Walker being a mummy's boy, boy did I have a hard time thawing the ice queen. I still don't think she believes I'm good enough for her precious baby, which is another reason that I want this promotion so badly. She did admit defeat when we finally got engaged though, acknowledging that I would officially become part of her family. I think she's still hoping that he will change his mind and reconnect with Carla Smythson - old family friend and barrister don't you know - but he's told me many times before that she was too boring for him. She doesn't have the spontaneous and mischievous streak that I do, which made me feel quite smug.

Grabbing my iPad, I have a quick look at last minute holidays and manage to find a break in Paphos in a fortnight's time. Cyprus again could be great for us. I skim through the hotel details and mentally check off Walker's usual rules and requirements that I have to meet in my head.

> 5* for Walker – check.
> Spa hotel for me – check.
> Good weather – check.
> Amazing food – check.

I remember this particular hotel well from our last trip, the dessert counter was to die for and just the luxury of the bar area practically had me salivating into my cocktail. I remember wondering whether it would cost too much to change hotels halfway through the trip. Permission was denied unfortunately. I grab my credit card and quickly book the holiday, knowing that Walker would never refuse a break in the sun and what use is being your own boss if you can't take a last minute break with your fiancée? I have holidays that I'm always being told to use up anyway so this is working out brilliantly. Clapping my hands I jump off of the bed and prepare for the meal with Satans little helpers – I mean the in laws.

Worst. Meal. Of. My. Life.
There were several times throughout

lunch that I wondered how badly the family would react to me stabbing Penelope in the hand with my fork, but, against my better judgement, I refrained.

"I do wish you'd try harder with my family Alexandra." Walker sighs breaking the silence. He's focusing intently on the dark country road ahead of us, oncoming headlights occasionally shining in and lighting up his perfectly structured face, his jaw tightly clenched. Shifting in my seat I turn and face him. I have tried and tried in all the years we have been together to get him to see it from my point of view, for him to acknowledge that his family clearly don't like me, but it's like he has rose tinted glasses on. Tonight, his mother practically called me a gold digger. Why, I hear you ask? Well, she believes everybody from Yorkshire, like my good self, are nothing more than uneducated Neanderthals who, and I quote, 'grab onto whatever and whoever they can to better themselves.' I did try to explain that some of the greatest people known to man were born in Yorkshire, Judi Dench, Patrick Stewart, the Brontes.....she threw The Ripper and Guy Fawkes at me. A little bit unfair really, I couldn't exactly defend the actions of a serial killer and a lunatic that tries to blow up Parliament.

"Why is it that I get chastised and am given my Sunday name after sitting through what was quite frankly, one of the worst experiences of my life, yet your mother can say what she likes to me and you say nothing?" I glare at him, hoping he can sense it given that it's so dark.

"My mother has been nothing but pleasant to you, Alex." He turns and looks pointedly at me at the use of my shortened name. "I just don't understand why you can't see that? She sees how happy you make me and loves you for that, she said that she has never seen me look as alive as I have done in the last couple of years and the trip to Cyprus was a lovely gesture tonight."

Grumbling I turn and sit properly in my seat, staring out of the window into the abyss, this is going to be a long drive home.

CHAPTER THREE

Thank God today is over.

I'm normally reasonably chirpy on a Monday. I'm always polite, always smiling, head down getting myself set up for the week, but today.....today was a different kind of Monday. I feel my face flush all over again when I think of how the day started but remind myself that John won't be there much longer.

By 8.00am I was sat at my desk working away, blissfully unaware that one of the worst meetings of my career was looming.

The Monday morning meetings at Mooney have always been something that I enjoyed attending. It's where we all put our ideas forward for the latest jobs that we have, the creatives always butt heads over something but compromises are always reached and I pride myself on usually being able to assist. To offer an outside perspective. This morning, John had come overly prepared for his presentation, which was bizarre in itself, but then when he mentioned PowerPoint, I began to worry. Did John even know how to do a PowerPoint presentation? Was he going to humiliate our entire team by making a royal tit of himself?

The answer was no. No, he wasn't going to make a tit of himself or the team. He was

going to make a tit of me by presenting a series
of photographs from various Christmas parties
where I was not only quite clearly shit-faced, but
I was throwing up in plantpots, losing my dress
or trying to climb to the top of the Christmas tree
to see whether I could be a real life fairy – not
my finest moments I must say. To make matters
worse, he didn't even try to apologise or make
up a story about how it was an accident. Oh no,
he actually wanted to use these pictures in a new
campaign that we had for drink awareness and
what could happen if you're spiked.

What a dick-weasel.

Naturally the whole point of the
'brainstorm presentation' was to make me lose
all credibility with the various heads of
departments and had nothing to do with him
wanting what was best for this campaign. There
were actual tears of laughter streaming down
their faces as mine continued to get redder and
redder, the humiliation was unbearable and I
could feel my own tears threatening. Of course
when I stood up to try put a stop to the looping
stream of photographs I had to go and knock
over a steaming cup of tea into the head of the
accounts department's lap closely followed by a
jug of milk across his paperwork.

I spent the rest of the morning hiding in
my office, only daring to show my face at
lunchtime because I was starving and forgot to
grab my salad from the fridge at home. This is

what happens when you have morning sex, your brain goes to shit. Having flashbacks didn't help me much either. I was that distracted that I didn't notice that the paving stone outside the sandwich shop had newly formed cracks in it and got my heel, my very expensive heel, caught in one of them. Cursing, when I bent down to untrap myself I felt a man walk straight into the back of me, his crotch meeting with my stuck in the air arse. I felt sick when I actually FELT him against me. Sicker when I stood up and realised it was John who had stuck his man bulge into me. He of course thought it was hilarious and said he'd always imagined having me doggy style.

I never did get that sandwich. A bar of chocolate and a cup of tea was as good as it got.

My day was then topped of nicely when I received a text from Walker. He was terribly sorry that he'd forgotten to tell me about Harriet's surprise birthday party that his parents were hosting. Tonight. Fuck.

But it's okay, because now I'm home. Walking through the hall I can smell the casserole that our housekeeper said she'd make for tea, it smells like all kinds of wonderful and I know I've got an unopened bottle of rosé in the fridge just begging to be poured. Hello silver lining.

I just need to work out how I'm going to eat, shower and get ready for this party all in the space of two hours.

"Ah, Alex my dear how was your day?" Mrs Atkinson greets me with a warm smile and a spoon to try the casserole. I do love her.

I pull up a chair at the breakfast bar and hand her the spoon back. "That is delicious, I'm so hungry. I forgot my salad this morning and the rest of the day....well to be polite I would say that it was hellish. I can't wait for the week to be over and were not even halfway through yet." I groan as I rest my head on the cool marble surface.

"Oh no, well, you go get a quick shower and I'll get this served up. Walker told me I had to make sure I got a move on with the food tonight because he didn't want to be late to his parents?"

"Well that's a bit rude. If we're late, we're late, he shouldn't tell people about things so last minute. It's a surprise party for Harriet and he only told me at four o'clock this afternoon!"

Nodding understandingly she taps my hand lightly. "Well you just show him how amazing you can look with only a few hours notice my love, show them all."

I smile gratefully. Mrs Atkinson has been with Walker for 12 years so knows everything about him, including how awful his family are and I know that I can always confide in her. She reminds me of Mrs Claus with her white hair, rosy cheeks and ever present red pinny.

Amazing hugger too. So cuddly.

Three quarters of an hour later I'm sat back with Mrs Atkinson devouring an enormous bowl of her infamous chicken casserole, my face and hair made up in record time when Walker steams through the door.

"What are you doing?!" He asks incredulously. "Have you even showered yet?"

I turn around and glare at him. "Yes I have thank you very much and now I'm eating." I lift my fork and gesture it rudely at him. "I have to eat Walker, I had no lunch and have had a really, really shitty day so don't start, okay?" I don't wait for him to answer; I turn back around and give my food my full attention as Mrs Atkinson scampers away sensing an impending argument. Thankfully she was wrong and Walker skulks off upstairs.

Finishing off my meal I load the dish into the dishwasher and glance out of the window into the darkness. I still don't know why we're bothering with an extension, it seems so pointless. All the disruption and upheaval and for what, a sun room and an extra bedroom. I wonder what I'd be doing now if I wasn't on this side of the project. What if I was sat at home with Luke after his long day working for another painful rich guy who makes unreasonable demands.

"Penny for them?"

Jumping, I turn and see Walker stood

behind me, looking heavenly in one of his many expensive suits. As he comes closer I smell my favourite aftershave on him. He looks ridiculously handsome, but then again I suppose I am biased, and I have always, always been weak when it comes to a man in a suit. Walker just seems to ooze sex appeal though. The way he walks, the way he smiles, but the way he always makes it clear to other women that fawn over him at parties that he's there with me just makes me want to pinch myself a little bit. He bats them away and slips his arm around me with a loving smile every time, and every time I see the way they look at me with pure contempt.

"Just thinking about the extension. What time is it?" The last thing I need is a lecture.

"We need to set off in about ten minutes, you have plenty of time." He gently pushes a curl behind my ear and kisses me on my cheek. "I'm sorry about earlier, I've had an awful day and then when I remembered this stupid surprise party I reached my breaking point." He kisses my nose and I relax against his chest, careful not to get my make up on him.

"It's okay," I whisper. "I had an awful day too, all I wanted to do was come home to you and maybe pick up where we left off this morning."

"Mmmmmm, that would have been amazing. What's happened today?" He lets me go, leaning back against the work surface and I can tell I have his full attention. This is the Walker I know and love, the one who will always make time for anyone no matter what their problem. We just got lost along the way somewhere but thankfully our Cyprus trip is next week. I must remember to book into the salon to be waxed within an inch of my life.

"John. He made a fool of me in a meeting in front of all the department heads, he showed humiliating photographs of me from Christmas parties and I've been a laughing stock all day. I forgot my lunch too so had to go out to get a sandwich but got my heel stuck in the pavement and John 'accidentally' walked into my arse, crotch first conveniently." I shake my head. I still feel sick when I think about that.

I see Walkers jaw tense, his fists clenched tightly by his side. "I'll kill him. Who does he think he is treating you like that, and he brings his crotch anywhere near you again and I will personally see to it that he can never use it again."

Shit. Glad I didn't tell him what he said about doing me doggy style.

"Well, at least he retires at the end of the month. Not long now." I shrug, noticing that I should probably be getting dressed. Oh well, that will just have to be another thing to add to the list of reasons Walker's mother hates me, ruining her favourite daughter in laws party.

"That's true I suppose. And everyone will

see how amazing you are in your new role when you get your promotion." He gives me a warm smile making his dark brown eyes crinkle and pushes away from the worksurface. "I'd better let you get ready. Don't be long will you darling?"

Jekyll and Hyde that fiancé of mine.

The Harrison house looks like it always does as we pull into the magnificent gravel driveway. Elegant, quiet and tranquil. The soft lighting glows from the downstairs windows of the Tudor style mansion, it always looks so warm and inviting, such a shame about the owners.

"Right, we'd best get inside before we end up walking in with the birthday girl." He gives my leg an affectionate rub and nods towards the door. "You look incredible by the way; I can't wait to get you home."

My insides leap in excitement. I wonder how soon we could leave without being rude. Maybe I could feign sickness? That could work.

I climb out of the car, careful not to flash next week's washing, as Walker takes my hand, squeezing it softly. I'm glad I decided to give my favourite navy dress one more outing before it gets too cold. I've always loved the way it hugs every curve but not in a provocative way, more in an, I'm confident in my body kind of way. Paired with a fitted black kick flare jacket, I feel pretty good. Tonight will be fine I'm sure. I'll sip champagne, make polite small talk, then Walker and I will go home and have more amazing sex and the stress of the day will melt away. What a plan.

"Walker, sweetheart, you look as dashing as ever!" His mother gives him a warm embrace at the door, her bony fingers clutching him tightly. "Alexandra." She addresses me coldly, her eyes skimming down me disapprovingly.

Just smile, just smile, just smile. I continue to chant the words in my head as we make our way through to the formal living room where everyone has gathered. I've only ever been in here once before and that was at the engagement party that his parents threw for us, begrudgingly I add.

The soft gold drapes are pulled back so that the stunning view below us can really be appreciated. That's the one thing I love about this house, it's so high up on a hillside that you really feel like you're on top of the world. I could gaze out of the windows in here for hours watching the city lights below or the stars above.

"They're here, they're here. Okay everyone, be very quiet," a voice calls from the other side of the room as everyone excitedly watches the door. I can faintly hear Harriet's soft voice getting closer and wonder what she'll make of all the fuss.

"Seriously Richard, your parents didn't

have to have us over and go to the trouble of cooking, your mother does so much for me anyway," I hear her say. Hmmm, his mother never does anything for me. Then again, I don't have a law degree.

"I know Retty but they wanted to, you know they adore you." Richard, Walkers eldest brother, has always cooed over Harriet, to be fair they are a cute couple but they do make me want to heave a bit. He's 43 and she's 40 today. It's sickening.

It makes me wonder where their other brother is though; I haven't seen him stumbling about tonight in his usual drunk state. Maybe his much older woman is keeping him occupied a lot more these days.

"SURPRISE!" The room erupts as Harriet squeals in delight. She may be 40 but she doesn't look a day over 25, life has dealt her a pretty great hand of cards. Her long chestnut hair is half pinned back showing off an impressive pair of emerald earrings, perfectly matching her eyes that are wrinkle free and unbotoxed, her teeth are so white that I'm more than a little jealous. But she is always so genuinely polite to me that I just can't not like her. She is so lovely and always tries to make conversation that I find myself thinking that maybe I should try and learn about things that she likes, just so that she doesn't feel bad for us having nothing in common.

"Alex!" She catches my eye across the

room and comes over to give me a hug. "You look lovely, thank you so much for being a part of this, isn't it so kind of the Harrison's to do this for me?!"

I'm about to remind her that she is in fact also a Harrison and that's the reason why they've made so much effort but there's no point. I'm just being grumpy because I recognise her dress from the pages of Vogue and know for a fact it's a sell-out everywhere. Sigh. Oh how the other half live.

"It really is," I agree with her. Which it is. They have opened their home to the whole family but it's not like anyone is likely to get so drunk that they throw up in Penelope's award winning garden or get over excited dancing to their favourite song and throw their red wine on the carpet. Not that I have ever done these things......

"I can't believe I'm 40! How depressing." She sighs as she takes a sip of her champagne and leans against one of the sofas. "Aren't you 30 soon?"

"I am." I nod gravely.

"Oh I remember my 30th. Richard hired a boat and we sailed around the coast in the south of France. We ate in St Tropez on my birthday night and he'd booked us into a gorgeous hotel, I forget the name now but it was fantastic. Have you any plans for yours?"

"No, we'll probably just go for a meal I

imagine."

"Ah I bet Walker has something up his sleeve, Richard says he gets so tired of hearing about how amazing you are every day at work and how lucky he is to have found someone as patient as you. Have you managed to set a date yet for the big day?"

"No not yet." I smile tightly.

"Well, you have plenty of time," she smiles back knowingly. "Everyone is always in such a rush for people to get married the second they announce their engagement, it's like they forget that it's about what the couple want. The pressure for me to have children was immense at first too, but now, well I think both sets of parents have resigned themselves to not having grandchildren from us."

"Thank you, it's nice to know someone understands."

"Oh I do Alex, I understand more than you think." She gives me a sly wink and slips away to mingle as Walker rejoins me with some older men that I've never met.

After the introductions, the small talk between the men drifts over my head. I have no idea what the words they are throwing around mean but I caught FTSE index earlier so it's obviously shop talk.

"So Alexandra, Walker tells me that you love the countryside?" George, an elderly balding man addresses me. Lies, all lies, I hate the countryside, although I do love the idea of a log cabin and an open fire, so romantic.

"Certainly do George," I throw a sideways glance at Walker who practically sags in relief.

"How do you fancy coming to the country house I own and doing a spot of shooting with Walker and as many friends as you like?"

"Shooting?"

"Yes, clay pigeon shooting. We do it all the time, brilliant fun."

"Oh, erm, thank you, but I'm afraid I don't agree with hunting or shooting animals for fun. I'm sure it's a lovely home you have though," I try in vain to cushion the fact I've just rejected his invite when I know he's a very important part of Walkers firm.

The four men stand and stare at me as the colour drains from Walkers face.

"Oh, yes, oh that's very funny," George laughs heartily as my smile is frozen to my face. "Oh I do love a woman with a sense of humour."

Walker stares at me and I frown. I don't know what's upset him so much, he knows I would never want to go shooting unless it was a water pistol.

Penelope and two other older women join the circle as George continues to laugh. "Spirited young lady this one, you must be thrilled to have her as a future daughter in law."

I manage a high pitched tense laugh as she looks from George to Walker and finally to me, her icy blue eyes cutting straight through me.

"Thrilled." She states. "What delightful anecdotes has she been telling you?" Her smiles is terrifying. I wonder if I could pretend to faint, I mean the floor isn't that far away, surely I wouldn't hurt myself too much.

"Oh we just invited her clay pigeon shooting but she doesn't agree with shooting or hunting animals!" He chortles again as his wine sloshes around in his glass.

Why does everyone look so uneasy?

"Have you ever actually been clay pigeon shooting my dear?" Something about the way she's looking at me makes me feel like I'm the prey of some wild animal. She's smiling, but I imagine the Big Bad Wolf gave Red Riding Hood the same smile before he swallowed her whole.

"N-no, I haven't. I don't think it's very nice." I pull my shoulders back in an attempt to hold my own and not back down.

"Of course you haven't," she shakes her head in disdain. "Aside from the likeliness of you managing to shoot a bird being slim to none in any event, I don't think you have to worry about the safety of the clay discs that are fired up into the air for you to shoot at during the activity that George is referring to. So I'm either to assume that you are mocking our dear friend here and trying to worm out of socialising with him, or that you are truly that simple. Which would you prefer me to assume Alexandra?"

Ah fudge.

Walker is livid by the time we arrive home. We didn't stay long after the clay pigeon incident. George was very kind about the whole thing and said Penelope was being a nasty old hag, didn't really placate Walker but he made me feel better.

"I cannot believe you would humiliate me like that Alex. I thought we were getting on well recently but this, this was unacceptable." His voice booms from every wall in the kitchen making me jump.

"I didn't mean to. I didn't know." I feel my face flame again, my voice shaking. Today has really not been my day, I just want to cry but I know Walker would think I'd done it to make him feel sorry for me.

"You are a bright, intelligent young lady, how could you not know?!" He sounds flabbergasted as he slams his hand against the dining table.

"I'm mortified Walker, and your mother didn't help matters! George would have laughed it way happily but she made me feel like an idiot and you stood by and let her."

"How am I supposed to defend you when you actually act like an idiot!"

I close my eyes and start counting before I explode.

"You call me an idiot again and it will be the last thing you call me, you got it? And she hates me Walker, that is why she did it. End of. You think I enjoyed being publicly humiliated, again? Today has been an epic bag of shite and all I wanted was for you to defend me, or at least not accuse me of humiliating you on purpose. Who the hell do you think you are speaking to me like this? You're as bad as the rest of them."

We both sit in a frosty silence for what's left of the evening, Walker nursing a glass of whiskey and me with a glass of wine. As I sit watching him, I start playing with my engagement ring and begin to wonder whether we really are worth fighting for anymore.

CHAPTER FOUR

After what has possibly been the slowest week of my entire life, Friday, and appraisal day, has finally arrived. I'm nervous, I'm fidgeting and my palms are sweaty but I look hot as hell even if I say so myself. Even Walker took a second look at me this morning as I was getting ready, his eyes following my every move and bend. Okay maybe I threw in some extra bends on purpose just to get him to give me some attention, because seriously, he has barely looked the side I'm on since Monday night and a girl has needs.

"Okay Alex, you're up." My lovely boss, Henry, pops his head out of his office and calls my name. This is it, finally the most important appraisal of my career to date. I stand up and brush myself down, straightening the hem of my new black dress and swapping my flats for my heeled pumps quickly before anybody notices. Isn't it weird how heels just make you feel more confident?

Taking a seat inside his small, cosy office, I look into Henry's kind eyes. His large black rimmed spectacles keep slipping down his nose making him that bit less intimidating, not that he could be intimidating if he tried. Henry Mooney is without a doubt the best boss I've ever had, it's just a shame I don't work directly for him and work for John instead, although that's hopefully all about to change. The nerves and excitement are twisting in my stomach. I haven't been able to eat all morning because of them. As soon as I leave this office, I'm going straight to the small deli around the corner for as many carbohydrates as I can possibly stomach. And chocolate. Obviously.

"Okay, I just want to start out by saying how much we value you here, you're a very important cog in the Mooney system and we would be lost without you."

"Thank you Henry!" I feel myself begin to blush, he's just become my favourite person ever. So sweet.

"But I feel I should address the elephant in the room first and foremost." Shifting slightly in his seat he looks away from me and begins to look uncomfortable. "You haven't got the promotion I'm afraid."

Bastard!

"Please don't be disheartened though Alex," he rambles on, "this just isn't your time. After a long chat with John we decided maybe you're not ready - yet." He looks at me sadly, I can tell he feels bad but I'm finding it hard to sympathise with him right now because I've just been screwed over.

"Who?" I snap, my temper starting to fray. I don't know whether to cry or laugh hysterically.

"I'm sorry?"

"Who got the promotion instead of me?" I demand, sounding a little harsher than I mean to, poor man is probably terrified of my crazy eyes right now.

"Susan."

"SUSAN?!" I scream. He at least has the decency to look contrite, he knows as well as I do that Susan is way under qualified for the job, it just doesn't make sense. John has thrown a spanner in the works the vindictive little slimeball, one last stab at my self-respect before he waltzes off into the sunset.

"I really am very sorry Alex. But I would like you to take on a lot more responsibility within the company and that will of course come with a pay increase."

I stand up to leave, my heart has dropped into my stomach and all I know is that I need to be out of this room.

"Okay, well, you have a think about it," he blusters on, shuffling his paperwork.

"I quit." The words come out before I have chance to catch them, a voice that sounds nothing like mine has taken over. It sounds distant. Empty. Dead.

"I'm sorry? Alex please be reasonable, I know you're disappointed but don't do anything rash!"

I shake my head and focus in on Henry,

considering his offer and thinking about whether I really want to take back what I said. I don't.

"I'm sorry Henry, consider this my one months notice. I quit." Calmly I walk out of his office and across to my desk where John is stood, smiling at me with that lecherous grin he has, and I begin to shake, tears threatening. I don't know whether they're tears of anger or sadness, but I know I need to get out of this place, and fast. Grabbing my handbag, I ignore John's smugness and go to leave. Just like that I decide on the spot that I won't be going back. Ever. All personal items can go in the bin, at least I'll still have my dignity intact. And I would have left quite calmly had it not been for that one comment. He just couldn't help himself could he?

"Boy I will miss that fine ass, shame she wasn't a better assistant if you know what I mean?" He laughs wiggling his eyebrows.

I close my eyes, count to ten, take a deep breath…..and punch him. Yes, I, Alexandra Jones, I turn on my heel, walk straight up to him, and punch him full on in the face. I won't lie, it felt amazing. A stunned silence fills the office floor and I catch Henry's jaw drop as he stands in the corner helpless. Sticking my chin in the air, I throw my handbag back over my shoulder and as gracefully as you can when your legs are trembling, walk out of the office.

Pulling up outside the house, I'm thankful to see that the building site that is my home is quiet. They must be out for lunch, but Walkers car's in the drive. I'm so thankful that he's home that I don't even question why, I just want to forget about Monday and our stupid argument and for him to hold me and to tell me I've done the right thing leaving Mooney Advertising, a place he had never liked me working anyway.

Walking inside I put my keys and bag on the table in the hallway and hear the shower running upstairs. Carrying my miserable self up to the bedroom I wonder what I'll do with my life now, hell what will I do for a reference?! I punched a man! For the first time I'm thankful for Walker's connections and hope I can abuse my fiancée privileges.

"Walker?" I shout throwing my jacket on the bed. "Hellooooo?"

"Oh Walker, oh baby!"

Giggle.

"Oh Lauren!"

Grunt.

I didn't know until that moment that it was possible to feel sick in your chest, but I do. My feet are frozen to the spot outside the bathroom door. I begin to shake as I reach for the handle and swallow hard, do I really want to see what's on the other side of this door? My heart is racing but I know there's no turning back. Taking a steadying breath, I slowly open the door.

Through the steam I see them. Lauren, Walker's 25 year old secretary, is naked inside my shower with her legs wrapped around Walker who is holding her up against the wall with his hips and grinding into her faster and faster. Her eyes meet mine with horror as I back out of the room and shut the door behind me. My head is spinning and I can feel the bile begin to rise in my throat as my pulse quickens, I need to get out of this house. As I go to leave the room I'm stopped in my tracks by a picture of us both on our chest of drawers. It was just after he proposed and we looked so happy, so in love. What went wrong? I choke back a sob and pull open the bedroom door, running for the stairs as I hear him shout my name.

As I pick up my handbag I hear him call me again. I turn around and see him stood at the top of the stairs in all his glory wearing nothing but a towel, his floppy blond hair soaking wet and dripping down his perfectly sculpted body that Lauren has been clawing at no doubt. The thought is nauseating and painful. No wonder he hasn't been interested in me lately when he has a 25 year old falling at his feet.

"Alex wait! I can explain!" He shouts again, very slowly making his way down the stairs, gripping his towel tightly.

Now you see, I have a very big problem with these three words, 'I can explain'. I've always wondered how, when you see or hear of a man getting caught cheating, how can you possibly explain yourself out of being naked, in a shower, with a naked woman, screwing her brains out? You just can't! Nobody can trip and fall out of their clothes, into a shower and into another person now can they?

"Leave it Walker." My voice is barely audible. "Just don't. Please." I hold my hand up so he knows not to come any closer. "Well done, you've ruined everything we had. I hope you're happy with yourself. Quite a show you've put on for the last four years, delaying the wedding when you never wanted me anyway did you?" I look up at him with bleary eyes, clapping my hands slowly as he stares at me like a deer caught in the headlights.

"Alex, baby, please. I'm sorry, this is nothing!" He gestures behind him in the direction of our bedroom. Our bedroom. Seems a little bit silly calling it that now given the circumstances. "I love you. You're my Alex. Don't leave me, please."

"You're only sorry because you got caught. If I hadn't come home today, this lie would have gone on for who knows how long wouldn't it? If you weren't happy why didn't you just say instead of us both wasting our lives on what I thought was a fairly happy

THE STORY OF US

relationship. Yeah, we've had our fights, our problems, but I loved you Walker." Swallowing hard I shake my head. "Don't call me." I turn and leave him stood there half naked and dripping on the carpet, pain lancing through my chest.

As I shut the door behind me, my day is topped off nicely when I come face to face with Luke. Just what I need. Thank you universe.

"Lexi? Are you okay?" His eyes are so full of concern that I break down in front of him, sobbing like a small child as he takes me in his arms and pulls me close.

"Walker.......secretary......shower......no promotion!" I just about manage to wail at him.

"Come on, get into the car I won't be a minute." Handing me his keys I walk down the path, head down so that all the eyes that are currently on me don't get a proper view of just how crappy I look. The last thing I need is them all giving Walker a slap on the back because of the mess his fiancée….ex fiancée looks.

I clamber into Luke's Dodge Truck and see him talking to the other workmen, pointing and nodding in various directions. I feel awful that he's missing out on work because of me.

When he finally climbs in beside me, he gives me a soft smile and starts the engine.

"I'll be okay Luke, what about your job?" As the heaving of my chest subsides I begin to feel worn out and it's not even one o'clock yet.

"Work comes and goes, plus I'm not sure I still want to work for him after this. Just relax, and breathe okay?" He strokes my cheek gently as I bite my lip. It's so good to have Luke back; it feels like only yesterday that we were planning our future, the places we'd see, the names we'd call our children. 13 years hasn't changed either one of us when we're together, we fall back into old habits, but we all know that following our hearts is a lot easier said than done, especially when one heart is currently broken.

We continue the journey in a comfortable silence thankfully, and as we pull up outside a small coffee shop, I'm amazed that I've never been here before and how on Earth Luke knew about it of all people. It has a gorgeous baby pink and brown overhang with Alice's Coffee House in swirled lettering covering three small outside seating areas. I really hope he isn't an outdoors freak these days because all I want is to sit in a dark corner and wallow.

He lets me out and thankfully guides me inside, his hand resting casually on the small of my back sending a tingle all the way up my spine. Coming here with him probably wasn't one of the smartest moves I've made today but then again, is it really the worst. I'm jobless, homeless and fiancé-less. Oh, and all this just a few weeks before I hit 30. Ugh.

"You still take your coffee black with one sugar?" As we find a table in the corner he moves towards the counter, catching me completely off guard by remembering how I take my drink. I really couldn't tell you how he took his which makes me feel quite bad.

"Erm, could I have a hot chocolate instead please? Soy milk, extra whip."

"We're not in Starbucks Lexi, but yes, I'll get you a hot chocolate." As he walks off I stare at his perfect bum again, it's an absolute joy to behold, it really is, but it still doesn't cheer me up.

I check my phone and see five missed calls from Walker, two missed calls from Henry and a text from Rosie telling me not to forget that it's my turn to sort the food for this month's girl's night in. There's no way that will be happening at my house this month, not that I actually have a house anymore, but I'm really not in the mood for a classic Kate Hudson romcom where she gets her happy ever after ending while I'm sobbing into my tub of Ben & Jerrys.

"Here, I flirted with the cashier to get you extra whip AND sprinkles. Got you a chocolate cupcake too, you look like you need it."

Smiling weakly I take a spoon to the cream and sigh, there's nothing like sugary goodness to fill your veins with hope. I take a bite out of the cupcake and moan; this is possibly the best cupcake I have ever tasted. Seriously, ever.

He waits patiently for me to make the first move but while I have a cupcake and a hot chocolate, I'll happily sit here in silence.

"So, want to tell me about it?"

"Not really." I push my cupcake away and sit back in the dark brown chair that encircles me. I wonder if I could live here? I would happily sleep in this chair. Meeting Luke's eyes I sigh. "I was a dead cert for a promotion at work, advertising by the way. I've worked my butt off for that job and can't remember the last time I got a full eight hours sleep - last Saturday doesn't count because I was rudely awoken by some inconsiderate workmen." He lets out a small chuckle as I continue. "My boss told me this morning that my supervisor has said he doesn't feel I'm ready for it. I deserved that damn job just for putting up with his shite, sorting out his mistakes and booking his hotel rooms for his lunchtime booty calls and he does this to me!" I see people turn and look at me as my voice gets louder, an old lady in the corner tuts at me before going back to her crossword. I guess not everybody wants to hear my tale of woe then. "I walked out this afternoon and got home early; unfortunately for Walker I caught him hammering his secretary in the shower. My shower. That just about brings you up to speed in a nutshell." I leave out the punching part, no need to scare him off so soon.

"Wow. So what happened to publishing? You were always such a bookworm, sounded like the perfect job." It's sweet how he doesn't dwell on the Walker situation.

"Yeah, it just never happened. Wasn't meant to be I guess. The dream was to be an author someday but I don't know, maybe that's a pipe dream. So how about you? What brings you back England?"

"It was just time I think." He takes a careful sip of his drink and smiles. "I wanted to come home, I missed a lot of things here."

I hide my face in my own mug so that he won't see the stupid grin that's starting to spread across my face.

"Why London though? Why not back home home?"

"Well, everyone's moved down here from Leeds now haven't they? You, Jason, Rosie. And, it's just closer."

"Closer?" I frown.

"Yeah." He shuffles in his seat. "Closer to mum, in France."

"Oh how are they both? I miss your dad's old tales and your mum's baking. Mine couldn't bake for the life in her. Remember that Christmas she did a homemade jam roly poly and tried to steam it but set the kitchen on fire, or the time she made me a chocolate birthday cake and forgot the flour." I do love my little mum, she is an amazing cook and even now I wonder whether I could get away with asking her to send me some care packages down, but baking.....disaster.

His expression darkens and I can't work out what I've said but I suddenly feel really uncomfortable, even this amazing hot chocolate isn't compensating.

"My dad died when I was 21, accident on the job. It's just been me and mum ever since. Last year she decided to open a little chocolate shop in Paris though and met an American guy, so when I knew she was okay and she was really happy, I took the plunge and came back here."

My heart constricts as I think of him losing his dad, they were so close that Luke even wanted to dress like him in his younger years. When I look at Luke now I can still see his dad in him, he has his eyes, such a rare colour that they're the first thing you notice on him, then his smile and the little dimples in his cheeks.

"I'm so sorry Luke, I-I don't know what to say. I wish I'd have known, I would have come to his funeral, he was a good man, he'd have been very proud of you, you know? Is that why you went into the building trade?"

He nods slowly and I take his hand. I just want to pull him close but I know that he doesn't need my comfort anymore, he's done his grieving, I think it's more me that needs the comfort as I think of the memories that I have of his dad and I feel the tears start to fall.

"Hey, hey, it's okay, oh God don't cry. Come here." And as he wraps me in a warm hug I break down and everything from the day comes out, all the hurt, the embarrassment, everything. He doesn't move as he waits for my tears to subside. He strokes my hair gently and I realise that I don't want to lose him again, whatever happens, I never want him to not be a part of my life. I just hope he feels the same way this time.

"Thank you," I sniffle in a very unladylike manner, wiping my nose with the sleeve of my jacket like a small child. "I wish I could have been there for you though."

"Don't worry, you didn't know and I never got in touch so...." He sighs as he checks his phone, types something then puts it away.

"So, how did you hear about this place?" It really is a cute little shop, the smell of fresh coffee and the sweetness of the cakes is heavenly and it's much more intimate than the chains of coffee houses. I think I'll bring Rosie back here.

"Hey Lukey! You never said you were popping by." A tall, leggy blonde with far too perfect skin bends down and plants a sloppy wet kiss on his cheek as I stiffen.

"Oh, Alice, hi. I wasn't expecting to be here. This is Lexi, an old erm, friend." His stuttering would amuse me if it weren't for the fact that I was horrified by what I was witnessing.

"Oh hi! Nice to meet you, I hope my staff have been treating you well?" She smiles a smile that doesn't quite meet her eyes, the warning in them coming across loud and clear.

Maybe I won't be bringing Rosie here.

"It's been just lovely, thank you. If you'll excuse me though, I really do have to go now, I have a lot of stuff to sort with Walker. Lovely to meet you Alice. Luke, I'll see you around sometime." Before he has chance to object I bolt from my seat and leave him sat with his precious Alice, my heart breaking a little as I leave my half eaten cupcake on the table. Rosie did warn me he could have moved on, but did it have to be with someone so successful and good looking. Dammit. I feel like such a fool, and now I've rushed out on my only ride home.

CHAPTER FIVE

Thank God Rosie came for me when she did, the heavens opened about ten minutes after I left the comfort of the coffee shop leaving me like a half drowned rat. The last thing I wanted was for Luke and Alice to come out and see me like that. Can you imagine, here's what you could have won Luke, aren't you glad you didn't?! The shame.

Rosie's house is so full of warmth. Memories cover the walls of the living room, pictures of us on nights out, pictures of their families, of growing up as a foursome, it really is a comforting sight knowing that sometimes the happy ending does happen.

I flop down like a ragdoll on to her pale fawn sofa, knowing she's probably going to go bonkers that I haven't waited for a towel to sit on. If the dye runs from my new dress I'm going to owe her a new sofa. Meh. I'll cross that bridge when I come to it, right now I just want to relax.

"Here, have this and tell me everything." Handing me a glass of wine she eyes the sofa where I'm sat but bites her lip. What a doll.

"Well, John screwed me over for the promotion, he and Henry don't feel I'm ready, so I quit, I'm officially unemployed. Then I went home and found Walker in our shower screwing

Lauren, you know, the 25 year old bimbo whose rack I wish I had? Then as I left the house Luke was there. I think I may have done something to seriously piss the universe off recently." I pause for breath and a quick drink. "He took me out for a hot chocolate where I ended up meeting his very stunning girlfriend and dear God Rosie, I didn't realise how much I missed him until then."

We sit in silence for a few minutes as Rosie processes everything.

"Oh, and I punched John and my hand hurts." I take a large slug of wine and shudder as it burns my throat. Now I know why I hate dry white wine.

"He has grown into quite a studmuffin hasn't he? He came over last night and went for a drink with Jason, my jaw hit the deck when I opened the door to him. He hasn't changed though has he, still has that cheeky grin and gives the best hugs." She starts to lift her glass to her mouth when she suddenly stops and frowns. "Hey, hold up, you PUNCHED John?! Wow, violent much."

"Well he deserved it," I mumble petulantly. "And yes, Luke does still give the best hugs. Shame he has Alice now with her long legs and evil eyes." I say her name childishly. It's not her fault really; if I had him I'd make sure every woman on the planet knew he was mine too. Hell, I'd make him have OWNED tattooed on to his forehead if I thought it would help. I just wish he'd have been straight with me from the outset and told me about her. I don't understand why he would keep it from me? If I'm being truly honest with myself, it's not that I really thought we could just fall into each other's arms like the last 13 years had never happened, but I think I got carried away at the thought of having him back in my life as my male sidekick and selfishly wanted him all to myself. I wanted it to be like the old days, the days where the only real worries I had were what shade of mascara to wear for a night out, or which pair of shoes made me look slimmer. The life of a teenager. The life I had pre Walker before he ripped my heart out of my chest and let Lauren stab her stiletto through it.

Nice to see my flair for the dramatic hasn't really changed since my teenage years.

"But seriously, Lukey?! Ugh. I hate her already!"

"Good. Thank you. If he brings her round here will you give her the cheap wine that takes the lining off of your throat?"

"Never! That's only for Jason's sister, I will however put laxative in her coffee because that's how much I love you." She winks making me laugh, she always has had a sinister streak and I know for a fact she would do this, because that's what best friends do. "So, what are you gonna do now about your stuff from the house? You going to go confront Walker and punch his lights out too, pretty sure he'd go down fairly easily. Or do you just want me and Jason to go?"

"Would you mind? I really don't feel strong enough to face him again yet, let alone Luke. Rosie what am I going to do, I'm jobless and homeless." The reality of what I've done hits me hard, at this rate I'll be moving back home with my parents which would absolutely kill me. And I realise that this may sound dramatic too but, well, this is my parents we're talking about. I love them dearly and would be lost without them but if I moved back home my independence would be gone. A 10pm curfew at nearly 30 would not do much for my already shaky street credit.

I flex my fingers on the hand I used to punch John and wonder how long it will hurt for. I don't know why some people get a kick out of it. God I hope nothings broken, that would be the icing on the very crappy cake now wouldn't it.

"You can stay here as long as you need to, mi casa es su casa…or something like that. Jason loves you anyway so he'll be fine." Pausing she takes a drink and I can see her mind working at rain man speed, her eyes go all crazy and frankly, this scares me because it usually results in me ending up getting roped into something that will scar me for life or get me nearly arrested. "Ohmigod, I've just had a brilliant idea!"

Here we go.

"Why don't you come to San Francisco with me next week? Jason has a ton of work so can't come but you can now your unemployed! Sorry." She touches my hand sympathetically and I wince. "I'll be busy a couple of full days with the photoshoot but other than that we could have the trip of a lifetime! Ten days in one of the best places in the world! What could be better?!"

"Sitting and wallowing in my pyjamas?"

"Pfft, not under my roof, and I know you're all out of options other than your folks," she narrows her eyes at me to challenge me but I have no argument. She has me.

"Well then, looks like my last wage is going on a plane ticket."

Giggling she jumps on me and kisses my cheek leaving a red lipstick print there before running off to tell Jason. Ten days in San Francisco, what have I got to lose?

"Sweet baby Jesus Lex." The door slamming wakes me from my glorious dream where I was sunbathing happily on a beach in Miami with Alan from the Hangover who wanted me to be part of his Wolfpack. I was to be the leader and the only female member because I'm the only one cool enough, obviously.

Now I'm awake though, back to reality and facing a very angry Rosie who doesn't look like she's prepared to take any prisoners. I don't blame her. I'm currently sprawled out on her sofa in one of her onesies holding a now melted piece of chocolate that has made its way onto my chest. I may or may not have gone a little bit Bridget Jones and eaten my own bodyweight in junk food whilst day dreaming about my own Mark Darcy before raiding her DVD collection. And now I feel quite sick. This is not going to go down well.

"Hi?" I smile feebly. My head is pounding. I cried myself to sleep after watching my fourth romantic comedy. Somebody should really start a petition to stop those things being made; they're bad for a single girl's health.

"Don't 'hi' me missy! Have you seriously been sat here all day with the curtains closed watching television? Please tell me that you didn't eat all of my ice cream?"

I lower my head and attempt to pick off the chocolate from her baby pink onesie, trying to avoid eye contact and swallow back down the sharp lump rising in my throat. I'm clearly in no fit state to be left alone at the moment. Jason offered to stay at home with me today and keep me company but I stupidly declined. I'm a big girl after all, I shouldn't need someone to keep an eye on me to make sure I don't do anything stupid, but at least Jason would have confiscated the remote control and hidden the chocolate like the good friend that he is. He always was the voice of reason in our group when we were growing up. Luke was the boy rebel, I was the one that always had to organise us wherever we went and Rosie was the wild child. Jason and Rosie have always balanced each other so perfectly; I can't imagine them without each other.

Their commitment to each other was finally sealed though when Rosie was involved in an awful car accident with her parents when we were about 16 and it left her fighting for her life. Jason refused to leave the hospital for the two weeks that she was in intensive care, it killed me having to leave him there but I had Luke and my parents to support me through it all, Jason needed to be there with Rosie's parents who both came off with minor injuries surprisingly. The day she came home was the day Jason proposed. They had no intention of marrying so young but it proved their love and their parents supported them completely.

I leant on Luke heavily during that scary period, he was all that kept me going and I clung to him like a child clings to their favourite blanket. I think that's another reason it hit me so hard when seven months later he left to go to France. It was all too much and so much never got thrashed out between us. I loved him, I hated him, I was confused and I was angry.

Basically I was a mess.

Thinking back to that time makes me think of Walker. For all his faults he would always be a pillar of strength when I needed him to be, I would have truly fallen apart when my aunt died had it not been for him.

Aren't memories a funny thing? It's always the good times that you remember when you've split with someone until you manage to get your head together. Right now, I've forgotten every bad time we ever had together, shower scene aside, and all I can think of is how much I love him.

"I miss hiiiiiiiiiiiiiiim," I wail at her.

"Miss who?" She sits down cautiously on the edge of the sofa making sure she's not about to sit on any chocolate.

"Walker of course! When will the pain stop? When will I stop feeling like I'm dying inside?" My chest heaves as my already puffy eyes release more tears. When will I start to hate him again? When I found him with Lauren, I wanted his balls on a plate, but now, everything hurts.

"Oh Lexi, come here." She pulls me close and strokes my hair gently until I calm down. It takes a while but I get there in the end. This emotional rollercoaster is draining, all I want to do is sleep, and eat, and hurry up and get to San Francisco so everything stops reminding me of the life I used to have.

When Jason gets home from work, we all sit together on the floor of the living room surrounded by pizza take away boxes and reminisce over old times. I don't know why but I've always felt a lot happier sat on the floor, especially when I feel sick, the way I see it is if you're already on the floor, you can't fall far can you?

"You know, you were too good for Walker Lex," Jason chews on my leftover pizza crust as I pick the mushrooms off of his slice.

"How so?"

"Well, he was an obnoxious snob who looked down his nose at your friends and family and you lost some of your sparkle when you were with him." He shrugs as Rosie looks at him nodding her head in agreement.

"He didn't look down his nose at you, he thought you were the most intelligent friend I had. I mean, he didn't love you," I laugh as I look at Rosie, "but you Jason, you he liked. He said so."

I frown as they share a look. You know that 'look' that some couples have where you're convinced they're talking to each other telepathically. It's unnerving.

"He did!" I insist through a mouthful of pizza. I have no shame.

"Babe, Walker tried to get Jason fired

once over. We were lucky that he'd been at the firm so long so the partners knew it was just Walker being a dick, but it made things quite awkward for a spell."

An awkward silence fills the room and it's suffocating. My mind whirs as it tries to process this new information.

"How? I mean, how do you know it was Walker?"

"My boss was one of Walker's old university friends, Walker told him that I had a drink problem, as did Rosie, and that they should be very careful who they choose to represent their law firm." Jason meets my eyes and smiles sadly. "We didn't tell you because you loved him and as long as you were happy and we still got to see you then it didn't matter. There was no real harm done." He shrugs as he takes a bite of pizza. Oddly enough I've lost my appetite now.

"You should have told me." I look between them but neither speaks. "You should have told me." I whisper as a new onslaught of tears starts, but this time, it's Jason who pulls me into a hug as Rosie rubs my arm affectionately.

"We didn't want to cause any problems between you. You hadn't long since got engaged," she says softly.

"Shit Rosie," I pull away from Jason and glare at them. "It was that long ago and you never said?! He could have ruined your law career Jason, what if that had effectively put a black mark against your name and no other firm would have hired you? What then?"

"Well then I would have told you," he says in a matter of fact tone.

"Is there anything else I should know?" I wipe my eyes and try to blink back any more tears.

"Apart from him ignoring us at your dinner parties and his patronizing manner, no, he didn't try screw us over after that."

"And why is that Rosie," Jason smirks as he looks lovingly at her.

"I may or may not have threatened to rip his balls off and display them on a pointy stick on our garden fence if he tried to mess with me or my family again. And that included you." She smiles triumphantly and I can't help but laugh.

"My wife, the epitome of class." Jason nuzzles her neck as I watch her giggle. I should be a lot angrier than I am that they kept this from me, but it was their life, their choice and the most important thing right now is that we all have each other, and that will never change.

It's been five days now since I've heard from Luke. It's like déjà vu and it stings just as much as it did back then. Then I remember that he doesn't actually have my phone number so that could be why he's not been in touch, at least that's what I'm choosing to believe. Of course I could text him but it just feels like one of those situations where I should let him make that move. Rosie told me she would pass on my number so that he'd have it though. That was yesterday. I check my phone again, as if two minutes passing by is going to make that much difference; he's probably busy having fun with Alice. Six months they've been together, six whole months and he didn't think to drop her into the conversation at all. I really want the chance to talk to him so that I know that we're okay before I leave for San Francisco tomorrow, I don't want any awkwardness between us or him thinking that I'm angry that he has a girlfriend. I mean, I'm slightly annoyed that he didn't tell me about her, but I don't want it to affect our friendship, not now I've finally got him back in my life.

Rosie and Jason went back to my house - or Walker's house now - earlier on today and I'll give Rosie credit where it's due, she did a great job of packing for me. She grabbed all the expensive knick knacks that were lying around AND even managed to do a bit of charity work while she was there. I do hope Walker feels as good as we did when he realises he will have dressed a lot of homeless people in Armarni and Hugo Boss with the help of the North London Action for the Homeless. I also hope he gives his toothbrush a good wash daily before using it, you can just never be too sure of where it's been. Rosie and I can though.

"So, pawn shop or eBay?" She holds up his gold Rolex and I gasp.

"Shit, he'll freak when he realises that's missing! He'll probably report it stolen, best just keep it."

Pouting she puts her head back into the black bin bag and pulls out a large photoframe.

"Here, I thought you might want this, you know, to burn or use as a target practice or something."

As I take the frame from her I smile, Walker in his graduation cap and gown looking as smug as ever. Yep, this will be perfect target practice for if I ever take up darts.

I stretch my legs out in front of me, wriggling my toes and survey the chaos around us. I didn't realise I had so many clothes until now, most of them I'd actually forgotten about. Luckily the spare bedroom here has a large wardrobe because I have a feeling I'll be doing plenty of eBay at some point in the future just to keep my head above water. Still, at least I don't have a mortgage to pay just yet.

"I still can't believe we're going to America tomorrow!" Rosie claps her hands with glee. "San Francisco is supposed to be amazing, and so romantic too, maybe you'll get lucky Lexi! Ha, lucky Lexi, I'm hilarious."

I arch and eyebrow at her and carry on

rummaging through the bin bag that contains what's left of my life with Walker. I haven't quite got round to telling her yet that I only booked a one way ticket. I don't know what possessed me but as I was booking it, I just found the courage from somewhere and realised that it's been a long time since I've done anything so spontaneous. I know she'll fret and panic when she finds out, but hopefully I can keep it a secret for as long as possible. I know that it might seem a bit strange and deceitful, but I don't want to give her chance to talk me out of it. We've always told each other everything but I feel almost guilty over this, like I'm running away from my problems. Rosie has always been a lot stronger than I am and I admire her for that, but I thought long and hard before clicking that button and I couldn't think of a good enough reason not to do it. After all, Luke has Alice so it's not like we stand a chance of being anything more than close friends. I'm seeing this as my chance to experience new things in life and come back a stronger person because of it.

"You can't shut yourself off forever, Mr Right is out there somewhere Lexi. You'll get your happy ending. I promise." And with a glint in her eye she pulls out Walker's favourite DVD box set. What an absolute legend.

CHAPTER SIX

Wheeling our trolley cases through the bustling airport I start to feel the butterflies in my stomach, the excitement bubbling inside of me has my adrenaline spiked. Families try to herd their children together, couples patiently weigh their cases at the stands, a pilot smiles at me as he wheels his tiny trolley case past us – hmmm hello Captain - the opportunities for people watching are just endless but I'm hot on Rosie's tail, weaving in and out of the lines trying to keep up with her as she navigates through the madness.

I've gone for the casual look today, leggings and a long vest with a cropped denim jacket, but Rosie, ever the stylist, has gone all out for this flight. Her bobbed black hair has been pinned back out of the way, large black sunglasses cover her eyes and sit on her full face of makeup. Her bright red lips make me envious every time I look at them. Although we both have the same porcelain complexion, my hair makes me over cautious and prevents a lot of colours from gracing my face. It's taken me a lot of years to embrace my colouring, I've been brunette, I've been blonde, but finally came back to my red head roots and so far, I think I'm working it pretty well confidence wise....or I was until last week.

Pushing that unpleasant thought to the back of my mind, we get rid of our bags - my two suitcases to Rosie's six. Although they aren't all hers of course. She has had to bring the clothes for the shoot as well as her own. And her shoe case of course. Sigh.

"Time for the duty free shopping." She claps, her eyes gleaming with excitement as she links her arm through mine, pulling me towards the fluorescent lighting of the shops. Now, as I'm currently unemployed I've been quite careful with my spending, essentials only has been my new mantra....but then I see the MAC counter and that bad boy is immense. My credit card can take one more hammering surely?

"Lex, come on!" Dragging me past my beloved MAC and through to the Chanel store, I get a sudden urge to buy a new perfume and you don't get much classier than Chanel. I've worn the same one for ten years so this new phase and new me should have a new smell - for the want of a better phrase. I run my fingers over the bottles trying to decide whether to go for a classic like Coco Chanel, or to try Chance. I can't see Rosie anywhere to ask for help either, she'll have honed in on the lipsticks I'm sure, and I refuse to approach the snotty shop assistant currently looking down her well made up nose at me from afar. Feeling like a shoplifter, I blush and spray a couple of different fragrances when

Rosie's head pops up from the other side of the stand.

"Bloody hell, don't do that you scared me!" I grip onto the glass bottle, thankful that I didn't drop it. I don't mind paying for something that I'll be wearing but I refuse to pay for something that the floor will be covered in.

"Sign of a guilty conscience that," she winks playfully. "Oooo perfume, which are you going for?"

"I don't know, I think I'm more drawn to Chance, it seems fitting too. Here smell this." I thrust the card under her nose as she walks around.

"I like it; I say take a chance on Chance. Get a wriggle on though, I want to grab a quick coffee at Starbucks." Honestly, we haven't even been in here ten minutes. The girl has the attention span of a goldfish.

I quickly pay for my new perfume and follow a skipping Rosie out of the shop when I realise that she has far too much energy for this early in the day and probably doesn't need caffeine. I'm sure she hasn't always been this perky. If she's on drugs, I want some.

Terminal 3 at Heathrow airport, whilst full of all kinds of awesomeness from Bvlgari to Caviar, Harrods to Yo! Sushi - although I do think they should put the Krispy Kreme after airport security for those of us that don't want to stand eating our doughnuts in the check-in hall, just saying - is also very much like a cattle market. There are literally no free seats at all in the main area, and it's a huge main area. Needless to say Starbucks is crammed too, I have the pleasure of being sandwiched in between a woman with crazy wild hair- I keep getting a mouthful – and a very lovely smelling teenager. Would it be weird to ask what perfume she's wearing? As the queue slowly begins to move, my feet start to throb and all I want is to rest them. Rosie must be feeling the pain too because she is shifting from foot to foot. I should add that while my feet are adorned with a pair of sensible but gorgeous French Sole pumps, Rosie has 5inch high Louboutins on. I've never been too sure about the whole suffering for fashion mantra. I do like my comfort, so you know I mean business if I'm wearing a pair of killer heels.

When we're finally served, I stand nursing my hot chocolate and begrudgingly have to admit that it's not as good as Alice's, they don't give sprinkles either. Sipping through the cup cautiously, my mind wanders to Luke. We still haven't spoken and I wonder whether I should text him first. A child running past and nearly taking me out snaps me out of my daydream, you really do have to be alert in this place, thank God we only have another 20 minutes or so before our gate opens. All I want to do is get my backside firmly settled in my seat, magazines and iPad at the ready, and relax for the whole journey.

As we queue to board I check my phone one last time and my heart leaps when I see that little envelope in the corner, then I see Walkers name.

Enjoy your little trip. I'll be in touch when you're back. X

I delete his message. After our blazing row the day before yesterday where he called me a money grabber, I have nothing to say to him anymore. All that's left in that house of mine now is my precious Mr Beefy who Jason has promised to collect while we're gone. We thought it best to catnap him while Walker wasn't there and as he goes away on the trip to Cyprus tomorrow with Lauren, it seemed like the perfect opportunity. Dear Mrs Atkinson won't be put in an uncomfortable position either because she always takes time off when we're away. Still, at least Walker had the decency to transfer me the money for Cyprus. Silver lining? I like to think so.

     As another text comes through I gasp. Luke.

Have a safe flight Lex. Sorry I've been quiet, had a lot goin on. Can't w8 2 see u when ur home. Luke xxx

Smiling goofily I save his message, until a wave of reality slaps me around the face and I remember Alice. I remind myself that it's time to move on. Luke and I are friends and that is all we will ever be.

11 long tedious hours later, we finally touch down at SFO International Airport.

"Wow, we're here!" I'm breathy with excitement as I hang out of the window of our taxi like an excitable dog while the driver shakes his head and laughs. Luckily we got a good humoured guy who has been telling us about the best places to eat and see, calling Alcatraz an overrated tourist trap. I don't say this to him but there is no way as long as I'm still breathing that I'm not seeing Alcatraz while I'm here. As we zoom past places that I've only ever seen on television, it all becomes very real and exciting.

"This is you ladies." Our lovely driver drops us kerbside and pops his boot open as Rosie fishes out some dollars from her purse. The plane journey hasn't affected her one bit, in fact I'd go as far as to say she looks like she's slept those 11 hours, unlike me who had a child kicking the back of my seat and a six foot giant in front that insisted on reclining his - even through our meals. The air hostess refused to ask him to put it up too advising me that 'it's his seat to recline' and she wouldn't be doing anything about it.

There's no way I'm travelling home with the same airline.

"Come on dolly daydreamer, this is us." Hopping manically on the pavement, Rosie is as eager as ever to get started on our adventure. Dragging my case from the road I look up dubiously at the sign above my head.

"What's a motor inn Rosie?"

"No idea, but I know a girl that stayed here before and she said it was great, not The Ritz but not Bates' motel. It's lovely and homey so suck it up and come on."

It's late afternoon by the time we check in to our room and start to unpack. I'm a lot faster than Rosie because I don't have as many fancy clothes, and if I'm being completely honest, nothing that's worth hanging up. Most of my things will happily sit in the drawers.

Grabbing a fresh vest and my cropped jeans I seize the moment and jump in the shower first, hoping that it's not one of those that leaks everywhere because of the weirdly long curtain that hangs down the outside of the tub.

No such luck. Crap.

As soon as Rosie takes her turn I hear her swear. I've left a puddle in there that could easily compete with the Thames I'm sure. I'm positive she'll sympathise though once she's done in there....I mean she'll still be pissed, but she won't kill me. I hope.

An hour later we hit the streets of San Francisco ready to explore. We decide to go ahead and investigate on foot to save some money after our taxi driver told us the quickest route to Fisherman's Wharf. I gaze in wonder at the sights we pass; the houses are unlike anything I've ever seen in reality before. They stand majestically with their large bay windows, each house painted a different colour to its neighbour. Don't get me wrong, they're all the epitome of class, I'm not talking Essex peach or sunshine yellow, the ones we pass are muted creams and pale pale blue. Flowers are blooming in every garden and we even get a wave from a lovely old couple doing their gardening. It's like a different world when you compare it to London.

"I've only seen one street and I never want to leave!" Rosie sighs wistfully.

"How many days have we got to explore?"

"Well, I have a full day on set Monday and Tuesday, then two sunrise shoots but they'll be finished mid-morning obviously, maybe some reshoots one day if it comes to it but at least five full days? You know you can always come on location with me to the shoot, you'll get to see Golden Gate Park and Haight Ashbury?"

Nudging me around the corner she links her arm through mine and smiles. "I'm glad you came and I can share this trip with you. You keep drifting away from me and becoming vacant since the Walker incident, are you really doing okay?"

Rounding another bend we both come to a halt. There it is. There in front of us is the bay, and it is mesmerising. Alcatraz sits hauntingly in the distance, cloaked with a thin veil of fog, a faint light twinkling from it as dusk begins to fall. Boats are too-ing and fro-ing to who knows where and a group of people speed down the road on Segways.

"Wow." I whisper.

"Yeah." Never has Rosie been lost for words in the 27 years I've known her, this moment is one I will treasure for a lifetime for so many reasons.

"Come on. Let's have our first diner experience." I drag her down the stairs to the side of us squealing and realise we're in Ghirardelli Square, home of some of the world's finest chocolate in my very humble opinion. So obviously I have to take a picture; did I mention that I'm a photo whore? No? Oh, I am, doesn't matter whether it's your lunch or a cute dog, I will get snap happy. My stomach begins to voice its discontent as the smell of food drifts under my nose so after I'm happy I've got a good enough photograph, we hurry inside noticing that there are very few tables available.

Lori's Diner is an old school 50's style diner with a delightfully tacky Betty Boop figure stood just inside the window to greet guests. It's hard not to fall in love with the place, even before we've sampled the food. The cream and red booths are mostly full, with numerous families chattering away as they eat their dinner. Everyone looks so happy to be here that I can't help but beam.

"What can I get you lovely ladies?" A young man stands beside us giving us his finest all American smile. I'm still too taken up with the retro decor in this place to care about the fact that he is a f ine specimen of a man and flirting terribly with us. What the hell is wrong with me? Surely I'm not resigning myself to a life with ten cats already?

"I'll have the Heart Breaker with a side of sweet potato fries and an Oreo Cookie milkshake please." Closing my menu I carry on gazing out of the enormous bay window that they eventually sat us in. I wanted to sit at the metal counter when we first came in but I'm glad Rosie put up a fight for the window seat.

"Bay Shrimp Salad with chilli cheese fries and a Cola Float for me please." I wrinkle my nose at the combination Rosie chooses but she simply raises her eyebrow at me, daring me to challenge her on it. I know how to pick my battles, this isn't one I want because I know what she'll bring up. I may or may not have once had the urge to try raspberry jam, ham and ketchup sandwiches. It won't be an experience I'll repeat but I had to do it, it was one of those moments of madness and I did enjoy it to be fair.

As I begin to stare out of the window again I start to think about the last couple of weeks. I meant what I said about a fresh start when I was sat in the comfort of my pyjamas back at Rosie's house, but being sat here right now really brings it home that it's such a big wide world out there. Sure my heart was broken by the man I planned on marrying, sure I cried my way through eight tubs of Ben & Jerrys in one weekend, sure I lost out on the promotion to a woman that has hair all the colours of the rainbow, but life goes on. It's true what they say, you have to pick yourself up, brush yourself off and dive into new adventures because you only live once and life is too precious to waste or take for granted.

Or count calories.

A little while later we sit nursing our food babies. That was without a doubt one of the best meals I have ever eaten. Absolutely foodgasmic. A new influx of people are starting to take over the diner so we decide to head out and explore the full stretch of the wharf, see how far we get. Paying the bill I slip a napkin into my handbag safely alongside my phone which is now on AT&T. Goodbye O2 you shall be missed.

"What are you doing you freak?!" Rosie hisses at me.

"Souvenir." I shrug and walk ahead of her back out into the still bustling Ghirardelli Square. I promise myself that I'll come back here soon and go into the Ghirardelli chocolate shop – well it never hurts to have a stash does it? I also need to have my picture taken by the fountain with the nymphs and maybe grab one of Kara's Cupcakes. I saw her on Cupcake Wars and was so impressed by her Karavan idea that I can't leave without actually sampling a store cupcake.

The strip down Fisherman's Wharf towards Pier 39 was every bit as impressive and cliché as I had hoped, as well as ridiculously cold. I really should have worn a coat, it is literally making my teeth chatter, not an attractive look on anyone. Even my goosebumps have goosebumps.

"Oh hoodies!" I squeal, as though I've never actually seen a hoodie before, this is what the cold does to you. You think you know what brain freeze is but you don't, not until you've walked on the front here and experienced this. This is ridiculous.

Rolling her eyes Rosie reluctantly follows me in, smiling though clenched teeth at the happy little Chinese man showing us his wares.

I've honed in on a black fleecy San Francisco one and as I take it in my hands and slide them up through the body I sigh. Warmth.

"I'll take it." I hand him $20 and put it straight on, sighing with pleasure and demolishing my hair in the process, but I do note Rosie's envious glare.

"I'll take the zip up one. God we're going to look so stupid." Throwing some money at him she sticks her tongue out and drags me back out to a much warmer sightseeing stroll.

When we eventually reach Pier 39 there's a hubbub of tourists bustling around, in and out of the Hard Rock Cafe, queuing up waiting for a taxi, standing watching the street artists in amazement. It really is the busiest end of the stretch.

"Well, I don't know about you but I can. Not. Wait for tomorrow! Can we do the Pier? See the sea lions? Oo oo visit IHOP?" I feel like a child experiencing Disney World for the first time, everything is so shiny and new that I just can't contain myself. Also, the fact that I am now actually on the same continent as the International House of Pancakes is almost too much to bear. I want to eat as many pancakes as my body can take, and then go back for more. I have a bit of a pancake addiction, I know and accept this.

"Sure we can Lex, anything you want." As she stifles a yawn I realise we've been up for nearly 24 hours and a cranky Rosie will be a bitch in the morning.

"Come on, let's call it a night, there's no real queue for a taxi anymore and I really don't want to walk any further." My cockiness from earlier on has ebbed slightly, my feet are killing me and I can feel a blister threatening.

As we hop in the back seat of the first taxi I gasp, it's the lovely guy from earlier who I now know as George. If I'd have spent more time with my head in the car earlier on I may have got this sooner.

"Home ladies?" He gives us a warm smile as we nod and takes us to our beds. Ahem.

CHAPTER SEVEN

I'm rudely awoken by the bed dipping and
bouncing beneath me. Slowly opening one eye I
see Rosie's perfectly manicured feet before me as
she continues to jump up and down in an effort
to get me out of bed. Cow. She always did this at
sleepovers when I refused to get out of bed
before eight in the morning. At Christmas, after
nights out, and clearly she still did it on the first
day of her holidays. Ok working holiday but
still, we were in San Francisco. The thought
makes me smile as I stretch my arm out and
nudge her onto her arse. We are actually in San
Francisco.

"You getting up then lazy?" She pants.
Clearly joining a gym wasn't keeping her as fit as
she claimed.

"What time is it? And why am I so tired,
shouldn't I be wide awake?" I begrudgingly
throw the covers back and slide my feet down
the side of the enormous bed. I do love a big
bed.

"You're always tired so no, probably not. I
got an email through this morning, James is the
photographer and wants to meet with me for a
quick coffee to discuss locations. You up for it? I
told him I would only give up my first morning
here if we could meet in IHOP just for you and

obviously he is dying to meet you."

I heard IHOP and a funny thing happened in my brain, suddenly I turned into Minnie Mouse on speed. The promise of food - pancakes especially - has always been the quickest way to get me to shift myself. I do love food.

Half an hour later and we were stepping onto the street to greet our first morning in the city, bathed in the early August sunlight. Slipping my sunglasses down onto my nose I take the map from Rosie who was looking altogether too confused for my liking. We could end up anywhere if I left it to her and as much as I wanted to visit Castro and maybe make myself a new gay BFF, I needed food and fast. A hungry Lexi was not a happy Lexi.

"Come on, up this way," I nod in a general direction as Rosie salutes me and grins. I don't know why she's looking so pleased with herself all of a sudden but it always worries me when she looks like she has a plan that involves me.

As we slowly climb the hill, I realise that as my determination to reach the top took over, so did my speed, and Rosie wasn't next to me anymore. Also, the hill was that steep that I was practically bent in half and my arse was sticking out. Lovely. Hearing a click and a giggle I spin around.

"Gotcha. That is absolutely getting printed off and going at the front of my album!"

Laughing to herself, Rosie turns around putting her hands on her hips and surveys the mountain we've just climbed. Okay, so maybe it's not an actual mountain, but seriously, I feel like I should have a flag or something for when I reach the top. Even the cars that we pass look like they're ready to roll down the hill as they park on the steep slant. All I can think is I hope they have good handbrakes. And insurance. And that I need a photo. Seriously has to be seen to be believed.

"Cow." Grumbling I decide to walk the rest of the hill backwards so I can keep an eye on Miss Snap-Happy and surprisingly it makes the walk easier. Huh, should have tried that first.

As we reach the top together I smile. And pant. But mostly smile. This is why I took the map. This is why I busted my ass climbing the hill. Looking to our left there's a clear view in the distance of Alcatraz, but before us is the most famous part of Lombard Street and a breath-taking view of the city. Tourists are gathered at the top of the world famous 'crookedest street', children laugh as they try to run down the road before any cars attempt the drive, a group of Chinese tourists stand in their suits with the cameras around their necks posing as their companions take their pictures.

"Well I'll be damned. This is amazing. Shit move, cable car at three o' clock!" Grabbing me out of my daydream, Rosie saves me from being crushed by the old wooden contraption that jingles past me, passengers hanging off the sides just like you see in the movies. I'm in a complete daze and London seems a million miles away.

"Come on," I grab her hand and drag her across the rest of the street so that we can take a closer look. A narrow red brick stairway leads down the side of the road allowing a safe path down for those of us that a) value our lives and b) don't want to get arrested for jaywalking. I'm still not sure of the rules and orange is NOT my colour.

As we make our way down the steps I realise that this is our first authentic San Francisco experience. Ghirardelli Square was one thing, and the bay front was amazing but the Pier was mainly shut, so Lombard Street is my official number one item checked off my list. Did I mention I'm a bit of a list geek too?

"I wish these people would buggar off so we could get a decent picture." Whining, Rosie rummages through her bag for her camera, her sunglasses slipping further down her nose as she frowns.

"It'll be fine, we always have Photoshop. Here, this couple look normal, let's grab them. Excuse me!" I do the internationally recognised smile and camera gesture, just in case they don't speak English. "Would you mind taking our picture?"

"Sure thing!" A gorgeous blonde gave me

THE STORY OF US

her best Colgate smile as she took my camera.
"So, where are you guys from? Australia?"

And just like that she ruined it for herself.

"Yorkshire, England." I smile and try not
to roll my eyes as hers became the size of
saucers.

"Oh my God, I love William and
Catherine, and that little Prince is so darn cute,
we were so excited for him to be born. Oh you
guys are so lucky." She was so close to clapping,
so close.

Yep, because Wills and Kate had the baby
were lucky. She wasn't wrong in all fairness I
suppose, I felt bloody lucky that I wasn't the one
that was pregnant, although I can't imagine
having a baby to the future King of England is as
bad as having one with Walker. Our new friend
seemed so excited though that I decided against
sarcasm that she might take offence to and just
smiled and nodded.

Grabbing Rosie around the waist we
stand in front of a stop sign for our photo, and I
silently prayed to whichever God was listening
that she wouldn't be the one to open her mouth
with some snide remark.

"Okay, say babyyyyyyy!"

Jeez.

"How about face palm?" Rosie said
innocently smiling and fluttering her lashes.

It was obviously too much to ask for.

As we carry on down the hill towards the

bay, I examine the photograph our excitable friend took and frown. This morning I refused Rosie access to my suitcase so that she couldn't take over and style me to death, and in the words of Julie Roberts, this was a big mistake. Huge. The picture staring back at me now shows a gorgeous girl with jet black hair looking very Parisian chic, and a redhead that looks like she's getting ready for a day trip to Blackpool. Nautical chic was not my friend.

"Come on, he's here already!" Dragging my hand she pulls me through the double doors into the warm, syrupy smelling heaven that was IHOP. I had died and gone to heaven. Seriously, I'm pretty sure I might have been hit by a cable car on the way here and this is where I've gone to rest in peace.

Following the direction that Rosie was waving in, my stomach churns a little. Two men sit at the far side of the restaurant in one of the corner booths and I let out a small giggle as they lift their hands awkwardly in response and smile. One looks like an extra from Baywatch while the other sits there looking quite bored and uncomfortable, his dark brown hair flopped over his face Johnny Depp style. He has a pair of cute and absolute geek chic black rimmed glasses on and a stubble covered square jaw that was begging to be licked. Swallowing the wave of teenage lust, I follow Rosie sheepishly through the busy tables and slide into the booth next to her.

"Rosie! So good to see you again." As they do the obligatory air kisses I shift in my seat feeling uncomfortable, and not just because I was most definitely sat in what felt like syrup. Ew. Note to self, put actual clothes on tomorrow, not shorts that barely cover your arse.

"God, how rude am I? James, this is my best friend in the whole world, Lexi, and Lexi this is the one and only James, absolute master and my favourite photog ever to work with. He moved out here last year, can you believe it? So jealous." Pretending to scowl at him she turns and looks expectantly at Mr Stubble in front of me.

"Nice to meet you. You're the IHOP girl then? I can highly recommend the hash browns here, I always get one on the side of a stack of originals." As James spoke, I realised that his smile was infectious as his playful baby blues bore into me. It's no wonder he and Rosie hit it off. "And this is my brother, Ryan. He's more of an expert than me with the city so he's my secret weapon." Once again pleasantries were exchanged, hands were shook, it was all terribly British of us.

As Rosie and James started talking animatedly about the fashion for the shoot and the direction they wanted it to go in, I tried to think of something interesting to say to Ryan, something that didn't involve the weather. I am a 100% cliché, I want to slap myself. Hard.

"So.....Ryan, what do you do out here? Are you a photographer too?" I was clutching at straws, I knew that, he knew that, hell, the child sitting across the aisle from me staring at my boobs knew that.

"God no." He scoffed. He actually scoffed. My mouth dropped. Pushing his hair away from his pretty, pretty face he sighed like I was asking him the final question on Who Wants to be a Millionaire. I mean seriously, it wasn't that hard.

"I work with music, nothing special." Queue awkward silence. That was it then. End of discussion. Although I wanted to know how the lucky bugger managed to get a visa to live here just by working in a music store, seemed a bit too easy if you asked me.

Silently pleading with Rosie to help me out here, I closed my eyes and prayed she would pick up my desperation with her spidey senses.

She did.

I love her.

"So, Ryan, you gonna be our tour guide for the trip then? Help a couple of damsels out yeah? Oh you could wear a little red jacket so that if we lose you we can pick you out in a crowd, you know, like those performing monkeys do on the tele. They are so cute!"

I bite my lip to stop myself from giggling nervously as he rolls his eyes. So rude. Still very pretty though and I still wanted to lick him. I might be recovering from a break up but I was still human after all.

"I guess so if you want? I'll be with you on the shoot anyway helping this damsel out so what's another two?" Sticking his fork in his pancakes he looks me straight in the eye and I feel my stomach flip. I just can't look away. His eyes are the most unusual shade of green that I have ever seen, I'd go as far as to say they were green with a hint of gold, they are mesmerizing. Eyes are my weak spot, my krypton.....maybe I would tag along with Rosie after all. It's not like there would be anyone there to shout at me for being on set anyway, aside from it being in the middle of a ridiculously busy city, she is the art director.

Thankful for the huge stack of pancakes arriving in front of me, I grab the warm maple syrup and groan with pleasure as I soak them in syrupy goodness.

"So, Lexi, what is it you do?" Ryan had obviously decided that the second I put a forkful of pancake into my mouth was the best time to start a conversation with me, and judging by the smirk on his face he'd done it on purpose. Trying to speed chew before I swallowed didn't do me any favours either; it just resulted in a coughing fit with tears streaming down my face. Composing myself I glare at him.

"I worked in advertising." There. See how he liked my blunt answers.

"Really?" He sat up straight in his seat; I had finally got his attention. "What did you do?"

"I was an assistant and did some copywriting." Rosie nudged me with her knee under the table, smiling her secret smile.

"Wow, so what did you actually do campaign wise, would I know any of your work?"

Hmmm, maybe he wasn't such a bad person. Maybe he was just one of those people that were a bit difficult to get to know? I used to be one of those, I was called a snob at school but I was just quiet…..times have changed now though.

"I'm not sure, erm, do you remember the adverts for the mobile phone network that had the jingle sung by all the different mobile phones?"

"Yeah….."

"Well, that was me." Blushing I look up again from my heavenly stack to gauge his reaction. Leaning back in his seat his mouth twitches into a small smile.

"Yeah, I remember it very well. I really hated that damn advert." Looking extremely pleased with himself he returns to his bacon and sausages while I secretly hoped he would choke on them. Definitely just an arse then.

I'd like to say my first IHOP experience was as wonderful as I'd hoped, but Ryan had tainted it and for that I would forever resent

THE STORY OF US

him. Who did he think he was with his hypnotizing eyes, his cheeky smile and his stinky attitude! I don't care how pretty someone is, there is no need to be so damn ignorant, let alone to strangers. I've also made a vow to stop calling him pretty. Not cool Lex, not cool.

I spend the rest of breakfast in silence as James and Rosie continue to map out their plans for the shoot and I hate that I'm so envious of her. She was chatting animatedly, clearly excited for the days to come, she loved her job and was the best at it. But what did I have now? I didn't even feel any satisfaction from knowing that thanks to Rosie, right about now, Walker would probably be covering himself in suntan lotion and would come away as smooth as a babies behind. It was worth the price of a new tube of Veet just to know how much of a pratt he'd look without a single hair on his visible body, ankles to chest. I just hoped he still used a different brand for his face or.....well that would be very unfortunate wouldn't it.

"Come on Dolly Daydreamer, let's get started on our first day of exploring." Slapping some notes on the table she kisses James again and grabs my hand. "See you tomorrow boys, bright and early!"

CHAPTER EIGHT

With a full stomach and the sun shining, I happily leave IHOP and the company of Ryan. I'm still reeling from his comment about my mobile network campaign. I loved that damn ad. Everybody loved that damn ad. Fact.

Calm down Lex, think of kittens and cake, let them take you back to your happy place. Taking deep, cleansing breaths I tilt my face up towards the warm sun. Heaven.

"Soooo, Ryan was cute right?!" Rosie elbows me lightly in the ribs.

Turning my head sharply I stare at her in shock. Was she actually present for any of that breakfast? I've seen less hostility at a January sale in Harvey Nichols.

"Are you kidding me?" I splutter. We come to a stop outside a small boutique and I'm temporarily distracted by the gorgeous denim shirt on the mannequin, I wonder how much it is? Or more to the point can I still pull off double denim? Second thoughts, can anyone still pull off double denim?

"Oh don't take his comment about your ad to heart, it did get a bit annoying after a little bit in all fairness Lex, even Walker muted it."

"Walker muted every ad of mine that came on to the television, he didn't want to 'encourage my fantasies' and used to ask when I was getting a 'proper job'." Oh Lord, I've become an air quote girl. I'm on a slippery slope now, where will it end, will I be saying YOLO soon? I really hope Rosie pushes me under a cable car before letting that happen.

"Well, okay not my best example," she frowns chewing her lip. "Let's change the subject, what do you want to do first, Pier 39, Alcatraz - though I think we've left it a bit late for early morning tickets - or do you just want to explore? Although hell will freeze over before you get me on a bicycle. Just putting it out there before you suggest it."

"I was not going to suggest that." I was absolutely going to suggest it, she's right. Luckily I have a list as long as my arm so other options are available. "Let's just relax on the Pier, I wanna see me some sea lions." Linking my arm through hers, we manage to navigate across the road and finally reach the famous Pier 39 and I'm so excited I may have even let out a little squeal. Ahem.

The Hard Rock Café sits at the entrance to the Pier, with the blue Pier 39 sign standing above its own. It really is the main thing that lets you know you have arrived at the Pier.

Stepping onto the giant Hard Rock Café circle printed onto the pavement I smile, everything is bigger and better out here, even a neon sign on the building isn't enough, they need one on the floor too.

"Photo op?" I turn to Rosie who already has her camera at the ready.

"Already there Lex, do your worst."

I pause thoughtfully. When you're in front of something of this scale there really is only one thing to do isn't there.

"STAR JUMP!" I shout as the onlookers watch us in mild amusement while we try to get the perfect mid-air shot and all I can say is, it's a really good job Rosie didn't choose to go down the photography path.

After about 20 attempts I finally admit defeat. My feet hurt from jumping and slamming back on the ground and I just want to get into the thick of the Pier now, I want to enjoy the atmosphere.

Strolling down the old wooden walkway, I gaze around like a child in awe as Rosie huffs and puffs her way through the crowd. That is until she spots a shop selling Betty Boop, then I lose her through the masses. Dammit. I try to edge my way through the little people, more commonly known as children, and successfully get to the entrance of the shop, but not before a child stomps on my toe for hitting her on the head –accidentally might I add - with my handbag. Rude.

"Lexi look!!!" Her little face lights up with

excitement as she holds up an enormous Betty Boop figurine.

"Bloody hell, put it down before you break it or something. You'll never get that back to the UK in one piece." It is a lovely figurine if you're into that kind of thing, and boy is my Rosie into that kind of thing. Her obsession with all things Betty started when we were about 14, she suddenly woke up one day and decided that Rosie wasn't a 'cool' name anymore, so everyone had to call her Betty. Well, I say everyone, everyone except her parents, but she didn't threaten to beat them like she did Jason, Luke and I, she just stopped speaking to them. Until she needed the money to buy a hair dye that is so she could finish the transformation. Such a rebel she was not. I can't even remember what she looks like with her natural hair colour anymore.

"I'll put it in my hand luggage!" She looks so excited that I can't bear to crush her spirits by telling her the price that's dancing from Betty's ankle as she sits in her bubbling glass of champagne. I think Jason would actually lose what bit of hair he has left if she paid $1750 for something so trivial. His reaction when she buys Louboutins is bad enough but he understands that. He really is quite a catch in that respect.

"Have a sleep on it yeah doll? Put Betty back and step away from the shelf."
Despondently she puts it back, pouting, and

follows me back out onto the Pier.

Leaning over the wooden rails I stare at the sea lions, letting the cool breeze from the sea wash over me. They are truly fascinating; I can't take my eyes off of them. The sign telling me not to harass, feed or approach them seems a bit pointless though, I mean all you have to do is smell them and you'd keep your distance. Still fascinating.

"Well, they're certainly.......different." I can tell she's trying really hard to find something positive to say about them God love her. Rosie has never shared my interest in sea creatures other than penguins but who doesn't love penguins?

"They just look so happy, not a worry in the world, basking in the sunshine and eating fish. Must be nice."

"Walkers a knob, don't let him get inside your head any more than he already has, he's not worth the brain power. Please? I promise I will find you a good distraction if you promise to block him out. Just for this trip at least." Taking my hand she squeezes it gently as I swallow the lump that's beginning to rise in my throat. I swore I wouldn't let him ruin this trip but everywhere I turn I see something that reminds me of him. Or Luke. I let out a small giggle at the irony of large, fishy smelling animals reminding me of both my exes. They would be mortified. Maybe I should take a picture and send it to them with the caption 'I saw this and thought of you'.

Sighing, I turn my back on the noisy sea lions and pull at my ponytail for the want of something to do with my hands other than wring them, one of my many tell-tale stress signs.

"It's not just Walker."

"If you say Luke I'm gonna push you in with those stinkers." She may only be a tiny figure of a woman but standing in front of me with her hands stuck firmly to her hips, Rosie Anderson was more intimidating than my mother. She was not to be messed with. "Dammit, I knew this would happen. You do remember why you came here don't you? What the final nail in the coffin was?"

"Alice?" I took a guess because to be fair, I think I was verging on a mental breakdown after seeing Walkers naked arse grinding up against his secretary in our shower. My poor shower.

"Yes. Alice. Hot, blonde Alice. We're here to have fun, well you more than me, but it's supposed to be a girly break, no stressing. I want you to be able to clear your head on this trip and at the risk of sounding like a therapist, I want you to just think about who you want to be and what you really want from life now because this is it, you have the perfect chance now. And what the hell, do a little flirting while we're here, get back on the horse. You know what they say, the best way to get over one man is to get under another."

She was right of course, she did sound like a therapist. But she was being a true friend, because only a true friend can shake you senseless by telling you what you don't want to hear while simultaneously trying to get you laid.

"Right, I've taken my sea lion pictures, let's get away from the stench and make a plan of action because tonight I want alcohol, and lots of it."

"That's my girl. Let's get stinking drunk like when we were teenagers again. How I miss those days." Rosie sighs as her eyes mist over.

"Yeah, those were the days when I'd have one bottle of blue WKD and then proceed to vomit all over my cream bedroom carpet. It looked like Papa Smurf had taken a shit all over." She doesn't pick up on my sarcasm, instead she chooses to brazenly stare at a hot guy walking past us while I silently pray she keeps her mouth shut.

My teenage years were not something I liked to reminisce over frequently. Luke left me when we were 17 so it was a pretty poor start to adulthood to be quite honest. Rosie plying me with alcopops did nothing to help matters either, it just made my parents think I was rebelling. I wasn't of course, I'd have been an awful rebellious teen - too polite you see - and as a result I lost my spending money for a month.

Should have opted for something clear like Vodka but like they say, hindsight and all that jazz.

As we carry on taking a stroll, we stop by the Ben & Jerrys shop to gorge on food that we don't really need and try decide what to do with our spare days. I'm hoping that Ryan is as good a tour guide as he is a smart arse. As she steers to conversation back to what I'll do when I get home I'm torn about what I should tell her, if anything. Fact of the matter is, she'll freak out at me staying here all alone anyway so why ruin a perfectly good holiday by telling her before I have to, right? I'm thinking maybe tell her as she's about to board the plane?

Chicken, moi?

CHAPTER NINE

"You can't wear that, your arse looks huge."

I glare through the mirror at Rosie's reflection as she stands behind me, hands on hips shaking her head. Sometimes I think it would be nice to have one of those friends that would just lie to your face and tell you that you look amazing, even when you look like crap. But no, I got me a stylist. Joy.

"Seriously, I love you too much to let your skinny ass go out in that, come here." I shuffle across the room and over to her wardrobe like a sulky teenager as she mumbles and mutters her way through the rack, every now and again her head popping back out to look me up and down.

"Do I really look that bad?" I realise that I didn't pack my most glamorous clothes for the trip but surely it isn't that disastrous? I don't know why I didn't, maybe I just wanted to fade into the background and not draw any attention to myself. Sighing I sit on the end of her bed and play with the hem of my vest. I wonder what Walker's doing right now. I hope Jason managed to pick Mr Beefy up and get him settled in without much fuss, he does always mange to rub him up the wrong way which usually results in fur flying and bloodshed.

"Here, this is perfect!" I look up just as the

fabric hits my head plunging me into darkness. Yanking myself free and trying to calm the static on my hair, I hold the offending item at arm's length and for once in my life am stunned into silence. As I carefully stroke the fabric I see Rosie smile smugly. "That dress is sold out everywhere, its silk and its Pucci so spill anything and you owe me £825."

"Whoa!" Placing the ridiculously expensive piece of fabric down on the bed - because it's so short it feels wrong to call it a dress- I question whether it's worth the risk.

"What?"

"You can't throw a dress at me then expect me not to be terrified to wear it when you tell me how much I'll owe you when, not if, when, I spill something down the front of it."

"We're not going clubbing Lex, surely you can manage to sit at a table and not dribble at 29 years old?" Sighing she pulls out the big guns, my weak spot, it's 'The' Shoes. Rosie has several pairs of shoes that I drool over regularly, much like her wardrobe, but the shoes in question are her pride and joy. Her very first pair of killer Choos. These are officially mine when she dies. Not that I want her to die just for a pair of shoes but they are pretty special. "You can wear the shoes?" She coaxes me.

"Sold!" Leaping up I grab the dress and strip off at a speed Superman would be impressed with. "So, where are we going that warrants you loaning me Pucci and Jimmy Choos?" I fluff my hair up briefly and top up my lipgloss. I do look pretty good in this even if I say so myself. Maybe I am ready to get back out there in to the dating world, or at least ready for a bit of harmless fun. Who knew that all it would take was an £825 dress to give me a boost.

"It's some rooftop bar in one of the hotels at Nob Hill, James said it has the best views of the City and they might even meet us there later, if they don't have anything else planned obviously." Just the way she brushes it off so flippantly tells me that we will most definitely be meeting them there.

"Are you freakin' kidding me?!" I shout like a banshee causing Rosie to freeze with her mascara wand mid-air. Okay, so it's possible I'm overreacting a little bit at the thought of facing Ryan again, but I feel ever so slightly upset that she didn't warn me. First he ruins IHOP and now he could ruin this. Now that my stomach is doing somersaults, a drink is the last thing she needs to worry about being down the front of her dress.

We spend the next hour in absolute silence as I watch Rosie Skype with Jason, only smiling when Jason is directed my way on the iPad. He assured me that Mr Beefy was fine and that yesterday they bonded over wrestling, which I took as Jason put the wrestling on and Mr Beefy went to sleep. Boys.

As they draw their painfully sickly Skype session to an end, I hear Rosie snivel and my anger fades. Her job often requires her to travel but it's usually just for a night or two in Europe, certainly never to the other side of the world. I move across to her bed and pull her into a cautious hug, aware of the fact that if she gets a single mascara or snot stain on me that I'll be landed with the dry cleaning bill. I wouldn't be able to pass the blame on this occasion, that would just make me a bad friend wouldn't it?

I stroke her hair softly as she lets out a soft sigh.

"Sorry I didn't tell you about meeting James and Ryan," she mumbles sheepishly.

I'm about to give her a snotty response when I remember that I still haven't told her about not coming home with her. Best not rock the boat when tonight is all about having fun.

"It's okay, I'm sorry I screamed at you. Bit of an overreaction. Hey, and maybe he won't be such a douche with some alcohol in his system?" Even I doubted my words, but they were all I had.

Climbing out of the taxi as carefully as possible so that my dignity remains intact and the guests staying at the hotel don't get a flash of next week's washing, I brush myself down nervously. So, this is Nob Hill. It is stunning and I can see why it's one of the most expensive areas to live in. Not that any place to live is really that cheap in San Francisco, even Homer Simpson says so, and if there's one thing I've learnt in my 29 years of existence, it's that television is always right.

As we get to the top of the hotel, I'm relieved that thankfully it's not that busy and we snag a prize table near the window. Waiting patiently for the sun to set over the Golden Gate Bridge, I order a Mojito and contemplate a S'more fondue. Well I am on holiday and this dress is very forgiving to say it's silk. Best not dribble though.

"Remember, you soil it, you owe me." Blowing me a kiss and raising her glass of rosé, Rosie gives me her million dollar smile that's bought us many a drink over the years and takes a sip as she admires the view. Dusk is falling and the sun slowly begins to set, the sky taking on a new life. Pinks and lilacs swirl as the orange glow fades and I have to admit, credit where it's due, this is a spectacular place to watch the sunset, I couldn't ask for a better experience on our first full night here.

"Well hey there handsome." Rosie whistles under her breath so that only I can hear. Turning around I see James and Ryan casually striding across the room and I suddenly feel overdressed. They both look effortlessly cool

and relaxed in dark jeans and a shirt. Especially
Ryan who looks to have chosen a particularly
fitted black shirt that hugs every inch of his
frame in just the right way.

"Hi ladies! Did you catch the sunset?"
James takes a seat beside me as Ryan sits next to
Rosie, directly opposite me again. Brilliant. Now
I get to get a better view of his handsome face
while he claws at my self-esteem and tells me
how shit I am. Another cocktail is definitely in
order if I have any hope of getting through the
night. Luckily, James is a gent and heads to the
bar to get the next round in as I play distractedly
with my straw.

"You scrub up well Jingle," Ryan smirks
as Rosie excuses herself to go help James. The
blood must have drained from my face as she
stood because she hesitates mid stand, the
concern evident in her eyes. I'm considering
suffocating her in her sleep tonight if she isn't
back within 60 seconds.

"Now there's some praise indeed, are you
always so complimentary or do you just save it
all up for special people like me?" I ask sweetly.

"You are quite special that's true."

Just as I'm about to take offence and come
back at him with another wise-ass remark, I look
up from my drink and straight at him and notice
the seriousness in his eyes as they cloud over.
My stomach knots and I swallow hard trying not
to let my nerves show but it's difficult. Speaking

is out of the question now, my voice would give me away if my body language hasn't already. He thinks I'm special? And not in an idiotic way or at least I think not. God I hope not.

We sit staring at one another for what seems like an eternity, my thoughts, along with my wits, are well and truly scattered. This man who made me feel like utter crap this morning, now has my heart pounding against my chest faster than it ever has before, my mouth is as dry as a rabbit cage and the butterflies in my stomach really are making me feel quite queasy. When did I last eat? I wonder if I should order that fondue for the alcohol to land on or just let it work its magic hardcore style. Eating is for wimps so they say. Of course that never works out in reality and you just end up lying in a pool of your own vomit outside a kebab shop at 3am while your best friend takes pictures so that she can tag you on Facebook. Or is that just me?

"Okay, another Mojito for you and Belvedere Martini for you Ryan." As she places our drinks in front of us, I take a second to admire my best friend. When we were growing up neither of us were very confident, if I'm honest, we were geeks - something Rosie refuses to believe to this day. Now though, here she is, the ultimate glamazon with a dream job, dream wardrobe and confidence oozing out of every pore. She claims that without Jason and his unwavering support she would never have got to where she is, but she has always had the quiet determination required to succeed in fashion, she fought her way up from the bottom of the ladder and now sits proudly near the top of the stylist lists for many of the fashion magazines that we grew up reading.

I take a refreshing mouthful of my new favourite drink and shudder as the cold hits my teeth.

"Easy tiger, maybe we should order a quick bite, I don't know how the people of San Francisco feel about vomiting in the street."

I scoff, since when did Rosie become the voice of reason.

"You haven't eaten?" His question takes both Rosie and I by surprise, or rather the tone does. I find myself colouring before him guiltily and if I thought my aim was any good, I would give Rosie a swift kick under the table, but sods law I'll kick Ryan instead.

"No, we didn't really have time for dinner before getting ready.....but we had Ben & Jerrys about three o'clock this afternoon." I glare at Rosie who just shrugs.

"Well I don't know about you James, but I don't fancy being responsible for two wasted women who weren't adult enough to eat before starting on cocktails." And just like that Ryan turns again. He makes my head spin with his moods and I'm seriously considering suggesting he seeks professional help, I mean who flicks between obnoxious arse and brooding hunk that fast? The mood changes on the table now as James shifts in his seat, not looking in our direction. I sneak a glance at Rosie who I can see is trying really hard not to snarl at him, his only saving grace being the fact he is James' brother who she has to work with.

"Bit uncalled for dude, they are adults. Do either of you want something to eat? I can call someone over if you like?" He tries his best, bless him, but the mood around the table now is as sour as Rosie's face and the only thing that can turn the night around is more alcohol. Watch out San Francisco, we're coming for you.

CHAPTER TEN

Sweet baby Jesus I'm dying.

I slowly open one eye, thankful that we had the hindsight to close the curtains before we went out last night. My head feels like I have Michael Flatly and the gang doing the River Dance against my brain and I'm not sure whether I dare open my mouth. Billy from Hocus Pocus flashes through my mind and I giggle.

"What's so funny?" A worse for wear Rosie appears from the bathroom, her hair resembling a scarecrow, her red lipstick smeared across her cheek making her look like the Joker. It's not a pretty sight at all.

"I can honestly say nothing is actually funny. My head feels like it's in a vice. I don't think I want to come with you today, I might just stay here until lunch then head out for a walk, see where the mood takes me."

"Whatever, just don't end up getting stranded somewhere or arrested, I don't have enough on my Visa to bail you out of prison." Oh a tired Rosie is a very grumpy Rosie. On this occasion though, I can smile, wriggle further under my snug bed sheets and zone out.

An hour later I hear the door slam. Hurricane Rosie has left the building. Glancing at my watch I notice that it's already after nine which means two things; one, I am really ready for some food and two, Rosie is very late for the shoot. Oops.

A quick shower and a raid of Rosie's wardrobe later, I step out ready to face the day ahead.

As I take a steady walk up Van Ness, I think about how I could quite easily call San Francisco home. There's something so calm and familiar about it, even through the hustle and bustle, it just feels like home. The only rude person I've met so far is Ryan and he's from the UK.

Pulling out my City Guide book, I have a flick through the pages. I have no idea how to get to most of the places I want to visit but thankfully this is turning out to be the best £13 I ever spent. I'm a geek, out and proud.

As I dodge through the traffic on and try to remember the route Rosie and I took down to the bay that first night, I wonder whether I should text my mum to let her know where I am. I should probably mention that I'm no longer engaged too. There's a conversation I'm not looking forward to. I know she'll be devastated, she always said Walker was the catch of my life and how most people have to punch below their weight for a few years before they land their Prince Charming. I think I'd quite like to try punching below my weight for a little bit, at least they'd appreciate me.

I realise now that I'm having a full conversation with myself in my head, this is not healthy. Although I've always said I get more sense out of myself. Chuckling away, I turn my thoughts to my grumbling stomach, maybe I'll find a nice coffee shop in Ghirardelli Square where I can sit and read my book and plan my day. This is a whole new experience for me, being a lone traveller, it's really quite liberating, which is a good thing I suppose because I'm going to be doing a lot of exploring alone in the weeks to come.

I don't end up sitting in a nice quiet little coffee shop where business men are tapping away on their laptops and yummy mummies sit catching up with friends over a civilized cup of herbal tea. I end up sat in McDonalds stuffing my face with one of their breakfasts. I regret nothing.

As I sit staring at my family size pancake meal, that's only for one, I realize that I'm going to have to practice some self-restrain soon with food or I'm going to be paying for an extra seat on the plane home because I've gone up ten dress sizes.

I sit people watching as I empty my plastic pot of maple syrup over my dustbin lid size pancakes – I'm definitely going to need more, how could they possibly think one pot would ever be enough? The queues are backing up the length of the restaurant now and I'm forced to listen to a young woman on the telephone to what I'm assuming is a doctor. I say forced, I'm just nosey really, but she has some serious itching apparently and isn't happy that she's got to let her boyfriend know that he could be suffering the same symptoms pretty soon....sounds like someone has been a naughty girl.

I wrinkle my nose as she moves down out of earshot.

"I like your hair." A little girl with big blue eyes and dark brown ringlets stands next to my table holding her dad's hand. I have to do a double take to make sure she's looking at me.

"Um, thanks? Yours is very pretty too. Did your mummy do that for you?"

"No, my daddy did it. Not this daddy, my other daddy."

I eye the man holding her hand suspiciously. He looks pretty normal but then again, what does a child catcher look like? Oh God am I going to have to make a citizen's arrest? Does that count over here? What if he's armed, what if he kidnaps me and we have to pose as a family to smuggle drugs across the border from Mexico and he feeds me nothing but bread and water. I would die.

"Your other daddy?" I ask carefully.

"Yeah." She tugs on the man's hand making him smile down warmly at her. He can't be a serial killer, he looks too friendly. "Daddy, doesn't this lady have pretty hair?"

"Now what have I told you about talking to strangers Madison?" He tilts his head disapprovingly as she pouts. "But yes, she does have very pretty hair. Honestly, my boyfriend is a hairdresser and he's making her as bad as him. Can you believe she's only four and is analysing everyone's hair that she meets. It gets a little embarrassing if she's telling them how they don't have the right hairstyle for their face shape, I don't even think she knows what it means, she just says it to anyone with bad hair."

I stifle a laugh as he rolls his eyes. Gay. Of course he's gay.

"Well, thank you Madison for telling me how pretty my hair is, I really appreciate it."

"You're welcome," she smiles a toothy smile back at me and looks up to her dad. "Is she Ariel?" She whispers in a not whispery voice at all. Kids eh?

"No petal, Ariel lives in the sea remember?"

Shaking her head Madison looks at me with a sigh. "No daddy, Ariel lives with Eric in a house now. Are you Ariel?" She narrows her eyes at me, her thick black lashes nearly hiding the bright blue shining back at me.

"I'm not I'm afraid, no. But I'll let you

into a little secret, she's my favourite princess and I hope to meet her one day too."

She laughs and gives me a big wave as the queue begins to move again. Looking down at my pancakes I notice that they're a little bit worse for wear now. Oh well, I've just been told I have pretty hair, nothing can dampen my spirits now.

Half an hour later and I'm ready to carry on with my adventure. I have my camera practically glued to my hand and am taking photographs of everything in sight, I'm so scared to miss an opportunity that I zone out into my own world. I stand at the edge of the curb to try and get the best angle for the Fisherman's Wharf sign by the fish market when I hear a roar and see a collection of lifesize branches coming at me. Screaming, my camera flies out of my hands and lands with a thud at my feet. I am furious as I turn around and am faced with a large group of people in hysterics and a man sitting back on a stool with his branches covering his face. I huff and pick my beloved camera back up, checking for any damage before standing next to him, tapping my foot angrily.

"I hope you're not expecting any money from me for that, my camera could have been demolished." I snap.

As he moves his branches away from his

face, I see the man behind the scare. His skin as black as coal, his hair in short neat dreadlocks with a fluffy white beard and he just sits grinning at me. Grinning. I want to scream.

"Oh relax England, it's the Bush Man, that's what he does, get a sense of humour." A young man from the crowd shouts at me. Rude.

"Yeah, he's like an institution in this city, stop being so obnoxious! Bloody English are so stuffy." Another man shouts.

I can't believe it. I'm being heckled. My face burns as I stare slack jawed at the crowd. I give the Bush Man one last cutting glare and storm off to who knows where, I just want away from the area before I do get arrested and Rosie leaves me there to rot.

I'm not sure how long I walk for but I eventually find myself by a beach. Turning to look behind me, I realise that I'm even past Ghirardelli Square. Maybe I'll just have a sit down on the sand, catch my breath and regroup.

Bush Man? I mean really, Bush Man? If he's that big a deal then why is he not mentioned anywhere in my guide book, tell me that angry mob! Okay, maybe they weren't an angry mob, but it felt like it. I dig my phone out of my pocket and search for this so called Bush Man.

Well I'll be damned. Not only are there pages and pages about him, but he has his own Wiki page and image after image appears in front of me. I also note that he's homeless. Huh. Well if he's that special to the city of San Francisco why doesn't someone help him out, give him a warm place to rest his head instead of shouting at people who take exception to being scared. Although I do feel quite bad now I must say. Buggar. Although it's not as bad as that time I huffed and puffed at a woman in the supermarket before snapping at her for being so rude and not moving fast enough. Turned out she was deaf. Cue awkward apologies and a red face.

Maybe I'll just stay here on the beach for a little while, out of the way of people and trouble. It's for the best. I can always explore later.

Finally getting back to the motel, I realise that I've only heard from Rosie once today which feels strange. I hope she's okay. I check my phone just to make sure that nothing has changed since the last time I checked it, all 30 seconds ago. Nope, still nothing. Sighing I switch the television on for some company and pick up my camera. I honestly don't know how I'd survive without my digital camera and the option of deleting and retaking a picture, the amount of unidentified objects I have in old photo albums is ridiculous, although I have a feeling I'd rather not know what most of them are. As a song I don't recognise plays out of the screen, a young gorgeous blonde smiles back at me and I flick slowly through all of the photographs from the day. I sometimes wonder whether I've missed my calling in life, whether I should have pursued a career as a photographer and writer rather than a job in advertising. In the end I just wanted to do something where I could be creative and advertising seemed to be well paid, eventually. As I get to the final picture of the day, I contemplate running across the road to the shop on the corner to buy a healthy tea of Cheetos and Pepperidge Farm Cookies. It's unbelievable how lazy I can feel without Rosie here to spur me on. I've lost count of how many miles I walked today but I know that I do need to devote a day to shopping downtown before Rosie heads home, mama needs her some new clothes and shoes.

I'm just about to grab my jacket when I hear Rosie's keycard slide in the door, either that or room service is really late.

"Honey I'm home!" Laughing she throws herself onto my bed and sighs dramatically. "What's for tea, I am starving. All the bloody models were eating like they'd never been fed and did they offer me so much as a single French fry, did they hell. So, I need carbs and I need them now." Lifting herself onto her elbows she realises I'm already half in my jacket. "Hey, where were you going?!"

"Just to the shop up the road, cookies and

crisps were my best idea," I blush.

"No way, we'll go out, just you and me, even if we go to Hooters it's better than all those E numbers. Give me ten minutes to get changed and we'll grab a taxi."

Grumpily I roll my eyes and sit back down, thankful that my best friend is back but not very happy that I'm going to have to walk further than across the street. My feet hurt and all I want to do now is curl up with a bed full of snacks and listen to Rosie tell me all about her day and how awful the models were – I need a boost, what can I say?

"Right, you and me have a date with some chicken wings and boy do I have some gossip for you! Come on, tonight is on me." And with a glint in her eyes and a wicked grin on her face she holds open our door. Show time.

So, it turns out that her gossip wasn't really gossip, more useful profile information. To call it gossip seems a bit mean. One of the models on the shoot today was a friend of Ryan's ex fiancée. Yes, fiancée. After four years of dating, their life plans had been made. They were like a real life Barbie and Ken apparently, she was prom queen, he was a British hottie. Everything was planned for the wedding too. Things were serious, deposits were paid, colour schemes were chosen, and then a very unfortunate incident took place in their bed with his fiancée and her yoga instructor when Ryan found them doing more than the downward dog. I guess when you compare it to my story I had a lucky escape.

Apparently, after the break up Ryan threw himself into work and still hasn't gotten over the hurt and humiliation, although it's only been three months so I don't blame him. The model, who's name Rosie couldn't be bothered to remember, had said he was a completely different man now and she had never seen him look so miserable. Personally I'd have gone with cantankerous but that's just splitting hairs. When Rosie - who has no tact whatsoever - questioned James, he told her that Ryan had been 'a bit of a dick' ever since and just didn't trust women anymore. They shared an apartment and James had told her how he was looking for his own place because he was sick of Ryan's moods and hearing different women in the apartment every weekend. Nice.

"So, you were right I guess, guy is a total douche." Ripping into a chicken wing Rosie gestures with it animatedly. "I bet his fiancée had her reasons for hooking up with Mr Yoga, affairs usually have an underlying cause other than the dude can't keep it in his pants." Realising what she's said her face drops. "Oh shit, I'm sorry. But I suppose if you thought about it, deep down you knew that things weren't right. Didn't you?"

"I guess so, still hurts though. Little bit of tact wouldn't go amiss." Dipping one of my fries in her blue cheese sauce I chew thoughtfully. Maybe I will go with her tomorrow, what harm can it do? It has to be safer than venturing down to Fisherman's Wharf again and it will be a bit of an adventure seeing somewhere else. Who knows, maybe Ryan will be there and actually start to be pleasant if I can get to know him better, maybe he'll see that I'm not a female monster like his ex. I'll give him one last chance. Yes. That's what I'll do. Good plan Lexi.

THE STORY OF US

CHAPTER ELEVEN

As far as bad ideas go, it really isn't one of my worst. Golden Gate Park is beautiful, what I've seen of it anyway. I even managed to get a sneaky photograph of a police man riding around on a horse by the Conservatory. The flowers that surround the Conservatory are spectacular, I became a bit obsessed with the clock planted in the centre of a flower bed and took several pictures. My dad would love it here.

The Japanese Tea Gardens and location of the shoot are truly a sight to see too, I'm dying to explore them in more depth but am terrified of getting lost on my own. I mean, how do you differentiate one lily pad from another? The place has that many ponds and fancy bridges that I'd need to tie a ribbon to the things I pass just so I can tell where I'm going and where I've already been. It's either that or a trail of breadcrumbs but I'm not convinced that they'd last very long, between the masses of people and birds, they don't stand a chance.

I've taken so many photographs today that I've lost count, so in that respect I'm really glad I came. On the flip side, I'm sat alone because Ryan didn't show up again today. Surrounded by beautiful people, I sit alone on a picnic blanket that Rosie tried to convince me I wouldn't need - like I wanted grass stains on my arse on top of everything else.

"Break for lunch guys? I don't know about you but I am starving." As everyone nods vigorously in agreement with James, I smile. He certainly knows how to command an audience, aside from being generally nosey with tourists, I've been carefully watching James and how he works, and let me just say, he is a great watch. His warm smile has all the models at ease, even I struggle to feel nervous around him. Pulling out my extra-large bag of Cheetos, I watch as he shows Rosie some of the photographs from the morning, her ooohs and aaahs signalling a good shoot so far and I couldn't be happier for her. This trip was a big deal, as creative director and stylist there was a lot of pressure on this going right. She told me last night over our healthy supper of cold Poptarts and Snapple, that if this shoot was successful, it could mean a lot more responsibility for her and potentially more exposure to top designers. Maybe even celebrities.

"They slacking off already?" I turn around just in time to see Ryan plonk himself next to me on the blanket before he sticks his hand in my bag of crisps. Bit rude.

"They've just broken for lunch, I can't imagine a hungry model is a happy model."

"So the rumours are true? Models do eat?" He feigns shock and I find myself laughing back at him reluctantly as he comes back in for a second handful.

"Apparently so. I don't suppose you'd like a Cheeto would you?" I tilt my head and raise an eyebrow.

"Sorry," he spits back at me. Men truly are disgusting. I brush Cheeto powder off of my - and by my, I mean Rosie's, obviously - gorgeous blush silk shirt and frown at him. At least he has the decency to look embarrassed. "Five years I've been out here and I never get sick of Cheetos. Have you tried the white cheddar ones yet? Amazing." My mind quickly tries to process that he's having a normal conversation with me, but it's no good, I'm in shock, so with my mouth slack jawed he throws a Cheeto into it and continues. "So, James told me that they might be able to get the full day shoots wrapped up today, maybe even a sunset one if they can convince the models to hang around. Does that mean more time for exploring?"

"Um, yeah, I guess it does," I swallow the last bit of Cheeto and smile. "You still our tour guide?"

"If you still want me I'm at your disposal. Rosie told James that you went exploring on your own yesterday, how'd that work out for you?"

"Good on the whole, I didn't get very far to be honest, I was on foot and then had an unfortunate run in with someone I now know to be the Bush Man." My pedicure is ruined too thanks to sweaty feet in ballet pumps but I miss out that bit of information, I don't think he'd sympathise really. "I'm a bit of a list freak though so I've written out the places I really want to visit."

"May I?" Gesturing to the list I'm holding, I hand it over to him for it to be met by a scoff. "All the predictable tourist traps then? Although credit where it's due, wine country is definitely a must see, and Alcatraz never gets old. Here." Handing back my precious list I feel like I'm back with Walker, being patronized for my interests, and call me childish but it really niggles me.

"So what would your suggestions be then Mr Know-it-all? Do you realise how arrogant and patronising you are? You don't even know me and yet manage to be so rude and obnoxious. Give a girl a break okay." My heart races after my little outburst and I see the shock in his face. Good. I'm glad I shocked him. I've let it build up and now, on our third encounter where I thought we were making genuine progress, he makes me feel like an idiot again. "And FYI, everybody loved that damn mobile phone ad." Yes, I really just went there.

"I'm sorry.....I didn't mean to be any of those things." Running his hands through his inky black hair he looks around like he's searching for something. "You know, you're not as quiet as you seem are you? Look, can we start over? Clean slate?" Standing up he brushes himself down and holds out his hand. Cautiously I take it and he pulls me to my feet. "Hi, my name is Ryan, and you are?"

Laughing, I play along with him.

"My names Alexandra, Lexi or Alex for short please. I don't often talk to strangers but you look reasonably normal so I'll give you a shot."

"Oh good. Well, I feel like I should probably warn you, I have been told I can be a bit rude and obnoxious so please forgive me if I ever make you feel that way, and feel free to pull me up on my behaviour. Sometimes I need a bit of a tongue lashing but I have been through a rough couple of months and am still getting used to integrating with people again. That's a whole other story though."

Surprised at his sudden change in behaviour, again, I secretly wonder why he has suddenly decided he wants a fresh start with me? I also make a mental note to Google split personalities when I'm alone; a girl needs to know what she's up against when agreeing to go exploring a foreign land with a stranger. One who sometimes needs a tongue lashing….ahem.

We fall into a surprisingly easy conversation as he takes me for a walk around the gardens, much to my visible excitement, and he explains that his move to America was his quarter life crisis. He grew up in Weybridge, Surrey with a relatively normal family life, just him, James and their baby sister, but then five years ago his parents called time on their 25 year marriage and it hit him hard. He looks so sad when he talks about the split. I can't imagine my parents ever not just being there when I decide I want to go see them, my dad pottering in the garden and my mum bringing him copious amounts of tea and biscuits. If I had to split my time between the two and not have them just there for me when I need them, I think I would have gone the same way as Ryan. Well, maybe not as extreme, who has the funds to just up and move to somewhere that requires a lot of time and effort to get through the red tape, to get a job, sponsors, to find a place to live - although it probably took his mind off of the divorce.

"Anyway Jingle, that's enough about me, what about you? Apart from an advertising job that you obviously feel passionately about or I wouldn't have hit a nerve with the mobile network ad, what else makes you you?"

"Well, I'm a Yorkshire girl, only child. Rosie has always been my sister, and her husband is like my brother. We all grew up together and I genuinely don't know what I'd do without her."

"So they're childhood sweethearts huh?"

"Yeah," I laugh. "Our parents had us paired up and married off before we were even old enough to realise that boys weren't just stinky and gross."

"A threesome? Cosy." He raises an eyebrow, genuinely confused.

"Ew, God no! There was another boy, Luke, but his parents decided to move to France when we were 17 so that ended our little romance. Anyway, we got older, all moved down south to study at university and never looked back really. London has been our home for the last ten years near enough."

"So why didn't Jason come here with Rosie then, did you just decide to make it a girl's trip?"

We've walked around in a full circle now, past the pretty lakes, tea shop and the drum bridge that I was dying to climb and have come back to the location of the shoot. Rosie is barking orders at the models, James is snapping away and laughing and an audience is building up watching the commotion. Sitting back down on the blanket I sigh.

"It was a break for me, she thought I needed it."

"A break from the high pressured world of jingles and doodles?"

I shoot him a glare and play with the grass beneath us.

"No, I walked out of my job after putting my life on hold for a promotion I was told I was pretty much guaranteed. I punched the man who's assistant I was. I came home to find my fiancé screwing his secretary in our shower. Oh and Luke came back from France before all this happened too, he was working on our extension and he has an incredibly hot blonde girlfriend now. It all just became a bit much at the time and a break was preferable over a nervous breakdown." I laugh bitterly as I count off the events on my fingers.

"Oh." He looks into the distance, an uncomfortable silence growing between us. "If it makes you feel any better a similar thing happened to me. My fiancée and the yoga instructor that I was paying for in our bed, wasn't the best thing to greet me after a long day at work."

"Doesn't make me feel better that you suffered the same heartbreak but at least I know I'm not alone." I offer a small smile and turn my attention back to Rosie, not really wanting to talk anymore because I don't trust myself not to cry.

"Yeah, me too. And for what it's worth, I think blondes are overrated."

CHAPTER TWELVE

It's been three days since the shoot in the Japanese Tea Gardens which means three days since I've spoken to Ryan. It's a strange thing the brain, I know I should be missing Walker, or even Luke, but I find myself missing the man that has intrigued me for the last week. A man who's moods were quite frankly irritating the hell out of me. That day at the Japanese Tea Gardens seemed to be a turning point though, we made a breakthrough and now….well now I just cannot stop thinking about him.

Rosie and James managed to get their sunrise shots and are going to work on the sunset one this weekend due to snappy models refusing to stay longer than they had to earlier in the week. I feel like a crazy person. I should not be thinking about Ryan this much. I'm going insane aren't I? Instead of leaving my heart here I'm going to be leaving my sanity.

"Penny for your thoughts?"

Chewing my lip I turn to face Rosie who is carefully applying a final coat of mascara.

"You don't want to know. So, we've managed to get through most of my list now, what about you? Where do you want to go?"

"I always want to know what's going on in that magical little head of yours. Enlighten me." Coming to join me on the bed she gives me her best, tell me or I'll beat it out of you face. It works.

"I really like Ryan. I haven't been able to stop thinking about him since that morning at IHOP and now I need you to tell me to pull myself together and go and get laid or something. I should still be devastated over Walker surely? I should be thinking more about Luke than Ryan shouldn't I? Ryan was so horrible that it's a bad boy thing isn't it, it's my brains idea of a sick joke." I don't stop for breath.

It takes me a few seconds to realise that she's laughing at me. Actually laughing. Not giggling, not a little chuckle. She's laughing.

"Something funny about your best friend losing her mind to a possible schizophrenic?"

"Oh Lex don't be so dramatic. I'm laughing because I think we've finally had a breakthrough and I now win a new pair of shoes from Jason. He said you'd be a mess over Walker for at least another month, I said this trip would wake you up and make you realise that both Luke and Walker are idiots and that there's plenty more fish in the sea. I'm also thrilled that you can finally see what James and I saw that morning in IHOP. The sexual tension is freakin' ridiculous, surely you must feel it?"

I am gobsmacked. She had a bet on me? I mean, yey more shoes for me to borrow but seriously, my two closest friends in the world had a bet on my heartbreak. I don't know whether to be offended or proud that Rosie knows me so well.

"I can't believe you had a bet going?"
I chose offended.

"Oh relax, you can have the shoes, I have too many anyway. The point that you're missing is that it's okay to feel this way about someone other than Walker or Luke. Sure, after hearing about his recent activities I was kind of hoping Ryan's dick might fall off as karma, but when I saw you guys sat on that awful blanket the other day – which I will burn as soon as I get my paws on it – I could just see how perfect you looked together. It was a bit sickening to be honest but I'm only jealous because I'm missing Jason." Standing to go retrieve her phone from its new home on the bedside table, constantly on charge, she scrolls down her screen.

"I'll leave you two alone if you're calling Jason." I lean down to fasten the straps on my sandals so that I can make a quicker exit.

"Stay put missy. James, hi. Listen, do you guys fancy going out somewhere tomorrow, after all you have been pretty poor tour guides, we've done everything ourselves since we've been here……….Oh don't give me that excuse, I've been at the same shoot, I know just how hard you've been working but I also know that your photos are that amazing you don't need to spend that long airbrushing. Come on, hit me with another excuse, I dare you."

Rolling my eyes I switch my own phone on.

A text from my mother asking why I haven't called. Oops.

A text from O2 confirming I'm abroad. Yeah, tell me something I don't know.

Ooo, a voice message! Hitting my voicemail button I wait for it to connect as Rosie hangs up looking quite pleased with herself.

"They're going to pick us up tomorrow morning and surprise us. I think that means he was too lazy to think on the spot but whatever. What are you doing?"

"Voicemail. You know I hate having that little icon on my screen." Hitting loudspeaker I wait for the message as I grab my perfume and give myself one last spritz.

"What the hell have you and that sadist friend of yours done to my sun cream?! Very mature Alexandra, very mature. Well, just wait until you get back, then we'll see who's laughing! I am furious. My arms and legs are bald!!! You are very lucky that Lauren gave me her cream for my face. And for the record, the locks will be changed by the time you get home so don't try coming around trying to make things right again. Lauren and I will be living together in that house and I have sought legal advice. Good day Alexandra."

As Walker's furious voice cuts off we begin to laugh hysterically. We must sound like a pair of hyenas because the people from the room next door actually pound on the wall, so of course Rosie pounds back. I haven't laughed this hard for months, and quite frankly, I'm glad that it's at Walkers expense.

"Oh God, I can't breathe." As Rosie struggles to gain composure, I dry the tears that are now streaming down my cheeks. Then I remember Walker's suits.

"Wait until he finds out that he only has three suits left in his wardrobe!" I clasp my hands over my mouth.

"What, you don't think he knows yet? What does he do, wear the same suit all week??"

"No, Mrs Atkinson always got his clothes out ready for him, you know, the cute little housekeeper we had. He'll only realise when he has to wear the same suit twice in one week. Boy will he be pissed."

"Oh that man is just beyond anything I have ever known. I wish I could see his face when he does realise that they're gone, and where they've gone." Handing me her baby wipes to clear up my face she shakes her head. "How did you do it Lex? How did you stay with that man for so long and not punch him in the face – which by the way, I'm still super proud of you for doing to John."

"Honestly? I think I was just working that

much over the last couple of years that I didn't realise how bad he was. I didn't see him that much really did I, which probably explains why he gave Lauren a little advancement in her career. You know, I blamed myself at first, worried that I'd been neglecting him for my own career, that I'd driven him into Lauren's legs. Stupid right?"

"She's a whore, you're amazing. Anyway, enough about that moron, we have an unknown day trip to prepare for tomorrow and we need you looking so hot that Ryan loses his mind! Fancy a trip downtown?" The way her eyes light up tell me that although the shopping expedition is for me, I won't be doing a lot of the choosing. Oh, what the hell.

Later on that night as I hang up my new purchases, my phone buzzes across the dresser. Expecting another tirade from Walker I ignore it and carry on stroking my new buys of the day. A shopping expedition with Rosie is never something to be taken lightly, but damn the girl is good. There were clothes today that she literally forced me into, and I'm not kidding, she came into my cubicle while I was in a state of undress and forced things over my head. It's a good job I don't mind her seeing my boobs too because one dress that I had refused to take in with my initially, turned out to look pretty damn good on me once she'd fastened me in. That along with a few pairs of jeans, more dresses and a handful of tops became my 'must wears' for whenever I was out with Ryan. Sigh.

Again my phone buzzes and I relent, it could be my mum after all.

Hey Jingle, be ready for 9am sharp tomorrow. There will be no tourist traps in sight either, you have been warned. R x

But where will I buy my fridge magnet souvenirs? And how did you get My number? Stalker. Lex xx

Please tell me you're joking? You don't actually buy fridge magnets do you when you go on holiday, because that's what my nan did! R x

Unfortunately this was something that I did do. I wasn't proud.

Of course not. And you still haven't answered my question. How did you get my number? Xx

I can't reveal my sources I'm afraid. I'm looking forward to seeing you tomorrow though. I like this truce that we have going on.
R x

Truce? You mean apologised for being an arse and held out the olive branch that i kindly accepted and didn't snap.

No need for the sass jingle. And snapping my branch.....ouch. R x

Despite my reluctance, I start to chuckle at the banter between us. Maybe we could become friends after all. I hoped so.

What can i say, you bring it out in me. Well you were a bit of a douche weren't you. You tainted my first ihop experience so you owe me a breakfast xx

I tainted it?

Dammit. Had I gone too far? I mean I am still a little pissed over his initial arrogance but in person he would have heard my tone, seen the humour in what I was saying. Now I have no idea what he's thinking.

Well yeah, a little bit. I thought you hated me. Don't be so touchy xx

I could never hate you. And you haven't seen touchy yet ;) r x

Are you flirting with me?! I am shocked mr.....hey what's your surname? Xx

I am flirting with you. And it's furrows. R x

Hmmm, Furrows, Alexandra Furrows. Mrs Alexandra Furrows. Has a nice ring to it. Bad Lexi, bad. Must not think about marrying Ryan!

Well mr furrows, i am shocked at your flirtatious manner......and look forward to more xx

You ain't seen nothin' yet r x

Haha well i need my beauty sleep, i have an outing with this strange man to prepare for tomorrow. Xx

Lucky guy. R x

Grinning like a Cheshire cat I hold my phone to my chest and notice Rosie stood at the bathroom door, wrapped in a towel and smirking at me.
"You're welcome." She winks, and turning on her heel returns to the bathroom.

As we walk out of the reception of the motel the next morning, we're greeted by a sleek black Range Rover, all tinted windows and gleaming trim work. It really is a thing of beauty. I subtly try to check my reflection but the window winds down and I see Ryan's grinning face.

"Your carriage awaits m'lady. Oh and your hair looks lovely, no need for any adjustments." Dammit he caught me checking myself out. I'm officially a loser.

Oh wait, did he....

I turn and look at Rosie, I'm confused. Leaning close she whispers in my ear.

"Just go with it. I'm doing some work with James." Patting me on the shoulder she blows Ryan a kiss and heads back inside. Dumbstruck, I look at Ryan who is still grinning.

"You gonna get in or what? I feel like a kerb crawler here."

Shaking my head, I make my way around to the passenger side, being careful not to get hit by an oncoming car. Why do they have to make things so difficult and drive on the other side of the road, I've never understood why all countries can't just be the same. Then maybe I'd be brave enough to get behind the wheel of a beast like this. And it is a beast. As I climb inside it smells like new leather and Ryan. And Ryan smells gooood.

"So, just so we're clear, if you try and kidnap me it won't be the wisest move you've ever made, I'll warn you now I punched a guy back home. And when Rosie gets upset, it's not a pretty sight."

"There's that sass again," he shakes his head laughing as he pulls out into the traffic.

"Hey, just giving you the heads up." I hold my hands up in mock defeat.

As we approach the Golden Gate Bridge, I am in awe at its size. It towers above us, rusty red beams stretching up towards the heavens and into the clouds, or fog maybe. I wonder just how tall it is. And where we're going. I wonder if he's taking me to wine country, he did say it was a good choice from my list, and what I would give for a glass of it right now.

Oh God, I'm having a full conversation with myself in my head again, this is not good.

As we approach the halfway point of the bridge Ryan plays with the stereo, flicking between stations.

"Isn't it like an unspoken rule that the passenger is the DJ?" I ask, mainly because I'm nervous enough on the wrong side of the road without him not concentrating properly. It's a long way down.

"Help yourself. I have a few CDs in the glove compartment too if you want to take a look?" He carries on watching the road again as I gleefully rifle through his collection, I think you can tell a lot about a person from their taste in music. Although I don't know what mine would say about me, mine is extremely eclectic, from soft rock to country and all the cheesy pop in between.

"Seen anything that takes your fancy yet?" My stomach flips as I glance at him, the grin spreading across his face making his dimples appear. Adorable. I shake my head to clear my thoughts, two can play this game.

"Jury's out, appearances can be deceptive you see, even the nicest of packages can have bizarre contents. Lucky for you I'm very open minded and like to give things a chance."

I continue to rifle through his collection and finally settle on Ed Sheeran.

After what seems like forever, we exit the bridge and he turns down a road that I hadn't even noticed.

"Hold the Ed, I want to show you something before we head to our destination."

Pulling up into a chaotic car park I arch an eyebrow at him and it's like he reads my mind.

"I know, I know, but this is a tourist trap that I highly recommend. Hey, I gave Alcatraz the stamp of approval."

"You did, that's true. So, what's this then?"

There are cars, children, a coach and a motorised cable car. I won't lie, I'm very curious.

As he grabs my hand I feel a spark shoot through me as his breath hitches slightly. Glad to see I'm not the only one affected. Friends, just friends, I keep repeating to myself.

"Here, look." As I follow his gaze, I can see why he wanted to make a pit stop here. The view is amazing. Angel Island and Alcatraz can be seen in the distance but the mist and fog mean that photographs would be a bit pointless, all you'd see is a haze which is disappointing. "On a clearer day, you can see across to the bay but it's still a great place to stop. I came here quite a lot to clear my head after.....well, you know."

"I can see why. It's beautiful," I reply softly. The mood feels quite sombre now as we both stand and reflect. There are a lot of truly stunning places out here in San Francisco and I feel a surge of excitement as I think about what the day may hold. I haven't felt this giddy with anticipation since Walker proposed. Sigh. I used to think that's what dreams were made of, that every woman deserved the fairytale proposal that I had and that pinch yourself moment like mine was. That when Walker had lit candles in our garden spelling out will you marry me, supported by a violinist playing my favourite song and food brought in from my favourite restaurant, that I was somehow owed it because I was a woman. It all just seems so obnoxious and ostentatious now though, nobody needs that. Don't get me wrong, it was like a dream and it must have cost him a fortune but, where did it get us in the end?

"What's that down there? It looks like some kind of army housing?" I look down to my left and notice a collection of white colonial style houses on a perfectly manicured lawn. Although lawn is probably underselling it, it's more like the size of Hyde Park.

"You're not far off. I mean, it's a hotel now, Cavallo Point, stunning accommodation so I hear but in 1866 it was somewhere that the US Army used as a military base. I don't know much more of the history to be honest, but the area down there is called Fort Baker."

"Wow, I'd love to stay there one day. I bet it's so expensive." Turning to face him I smile shyly. "I'm a bit of a history fan, anything with a story behind it fascinates me."

"Well, maybe one day hey? You never know what can happen." As we fall into a comfortable silence I think about Rosie, the sneaky little thing. I wonder what else she's been plotting behind my back.

Catching Ryan look at his watch makes me frown.

"You in a hurry to get rid of me," I joke.

"Don't be ridiculous. I was simply looking at my watch. Come on, we don't have far to go now."

He's still not telling me where we're heading and it makes me growl in frustration.

"Did you just growl at me?!!" He asks

incredulously.

"Might have done. Why won't you tell me where we're headed?!"

"Because I thought it might be a nice surprise. Don't you like surprises?"

What can I say to that? I love surprises, I can't lie and say no because, well, firstly it's a lie and secondly I think I'd offend him.

"I like surprises," I grumble.

As he takes my hand again, it feels more comfortable this time, it feels right. So I let him take the lead and behave myself, no point spoiling what could be a perfectly lovely surprise, after all, this viewpoint was gorgeous.

CHAPTER THIRTEEN

Ryan's excitement is palpable as we pull into an off road parking space by a harbour. He was right, we weren't far and as far as surprises go, this one looks pretty good.

"Welcome to Sausalito." His grin almost splits his face it's that wide and I can't help but mirror him.

As we make our way on to the sea front I get the chance to fully appreciate the location. It is stunning.

Boats of all shapes and sizes are docked in at the harbour, bright and colourful shops line the whole stretch ranging from clothing to books with seafood restaurants and deli shops in between. People bustle in and out carrying their bags and although it's busy, there isn't the same kind of chaos that there is back in the Fisherman's Wharf area. It seems peaceful almost, and at the risk of sounding like an absolute cheeseball, I'd say it's enchanting.

"A lot of locals come here for a more peaceful shopping experience, it's mainly boutique shops but still, it's quite special I think." He looks at me, his expression filled with apprehension, like he's waiting for my approval almost. He really is a bit of a cutie.

"It's gorgeous. Thank you. I would never

have even known this place existed."

"How do you feel about walking?"

"How far are we talking?" I joke nervously looking at my feet. I've only just rectified the massacred pedicure, I love walking but the thought of having to redo my feet yet again is soul destroying. I'm a big ol' girl, I know and accept this.

"Not that far, just down the rest of Bridgeway to the park, you have to see the park." He nods into the distance and I decide that my little tootsies can probably manage the walk to the end of the stretch. I try to remember the last time Walker was so excited about something in this way but for the life in me I just can't. I'm coming up blank. Rolling my eyes I agree, and we start to take a steady walk on the front, the reflection of the sun making the water sparkle all the way across to the city skyline.

"So I was thinking, if you like, we could grab a bite to eat from one of the delis after the park and sit out here. Plenty of people do it, look." Following his eyes I notice an old couple with their little picnic box sat neatly in between them, and I have to chuckle when I see the blanket they're sat on. "I noticed that too." Frowning I look at him questioningly. "The blanket, it's just like the one we sat on in the Japanese Tea Gardens."

"Okay now that's a little bit weird. You read my mind again."

"I know," he replies smugly.

Twisting my mouth to suppress a grin of my own, we carry on down the front. I marvel at every shop we pass, they all look so quaint, each one has an old style Victorian front, much like the houses back in the city.

"Do you come here a lot?" We dodge a rogue dog that tries in vain to hump my leg as Ryan dodges the question. He thinks I don't notice too I'll bet. Foolish man.

"Think you've made a new friend there. So about lunch?"

"So, about coming here a lot?" I fire back at him.

"In all fairness, you didn't answer my question, you just got all misty-eyed over the old people and their blanket. Don't think I didn't see the envy in your eyes for that get up."

"It was a nice blanket! But yes, food out here would be lovely, thank you."

"Good. Well then yes, I do. Did." Sighing he runs his hand through his hair, something I'm learning is his little stress or frustration sign, and we come to a stop. I look around. I may only be a simple tourist but I'm pretty sure this isn't a park. "My ex and I lived here in a house up there in the hills." He points up to some enormous houses set back in the distance. Mansions, they're frickin' mansions. I pick my jaw up and give him my attention again. "I would have stayed in the area but I don't know, it just seems more like a place for couples or families, not a single guy. So back to the city I went. I just love it here so much though, there's something so soothing about it and the view of the city on a night, just spectacular."

I have no idea how to respond. He constantly surprises me.

We carry on walking in silence. Nice one Lex, push him to answer a question that covers you both with a nice blanket of awkward. What a tit.

"This is it." I look up from the pavement and am greeted by a glorified garden. This also, is not a park.

"This is what?"

"The park. Vina del Mar Park."

"Ryan, I know you've been here a while, I appreciate that, I really do, but this isn't what one would normally classify as a park." I smile sadly at him, shaking my head.

"Very funny, come on." He grabs my hand and pulls me into the small area of garden. There is no denying its beauty, a large fountain stands in the centre alongside an enormous stone elephant with lamps on top of its back. I bet it's lovely at night. And romantic.

For such a small area, it seems quite popular. I'm discovering people really like their picnics out here.

"Okay, joking aside, it is very......" I'm searching for the best word to describe how I feel. Pretty, lovely, nice, none of them do the place justice. "Serene?"

Now I feel like I'm humouring him.

"Serene?" He looks confused. My bad.

"I can't think of any words that would do it justice, and yes before you say anything, I know that I'm the one in advertising and I should be able to think of words at the snap of my fingers but -" I'm just about to get very deep with Ryan - ahem - when I feel something thud against my leg. I see the horror and glee in Ryan's eyes as I slowly look down. The dog from earlier on is having its way with my leg and I'm frozen in disgust. My brain is screaming at me to shake it the hell off but I just. Can. Not. Move.

I look to Ryan for help and see the tears streaming down his face as he struggles to keep his composure.

"Hey asshat, little help?!" I know if this was Rosie I would be on the floor struggling to breathe so fair play to Ryan, at least he's still standing. "Where is the God damn owner! You and your bloody park idea." I'm beginning to shriek, I think I might be finally getting through to the dog though at this pitch. Well, either the dog or some faraway dolphins.

Cautiously leaning in, Ryan tries to coax the dog away from my poor leg as a flustered young girl runs up to us.

"Oh my God I am so sorry, Grizzle get off her leg. Oh God, Grizzle please!" She pleads. Her cheeks are crimson, she looks so embarrassed but I'm really struggling to sympathise right now.

I look from the girl to the dog. Firstly, Grizzle?! It's a frickin' Shih Tzu, not a Pit Bull, and secondly why isn't she just picking it up!

"Hey, can you not just lift it up, I mean it's the size of a stuffed animal." I snarl at her. Pretty sure my lip curled too, mirroring the dog as I give it one last shake. "Little buggar has a serious grip!"

Eventually Ryan mans up and prizes the little snapper away from me. Vicious little thing is Grizzle. I assess the damage to my calf and aside from a lot of drool, it isn't too bad, just a couple of scratches. At least I've had my Tetanus jab.

"I am so sorry, he hasn't done this for ages." She grabs him and quickly clips his leash to his collar. "If it's any consolation, he doesn't try hump just anybody's leg."

"Thanks." I snap, glaring at Ryan just daring him to make a smart comment.

"Thank you, I'm sure she'll be okay. Come on Jingle, let's get you cleaned up." He rests his hand at the small of my back and tries to guide me away from Grizzle and his young owner. I have no idea how she lost control of him, he really isn't that big. Grumbling and muttering under my breath, I let him lead me to a bench next to the fountain.

"Here." He pulls out a handkerchief, runs it under the water and gently dabs my leg making my heart leap into my mouth. His tenderness is completely off balancing, it makes me feel quite gooey.

Oh God I'm losing it. Come on Lex, snap out of it. You fancy him, obviously, don't swoon so soon.

He stands up slowly and meets my eyes. Heart, you're done for, just accept it. I can't process my thoughts, his proximity is intoxicating and I feel quite delirious.

"You should be okay until we get back to the city," he whispers.

"Thank you," I manage to choke out.

Oh boy. Am I in some serious trouble here.

"So I - " he starts.

"I really enjoyed - " I begin.

We both laugh. It's certainly been a day that I will remember forever. For more than one reason. Bloody Grizzle.

"You go." I tuck a stray piece of hair behind my ear as we climb into the car. The temperature has started to drop as the afternoon has drawn to an end and I'm tempted to take my hair down, just to warm my ears up if nothing else.

"I was just going to say that I had a great

time with you today. You're not too bad after all," with a wink he starts the engine and it makes me giggle.

"Why thank you, I think I'll dig deep and take a compliment from that."

"You should, I meant it that way."

I wrap my arms around myself, partly to warm myself up, partly to help contain my elation. Every time he says something nice it makes me feel a bit giddy inside, like when you're at school and you find out one of the cool boys fancies you.

"Well I was going to say I really enjoyed myself today too. You certainly know how to show a girl a good time and I'm happy that I was that girl and not some other floozie." I meant it as a joke of course, but as soon as the words leave my mouth I want to bite my tongue off. I curse to myself and look out of the window at the passing scenery.

"What floozies?" He sounds confused, either that or he's just buying some thinking time. Hmmmm.

"Um, oh God this is awkward. So, James might have told Rosie that you've had an, erm......difficult few months and have had a fair few lady visitors lately." I'm blushing like a fool and inwardly dying of embarrassment.

"He did, did he? Well, what James failed to mention, clearly, was that although it may have seemed like there were a lot of different women, the fact of the matter is that there were only three. I mean, okay so three is still a bit shit but they were all doing the same, we weren't exclusive and it was just a release."

"He said you were drinking a lot too."

Dear God what is wrong with me, make it stop! Why choose this subject to develop verbal diarrhoea?

"My, he has been quite vocal about me hasn't he? Yes, I drank a lot because I was upset." We're silent for a minute or so when something hits him and I catch him glancing quickly at me with a smirk on his face. "Why was Rosie asking about me anyway?" He asks raising an eyebrow.

"Whoa there sailor, I didn't ask her to if that's what you're digging at. I thought you were an arse." Folding my arms indignantly, I turn my body away from him laughing.

"An arse huh?" I can't believe that he finds it funny. I'd be hurt if he thought I was an arse. Just how thick is his skin.

"Yeah, arse."

"Well I'm sorry. I hope I can make it up to you?"

"Well I've already told you that you owe me another IHOP trip. That's a start."

Wrinkling his nose he signals onto the Golden Gate Bridge and once again the city is in sight.

"Can't we do better than a stack of

pancakes?"

"No! I was so excited about my first IHOP experience and you really upset me that morning, it ruined it for me." I'm nervous that something will come out of my mouth that will upset him again but what the hell, may as well be honest right? Best start as any to a relationship, whether we'll just stay friends or something more.

"I am sorry." He says it so softly it shocks me. He sounds so sad that it makes my heart constrict. "I didn't mean to be so obnoxious that day, it had been a really rough night the night before, I'd had a huge fight with Rachel and I was having a bit of an 'all women are evil and none of them can be trusted' kind of day. You just turned up so happy and chirpy and so God damn sexy that, God this will sound so awful now but, I just didn't see why you should be so happy when I wasn't. I am truly sorry Lexi."

Wow. This honesty thing stings a bit.

Sighing I realise that I don't want to be mad at him. We've had some fun since our clean slate and I couldn't be happier for it.

"You think I'm sexy?" I ask shyly.

"Out of all of that, that's the thing you choose to question." Shaking his head in disbelief he laughs. It's such a deep, manly laugh that I could listen to it all day.

"What can I say, I'm a sucker for a compliment."

As we weave our way back through the city on the short drive to the motel, we fall into an easy conversation about various landmarks. Rosie would find this kind of thing beyond dull but I love learning whatever I can about a place. San Francisco has a fascinating history and there are still so many more places I'd still like to visit. I'm hoping Ryan will be my guide for what's left of my list, after all, it never hurts to have something good to look at while you sightsee.

CHAPTER FOURTEEN

"Oh good, you're back!" Clapping her hands Rosie greets me with a huge smile and jumps onto the bed. "Tell me everything, leave no stone unturned, I want all the gory details."

Sometimes I wonder if our friendship will ever evolve from our teenage years, and then I realise that I really don't want it to. Rosie and I have shared everything from first kisses to pregnancy scares. Thank The Lord I never did get the chance to procreate with Walker, it sends a small shiver up my spine when I think of being tied to him for the rest of my life.

"Well, we went to Sausalito, had a picnic looking out towards the city admiring the skyline, he apologised for being so mean when we first met - I told him he still owed me another IHOP experience - oh, and a dog had its wicked way with my leg. I felt very violated." Popping open a bag of Cheetos I attempt to tot up in my head how many bags I must have gone through in my short time here. It's impossible. I'm quite surprised that my fingers aren't permanently stained orange. Maybe I could start a new trend, move over green fingered folk, orange is the future.

"Hey, back to me missy." Snapping her fingers in my face she startles me. "I can always tell when you're laughing at your own jokes you know, you big geek. So, will you be seeing the dog again, did you get its number or did you just use and abuse it, breaking its poor heart." Oh I am glad she finds this so amusing. I could be mentally scarred here and she'd still laugh at my expense. Although I'd probably laugh at her.

"Oddly enough Rosie, no, I won't be seeing the randy little fuzzball again." Hands on hips I try my unamused face on her. Doesn't work.

"Oh please, you've used the same face for years and each time I'll tell you the same thing, you just look constipated. So, Ryan. It went well then yes?" Invading my bag of Cheetos I squeeze her hand and snarl. I'm very protective over these little puffs of cheese, Ryan caught me off guard, he got lucky. "Ouch, jeez Lex, vicious much?!"

Pulling out her hand and surveying the damage, she shoots me a look that tells me I'm going to pay for that at a later date. We have this long standing and frankly cruel game that happens quite a lot. Jason is getting very tired of it but fair play to him for putting up with it for so long. Walker used to lose it, seriously I'm talking Crazytown. There were arguments, tears, tantrums, and like I say, Walker used to get pretty angry too.

Examples of our games? I messed with Rosie's alarm on her phone one day, she screwed with every clock in my house. I hid her favourite work trousers, she pulled mine down in the middle of Topshop. The lesson here kids is that Rosie always wins. Always. I'll probably wake up tomorrow with Cheetos stuffed up my nose or down my pants. Not sure which is worse.

"As it happens, yes, I had a lovely day and Ryan was very sweet. He's going to take me to Castro tomorrow, do you mind?" I pour her a few Cheetos out into one of the plastic coffee cups next to the kettle. I wonder if people ever actually use them or are they just for display purposes, you know, like the obligatory bible in your top drawer.

"No, not at all, I'm just glad to see you getting your flirt back on. So, while you're in a pro-Ryan mood, James invited us to their apartment tonight for a few drinks if you fancy it? Seriously, you will love it there, the views are epic!"

"He never mentioned it?"

"No, James and I were discussing it today and thought it might just be nice, you know seeing as the last time we were all together Ryan was a douche and James called it an early night didn't he so....."

"Okay, sounds like fun."

"Brilliant. I'll let James know then I need to Skype Jason, you want in to see the Beefster?" Phone in one hand and iPad in the other, she is the master of multitasking. I am in awe.

"Hell yes, I've missed my little man so much." The only consolation about being so far away from Mr Beefy is that he's with Jason. I would never have left him with Walker this long, apart from the fact he would probably have had him shaved by now because of his stupid allergy. I used to wonder why Mr Beefy never seemed to bond with Walker, but like they say children and animals are the best judge of character. Should have listened to the cat.

An hour later, I've been suitably scalded by Mr Beefy for not being around to listen to his daily tales from the litterbox and obviously forgiven again because I got a lick of the lens and a purr before I said my sad farewell to his fluffy little face. I do miss him. I wonder whether it would be cruel to ship him out here for the duration of my stay. Note to self, Google that tomorrow.

"Come on then hot stuff, let's get you sexified for Ryan." And with a swift slap of my backside, Rosie guides me over to her wardrobe.

As I release the final curl from my GHDs, I survey my appearance and I'm impressed. With the help of Rosie's wardrobe, it's amazing how effortlessly sexy I can look. We've managed to pull together an outfit of baby pink and grey print shorts, a cream cashmere sweater and my ever faithful nude Topshop ballet pumps. I was allowed to dress my own feet so that must mean she trusts me. Spritzing my new Chance perfume I give Rosie a twirl and she whistles.

"Sexy mama! If Ryan's jaw doesn't hit the deck tonight then I officially declare him gay. Just saying. Ooo, James will be here soon, I told him to swing by around eight, the apartment isn't that far really but I couldn't be bothered with the walk."

I don't blame her. I've never walked as much in my life as I have done since we landed here in San Francisco, but my bum thanks me for it, especially now that she's out for the world to see in these tiny shorts. At least I know, or I hope anyway, James' sofa won't have maple syrup on it like the last time I wore shorts. Shuddering at the memory of a sticky bum, I wander out onto our balcony overlooking the main road. I should really tell Rosie soon about my not returning home with her. I'm being a bad friend aren't I? She invites me along and how do I repay her? I can just imagine the conversation, oh Rosie, funny story, did I mention that you're flying that hellish 11 hour flight alone back to the UK? You won't get to spend my birthday with me either even though it's been tradition since we were three, oh and be a doll won't you and take care of Mr Beefy for me until I can fly him out or return home. Best steer clear of any balconies when I'm telling her. She can be pretty feisty when she's angry.

    I check my phone for messages while Rosie applies the finishing touches to her ever flawless makeup. I wonder if Walker has left anymore delights for me. My eyes light up when I see a text from Luke.

> **Hey Lex. Hope ur havin fun out there n keeping Rosie in check. Miss u. Remember to bring me an awful keyring bk xx**

I laugh a little at his joke. From around the age of 11, whenever Luke or I would go on holiday, we took the pressure off of gift giving by buying each other the tackiest or plain ugliest keyring we could find. I still have my collection stored in a memory box back at Rosie's. I'm fairly sure I have around 20 key rings from the many trips Luke went on, and then the last one he posted to me from France. If I'm honest, I'd completely forgotten about that tradition until now, after all I was 17 the last time I received one. Walker would rather have a nice aftershave or piece of art. Absolute polar opposites in so many ways.

As we pull up outside the apartment I freeze.

    "THIS is the apartment they live in?!" Standing on the pavement as James parks up, I crane my neck upwards. The building before me has an entrance that you'd expect to find in a Park Avenue Apartment block in New York....or at least on the Gossip Girl set. A large glass double door sits under a gold frame and the only thing missing is a doorman.

"Yeah, pretty cool huh? Why do you think I wanted to store all the shoot clothes here this time? It's mahoosive."

"Rosie?"

"Yeah?"

"I'm nervous."

"I'm not surprised." And with a devilish grin she takes my hand and pulls me through the door.

After a grand tour of the apartment, and it is grand, I take a seat on the enormous L shaped sofa. Sinking back into my seat I take a sip of wine and survey the living area. Dark wooden bookcases line a whole wall with various photography books housed there, a few I recognise, a few I don't. I also notice some old classics too such as Dickens….interesting.

"Have you been out onto the balcony yet?" Ryan sits carefully next to me for which I'm thankful, it's such a squishy sofa that one false move and the frighteningly pale, cream material would have nice little pink patches from my rose.

"No not yet, I can see the view is amazing from here though. How long have you lived here?" If in doubt, revert back to small talk.

"Come on," he laughs, hauling me up

from the seat. I see Rosie raise her eyebrows as I follow him out to the balcony and as soon as we hit the cool air my breath catches. It's true that the view did look amazing from the inside, but standing out here under the night sky, it's truly breathtaking. The balcony hugs all three sides of the apartment meaning the views are varying and all equally as compelling. From this side there is the view of the bridge, lit up and standing proudly across the water connecting the city to Marin County, there's no surprise really that it's one of the seven wonders of the world. As we stroll around the corner, Alcatraz sits hauntingly in the distance, just remembering our trip there through the day sends shivers up my spine. Rosie didn't stand a chance in getting me onto that island at night. Not a single hope in hell.

"And finally we have a view of downtown. I love this place, the second I saw it I knew I had to have it. What do you think?"

"Me?"

"Of course you, there's nobody else out here." Laughing he leans against the balcony making my stomach lurch. He's one dodgy railing away from face planting a passing car ten stories below us. Hello vertigo my old friend.

"It's amazing," I breathe hoarsely. Ryan looks, and smells, gorgeous tonight. The butterflies I have flapping around in my stomach are killing me, they behaved themselves today so what are they playing at rearing their ugly wings now? I blame the view. It must be the view. Views do funny things to people. They up the romance factor and now I want to throw up. Breathe Lexi, come on you can do it. In through the nose, out through the mouth.

I can't tell whether Ryan is confused by my expression or entertained, but he takes a small step towards me and I am one more step away from hyperventilating. My heart is in my mouth.

Before I have chance to think about it, he takes that final step, cups my face and kisses me. The second his lips meet mine it feels like a bolt of electricity runs through me, his mouth so soft and warm that I melt into it. I even see fireworks, true to life frickin' fireworks.

When we finally separate it takes me a few seconds to catch my breath.

"How's that for romantic eh, fireworks and that view." He smiles softly, his hand still cupping my face, his thumb stroking my cheek.

"You saw them too?" We are officially soul mates if we're both such hopeless romantics.

"Um, yeah, can't really miss them exploding over the bridge." He looks baffled as I turn around and feel my face heat. Thank God it's dark because I'm fairly certain you could fry an egg on it right now. How am I mortified, let me count the ways. I don't even know how a grown woman who knows better, can actually think she has seen fireworks from a kiss. Gah get a grip girly.

Slowly I see it dawn on him what I meant and I scramble for something to say so that he doesn't kill me off by saying it out loud. He does look pretty smug all of a sudden.

"So, how long have you lived here then?" I take another sip on my wine as I stare out at the bridge, the cold glass against my tingling lips is heavenly.

"About four years," he frowns. "Fell in love with the views the second I walked through the door. Locations perfect too. Look, Lexi, should I not have done that? I'm sorry, I just, I've wanted to do it all day and.....I'm sorry." The words tumble out of his mouth in such a rush I have to take a second to process them.

"Oh Ryan no, no don't be sorry! I was just embarrassed, but please don't be sorry."

"You're not mad?"

"If I was mad I wouldn't do this," and with a newfound confidence that only the fuzz of alcohol and lust can bring, I pull him close and kiss him like my life depends on it. As he puts his arm around my waist to pull me closer I melt against his chest and the muscles that I hadn't known existed until now.

"Hey, keep it PG out there kids!" I hear Rosie bellow from the living area and feel Ryan smile against my lips. Resting my forehead on his, I start to giggle. I tend to giggle when I'm nervous and on my merry way to being tipsy. Don't you just hate gigglers?

Guiding me back indoors he rests his hand casually around my waist, slowly moving his thumb up and down rhythmically as we join James and Rosie's conversation about the shoots final set up and I can't help but think how right this feels. How at ease I am all of a sudden with him when I've only known him a matter of days.

"I'll be sad to finish this shoot, it's been so special and different for me. We should totally do another one together soon, a year is too long." Rosie gushes.

"Let's just get this one out of the way first crazy lady. Although I have had fun this time, it's been nice being able to socialise with you again like old times, shame Jason isn't here."

"I know, he is gutted about not seeing you, so you kind of owe it to him really to come home for a shoot?" Topping up her glass she offers me a refill but I sensibly decline. I want to remember tonight.

Listening to the easy conversation and banter between the pair makes me smile. I remember when Rosie first met James, she was so nervous because it was her first big shoot that she threw up the full night before and obviously got no sleep. Luckily, James is a real gent and can make anybody feel at ease. He took Rosie under his wing and they became good friends.

Eight years later they're still a great team and he even got an invite to Rosie and Jason's wedding but 'unfortunately' - yeah right - was in Australia. Jealous, me? Never, ha! Of course Rosie never gets a look in when he gets together with Jason so that's when she usually leads me astray which is probably why I've never met him before now.

"Do you still want to go to Castro tomorrow?" Ryan leans in to me; he's so close that I can feel the heat from his breath which gives me goosebumps everywhere. Mind - mushed. My brain takes leave whenever I'm near him, which is inconsiderate if you ask me because being able to string a sentence together is usually a helpful skill to have.

"Definitely, I can't wait. What girl doesn't love cookies and gay men?" I give him a playful nudge as he feigns offence.

"And here's me thinking that it was my company that you enjoyed."

Oh Ryan, if only you knew. After tonight, I know now that I am dangerously close to falling for this man, this man who last week annoyed me to the point of explosion, who offended me and stole my Cheetos. What a difference a week makes.

CHAPTER FIFTEEN

The second we walked through the door last night we both collapsed into bed, neither one of us even bothering to remove our makeup. So it's unsurprising that I didn't hear Ryan text my phone.

You looked amazing tonight. Just thought you should know ;)
pick you up to tomorrow around 10? R x

It was a lovely message to wake up to and makes my day start on a good note. Quickly typing him a reply, I hear the shower in the bathroom and realise just how desperately I need a wee. I wonder how long I could hold it for? I strain my ears to try work out what Rosie is singing. She has a whole shower routine you see, right down to the playlist she belts out and right now, if my calculations are correct, she's just about ready for getting out.

As I lock my screen I notice the time. It's just after 9am. Shit.

I jump out of bed and bang on the bathroom door, crossing my legs and doing a jig. The noise the shower is making is going to finish me off.

"Come on Scary Spice, I need a wee and Ryan will be here soon!" I bang again just to get my point across. I'm going to be so late.

"Okay, jeez, I think you're Scary Spice today." Rosie comes swanning out of the bathroom, wrapped in towels and followed by a cloud of steam. It's like a sauna. I've always said she has her showers too hot.

There's no time to wash my hair so I decide on a simple look today. Leggings, a nice long vest, high ponytail and minimal makeup. It's the only way I'll be ready in time.

40 minutes later, a new record has been made.

"Well normally I'd say you should make more of an effort but to be honest, you look gorgeous like that. What foundation are you wearing today?"

"A ten hour sleep effect one, the natural look was all I had time for. You sure I look okay? I mean I know I'm going to be pretty much surrounded by gay men, and Ryan knows I scrub up well, but I still want to look.....alive?" I brush myself down as I analyse my appearance in the mirror. I'm sure I look perfectly acceptable for a daytime date, and back home this is my every day wear, but something about Ryan just makes me want to be more. I look forward to seeing his reaction when he first sees me, I enjoy the look of appreciation on his face as he moves his eyes up and down my body with pure lust and need. I may also put a little extra wiggle in my step when I know he's watching.

"You look perfect. Now go on, get

yourself out there with that guy who is clearly nuts about you, but make sure you bring me back a gay BFF and plenty of cookies you hear me?"

I laugh nervously as I grab my bag and head out of the door.

"Will do. Love you."

"Love you too Lex!" She shouts back as I close the door and take a deep breath.

Castro is everything I hoped it would be and more. Rainbow flags hang from shops, lampposts and houses, everyone has smiles on their face as they strut around holding hands with their other half, and when I walk into one boutique shop, Liza Minnelli is blasting out of the speakers. I never dreamt that it could possibly be just as cliché as I had hoped. Of course to be fair there are a lot of humble, discreet shops but I'm so glad I got to see some wacky things too. The only thing I'm truly sad about is that I missed the parade in June because let's face it ladies, who doesn't love to see half naked men shaking their tail feathers down the street with pride?

Of course, I've also heard reports that Castro houses a few of San Francisco's best eateries so colour me happy, you can always guarantee a smile from me when I'm getting fed.

"So, how are you liking Castro?" Ryan

brings me back out of my daydream of a land of eternal food, wouldn't that be amazing?

"I love it!" I gush, giving him my cheesiest grin as we approach the infamous Castro Theatre. Never one to miss a photo opportunity I pull out my camera and snap away. The building is so far beyond magnificent that no words will ever do it justice, I snap it from every angle possible, even risking life and limb to cross the road to get it from the front, much to Ryan's amusement. Mid snap I lower my camera as a wave of desperation comes over me. Tonight, the Castro Theatre is showing Fiddler on the Roof, one of my all-time favourite musicals that Rosie and I used to watch over and over again growing up. I can't believe we could watch it in such an iconic place tonight.

"Hey, earth to Lexi. You ok?"

"Fiddler on the Roof," I say, clutching his arm. Of course I expect him to be a mind reader.

"You like Fiddler on the Roof?" He guesses.

"I love it! Rosie and I know every single word to every single song. I can't believe they're showing it here tonight! I wonder if we could get tickets? Oh God Ryan, I can't not see it." I have to tell Rosie, we have to come back for this. Failure is not an option.

"Well then, tonight Cinderella, you shall go to the…..really old theatre. Excuse me ma'am, would you mind taking our picture with the theatre behind us?" Before I have time to process what he's said, he's prized my beloved camera from my grasp and has handed it to a lovely old lady with a very brave blue rinse. Rock on sister.

As he pulls me closer, we both give our best photograph pose, although I think maybe I'm showing more teeth than is acceptable, but when you've just realised you'll be able to see one of your favourite musical films in a classic theatre, and you're pulled close to a man who could give Matt Bomer a run for his money, what else is there to do?

"Thank you." He takes the camera from her and flicks onto the picture of us both, our first picture together. When I take a closer look I hardly recognise the person before me, I'm positively glowing.

"You're very welcome, such a lovely couple." As blue rinse smiles at us, I feel my heart rate speed up. Could we become a couple? We obviously look like one. And that picture certainly screams lovebirds. Is it wrong that I'm hearing the bridal march in my head? It is, isn't it?

"Thank you," I murmur as I take my camera back. "And you Mr, it's a good job I didn't mind you handing my camera over to a random stranger isn't it?"

"She's old, she wouldn't have got very far. Anyway, it's a great picture, surely it was worth it? Something for you to remember me by when you get back home." He gives me an adorably sad smile and I feel a pang of guilt.

"Come on, where are these cookies at, mama needs some sugar."

"Sweet mother of mercy that is good," I groan in pleasure. With a mouth full of naughty I am in the ultimate happy place. Ryan is a God.

"I told you didn't I, trust me and I will take you to places you could never even imagine."

And boy has he.

Hot Cookies sits right on Castro Street, just seconds away from the theatre, and as soon as Ryan came to a stop outside the small shop front I knew I was going to love it here. The selection of cookies was out of this world, but it's not just that, above the counter were a collection of risqué photographs of men and women sporting the bright red Hot Cookie Y-fronts that also hung above our heads. Hopefully they were different Y-fronts or that would be pretty unhygienic. This is without a doubt the coolest cookie shop I have ever had the pleasure of visiting. Absolutely brilliant.

I've just eaten my third snickerdoodle cookie and am about to make myself sick with a fourth when I think of Rosie. I mean, I did buy her a pound of white chocolate cookies and an edible penis shaped macaroon but if I don't save her snickerdoodle, then her wrath will be pretty scary.

Of course Ryan found it highly amusing when I bought a chocolate covered penis – insert crude joke here, he did – but it screamed Rosie.

"You want half of my double choc chip? I'm all cookied out." As he lays back against the car seat, he pats his stomach in satisfaction and lets out an almighty burp that I swear shakes the car.

Okay, so maybe it didn't shake the car, but it was so loud it left me speechless.

"Absolute pig. But yes, yes I would." I take his cookie and happily munch away as I people watch. There really are some fascinating sights here. My ultimate favourite so far has to be the guy that's just walked past us wearing a bright yellow t-shirt on with 'I'm the pink sheep of the family' emblazoned proudly across his chest. Along with a pink sheep, obviously. God bless America.

"What you thinking?" Ryan asks as he turns his body so that he's facing me, giving me his undivided attention.

"I'm not going back home next week." There, I've said it. My secret is out.

I daren't look at him so carry on staring out of the window at a lovely gay couple that are approaching us, stopping every now and again to look in the many shop windows. I say lovely, more interesting. One half of the couple looks like a middle aged, kind of on the chubby side, book wormish man, while the other has a pair of skin tight leather trousers on and his hair spiked up into scary looking multi-coloured points. Definite polar opposites but none the less, they are holding hands and chatting away happily to each other, blissfully unaware that a fascinated English girl is staring at them. I know I shouldn't, and I know it's rude – my mother would probably wag her finger at me – but I can't help myself. It makes me want what they have. Not multicolored hair of course, but the unconditional love and soul mate to share your life with. No judging, no criticizing, just love.

"Where are you going then, back up to Yorkshire?"

Men. Such simple creatures.

"No, I mean I'm not boarding the plane with Rosie next Tuesday."

"Wow. I mean, are you staying in San Francisco? Because that would be brilliant! When did you decide this?" His eyes shine as he bites his lip and smiles.

"I am, and the day I booked the flight. I haven't even told Rosie yet either which makes me a very bad friend and a very cowardly one too. I've had so many chances to tell her but I just couldn't find the right moment. I keep clamming up. This is probably the first time in my life that I don't have a plan in my head. I am literally winging it. What am I going to do?" I search his eyes for an answer but all that happens is my stomach somersaults and I kiss him. I am so weak.

He laughs as we finally come up for air.

"Wow. Again. Keep kissing me like that and I'll never let you leave. But I do think you need to let Rosie know, she's your best friend isn't she? Surely she'll understand. And being really spontaneous every now and again is a good thing, trust me, I should know. Look where it got me."

He has a point. He upped and left England on a whim all those years ago and now he's happily settled here in the most amazing city I have ever been to.

"I don't even know where I'll stay once she goes. I wonder how cold it would be under the Golden Gate Bridge on a night?" This is the major stumbling point in my master plan. Where will I lay my head at such short notice? San Francisco is notoriously expensive and getting a last minute room when you can't even tell them when you're likely to be checking out just screams weirdo.

"Don't worry about that, you can always stay with James and I." He looks at me like it's the most obvious answer in the world. He doesn't realise that it is basically like moving in with someone after only a week of knowing them. That doesn't happen in the real world. But then again, in the real world do people just book one way tickets to America after a bad break up and the loss of a job and not tell their friends or family? My guess would be no. Most people would call this a cry for help and say that I should go see a therapist or something. It would probably work out cheaper.

Now I'm saying what I've done out loud, I realise how crazy an idea it was. Who was I kidding? I should just go back to the motel and book myself on the same flight as Rosie and nobody would ever know any different. Except I don't think I want to. Confused? You will be.

"Okay, well I have a really good friend who has a house that's just sitting there empty at the moment. He has no plans to move into it any time soon and I know he'd rather it go to a good cause than stay empty so what about checking that out?" He must have seen the look of horror on my face when he suggested living with him and thought better of it. I don't really want to get to know his bad habits so soon in the relationship.

"How good a friend? And why is this house empty? No offence but I've seen some of the houses in the less than affluent areas shall we say and I do not want to get shot."

"Firstly, San Francisco is one of the safest cities in the world for women – fact. Secondly, he is a very, very good friend who would want you to stay there as long as you needed to. Thirdly, you will not get shot unless you seriously piss a member of the Triad off, and even then I think that would be extreme. This house is in Buena Vista, one of the nicest areas in San Francisco, and to give you an idea of how nice the house is, it not only has a gym, an office and a rooftop terrace, but it has a library as well so can you at least have a look before you rule it out?"

Holy fudge cake.

"Ryan I'll never be able to afford to pay him anything like what he'll need for the mortgage for that!"

"Rent free." And it's as simple as that. There's no, it's okay I'll check with him how much he'd want, or, we'll have a chat with him and see what he thinks. Just two words. Rent. Free.

Now you would think I would be jumping for joy at the thought of this, but it seems too good to be true.

"What's the catch?" I narrow my eyes and study him carefully. There has to be something. His friend is probably an ogre who wants to be able to call on me on a whim to accompany him to functions, I'll become an escort girl just to pay for a roof over my head. The thought makes me shiver.

"No catch. I can speak for him and he insists you have it. If you like it of course."

"Can you at least check with him first?" I sigh. The last thing I want it to be thrown out on my ear when he suddenly decides he's coming home in a few weeks' time or something.

"Fine, I will call him later."

"Why not now?"

"Because he'll be busy." Starting the engine he glances at me and gives me a wink. "Just promise me one thing though, that you'll tell Rosie? Then at least she gets the chance to see where you'll be living, she'll feel included and involved. And you're probably overthinking it, she'll probably be absolutely ecstatic for you."

I hadn't thought of that. Why is it that men can be so simple at times and yet have moments of wisdom like this? So I make a promise in readiness for my deal with the devil. I will tell Rosie. I will tell her tomorrow.

As I clear my head of Rosie, another thought hits me. This is our official second date. Our next date is the big three. THE date. I may be being presumptuous here but it doesn't stop my mind reeling. Be still my beating heart. I can't contain my glee and as I think of a naked Ryan, my smile practically splits my face in half.

CHAPTER SIXTEEN

Today is the day I tell Rosie. At least that's my plan. I really hope she takes it well.

We had such a good time last night watching Fiddler on the Roof in Castro with James and Ryan. Drinks afterwards were as fabulous as you would expect them to be and Rosie succeeded in making a gay BFF when she insisted on dancing on the tables in a karaoke bar, despite there being somebody else on stage with a mic at the time. The men in there actually bowed down before her, I was suitably impressed. Well, I say all of them…all of them except the drag queen that was on stage at the time of her little performance. Rita Teeta and her sidekick Glitter Puss were not amused, they wanted to get their Gaga on and she ruined it with her Katy Perry medley. I feel I should tell you that at this point that she didn't have a clue what the lyrics were. She free styled.

I giggle as the memories of Ryan's face come flooding back. He looked genuinely terrified. He got chatted up a lot last night. He started off loving it, lapping up the attention, until one of them grabbed his bum. As we all struggled to breathe from laughing, he took his bat home and sulked for a while until I convinced him that all he had to do was stand a little bit closer to me. James however, James was on his own. Rosie was having too much fun to care about how many men hit on him.

"What's so funny?" Rosie looks at me from above her huge sunglasses. Today is a girls only day and I've suggested a walk to the pier so that we can get a ferry across to Sausalito. Neither of us fancied driving today after last night's antics so going over the bridge was a no go unless she gave up her fight against the bicycle ride across it.

"I'm just thinking about last night. I had so much fun, thank you."

"You're welcome. You should know by now that you'll always have an awesome time with me. Franco text me earlier as well saying how utterly *faaaabulous* he thought I was and that he's adding me on Facebook." Scrolling through her phone Rosie shows me a picture of them, faces squished together with identical perfect pouts. They do look fabulous. She shows me a couple more pictures that I don't remember being taken and then one of Ryan and I. I love that I'm going to have the chance to get to know him better now that I'm staying longer, but I wonder how much I'll miss home. Or more Mr Beefy, Rosie and Jason. And possibly Luke.

"You'll have to send me those, I love them."

"You should do, you two look gorgeous together. Oh imagine your kids. They would be so stunning it would make me ill," she chuckles at me as I frown back at her. "Just kidding. But seriously, super cute. What will you do when we leave, I mean, you'll stay in touch won't you? Maybe he'll move back to the UK?"

It's now or never. I make sure we've crossed the busy road before I tell her. Just in case.

"I kind of have a confession. You're not going to be happy, in fact I think you'll be pretty pissed but I hope you understand why I did it." I chew desperately on my lip and sense her coming to a stop next to me.

"Lex, what have you done?" Her voice is dangerously calm. I man up and turn around.

"I'm not coming back with you on Tuesday. I only booked a one way flight." I look at my feet as I feel a lump start to rise in my throat.

I hear her laughing and look up in shock, tears forgotten.

"Good one! You had me going for a second there. You'd never leave Mr Beefy for longer than you had to, come on, give me some credit." Linking my arm she drags me further down the road and back on track. I could just laugh with her, but that would be wrong. So I pull us to a stop and take a deep breath.

"I'm serious Rosie. I'm not coming back with you. I know I should have told you when I booked my flight but, I didn't want you to try and talk me out of it and then the longer I left it, the worse I felt about not telling you."

The look in her eyes tell me she knows I'm serious this time, and the fact she storms off ahead of me tells me I'm in for a treat of a day.

The walk to the pier and the ferry trip across to Sausalito were spent in silence. I avoided her on the trip across because she knows I'm not a strong swimmer. Better to be safe than sorry.

I cautiously approach her as we wade our way through the small crowd of people and pull my cardigan tight to block out the cool September breeze that's already nipping away at my face. San Francisco is an amazing place but dear God when it's cold, it is cold.

She still doesn't talk but sits down on the same bench the old couple were sat on when I came with Ryan, so I follow her lead.

"You'll come back won't you? I mean, you'll only be out here like what, three months max yeah?" Rosie stares out at the sea and a pang of sadness hits me. We've never been apart for this long. I know Skype is a wonderful thing and I'm sure I'll abuse the wifi in the house profusely but, nothing will be the same as having my best friend by my side.

"Yeah of course I will, I mean what else could I do out here? Let's face it, who's going to give me a visa?" I laugh, nudging her a little.

"And anyway, who knows, it might not even be three months, I might decide after another few weeks that it's time to come home."

She smiles at me sadly and I see her eyes start to water.

"You have to take chances in life, I know that. You needed to do something drastic but I just expected maybe a haircut or career change, not a possible emigration." She takes my hand and gives it a gentle squeeze and we sit for who knows how long just watching the world pass us by. Thankfully, the dogs of Sausalito have decided my leg isn't attractive enough for them today so we're left alone in our own thoughts, contemplating our lives without each other temporarily. It's something I can't even begin to imagine.

Taking me by surprise she pulls me into a tight hug and I wonder how long I can stand it before she crushes a rib. I want to wince in pain but it might spoil the moment.

"Well, I'm just glad you have James and Ryan here to look out for you. They're both good guys, I know you'll be fine. And hey, maybe you can explore the possibility of 'more' with Ryan now? It seems a bit more realistic if you're staying. I bet he'll be over the moon when you tell him you're not leaving." Popping a Lifesaver - or a Fruit Polo if like me you just have issues adjusting, yeah Starburst I'm talking about you - into her mouth she gestures animatedly. "Oooo when will you tell him? James said he's pretty smitten with you!" She prods me cheekily. She'll be doing more than a friendly prod if she finds out he knew before her. I'm thinking definitely a nudge overboard if we take the ferry back again.

"Well that's always nice to hear," I laugh weakly.

"James thinks you're a sweetheart too. I mean I told him of course you are, you're my best friend in the whole world."

Dear Lord make her stop. The guilt is eating away at me. I wonder if she knows he knows, she has got weird mind reading abilities at times.

"Again, always nice to hear." As she offers me a Lifesaver I take one for the sole reason that it might make her stop talking to me. I don't fare well with fruity sweets and speech. One word - drool.

"So, this is the place you got violated by a dog," she cackles. And just like that, my Rosie returns, the sombre mood has lifted and so has the weight from my chest. I mean in the grand scheme of things, three months out of forever isn't that long is it? Really? It will be fine I'm sure. Eeek.

Did you tell her yet. R x

yeah, i told her this morning before i took her to sausalito.
Public place meant less chance of murder xxx

Such bravery. Do you still want to look at the house tomorrow? X

Please, if your friend doesn't mind? Don't tell rosie you knew first though pls, it would kill her, and she would kill me. Xxx

Again, so brave x

I'm not hurting her feelings Ryan.

Fair enough, and of course its fine, my friend has given me the keys x

Thank you xxx

Oh, did she like her cookie? ;) x

She did, and i'll show you just how much......xx

I quickly find the pictures that I took of her last night as I handed her the bag of goodies. As soon as she saw the penis one she demanded I take her picture with it, so in true Rosie style she posed in various positions, some hilarious, some enough to make a hooker blush. I send him a tamer one where she's holding it up against her skirt like a ladyboy. Classy bird is my Rosie.

Oh my. How old is she again? X

Old enough to know better, young enough not to care! But that is nothing, there are some seriously x-rated ones on my phone. Xxx

Remind me to look through your phone tomorrow then lol x

Filth! Xxx

You have no idea ;) x

Checking my watch I try to work out the time back home. Rosie decided we should call in to see Ryan and James on the way back to the motel to let them know the good news. I'm not sure if it was a test but I think I passed with flying colours. Ryan had played dumb as promised, and I don't know whether or not he had told James but he looked suitably surprised too when Rosie blurted out that I was staying in San Francisco for the foreseeable future. All of this happened before we had actually crossed the threshold.

I stare across the living area at Rosie and Ryan in the kitchen, cups of coffee in hand, conversation flowing happily. I smile to myself at the scene. Rosie couldn't even stand to be in the same room as Walker for longer than an hour before she excused herself and found someone with more personality to talk to. Her words not mine. She would usually end up sat next to Mr Beefy holding quite a conversation with him. Apparently they shared the same love of take outs and long walks in the park. Again, her words not mine. No wonder Jason used to be jealous of him, he is quite a ladies man is my little boy.

As I turn my gaze, I watch the sun blaze out over the city. The view from this apartment never gets old. Sighing inwardly I decide that it's now or never. I need to make the call back home to my parents.

"Hey, do you guys mind if I just make a quick Skype call back home before we eat? I think I should let mum and dad know that I won't be coming to see them any time soon."

"Sure go ahead. James has just gone to pick up pizza, my iPad is in my bag if you want it?" Rosie shuffles across to me while trying to dig deep in her large, battered cream satchel. That thing goes everywhere with her, she must have had it about five years now and it only cost her £20 in the sale from Topshop. Talk about value for money. "Here." She thrusts her shiny white iPad into my hand and heads back over to Ryan.

Walking over to the balcony I start to open up Skype but decide maybe Facetime would be better, mum knows how to use that on her phone. I swallow nervously as I wait for the call to connect, praying they won't be in the middle of a film or having an early night. You just never can tell with my folks.

"Hello?" I hear my mum's voice ring out from the screen before I see her.

"Mum, it's me, just give it a second to connect."

"Brian, Brian get over here it's Lexi! She's calling from America so hurry up, we don't want it costing her too much money." I smile at my mum's panicked voice. I think about trying to explain that the call is actually free because I'm using wifi but decide against it. It's more of a headache than it's worth. As the screen flickers I see them both with their heads squashed together trying to make sure they fit in the screen. I love them so much.

"Hi guys! I haven't disturbed you have I?"

"No, no of course not. I was only knitting and your dad was watching some nonsense on the television." My mum purses her lips and it makes me smile.

"It's not nonsense, it's the new Hawaii 5-0, have you seen it love?"

"Oh I have, yes. I didn't realise it was back on, is it a new series?" I don't tell them that I only started watching it for the eye candy, I think my dad probably has an idea and is secretly pleased that I haven't told mum just how hot Steve and Danno are these days.

"No, no, love, just repeats. So, how's America? Are you looking after yourself? Do you have enough money? Are you taking lots of photographs for us?" My dad and I have always been very similar, not that I was really a daddy's girl growing up, but I think that's where I got my creative flare from. I look a lot like my mum but have a lot of my dad's personality, best of both worlds I've always said.

"It's great, you guys would love it here, honestly. I'll email you some pictures tomorrow." That statement is aimed at my mum. She is a whizz on the laptop, phone not so much, but her laptop is like another child to her.

"Why don't you just bring them up when you get home? It would be lovely to see you, especially after recent events. Come and have a week or two up here, clear your head before you head back to the big smoke." My mum, ever the optimist that I'll move back to Yorkshire. I look at her hopeful blue eyes and it breaks my heart. How am I going to last out here without my best friends and family so close. Shaking my head I try to control my errant thoughts. I'll cope the same way I always have. The same way I coped when I moved down to Uni. I'll just adjust. Keep myself occupied.

"Yeah, about that," I glance over my shoulder and catch Ryan's eye as he smiles warmly at me. "I'm not coming back with Rosie. I'm staying out here for another couple of months, just to spend some time doing the things I love and taking time for me. I thought you should know." I stare back at the screen, unsure whether it's frozen or whether my parents are just in shock. A good 30 seconds pass before my dad speaks up.

The screen wasn't frozen.

"Are you sure that's what you want love, will you be okay for money? Where will you stay?"

"I'm sure dad. Money is okay at the moment, I have enough to keep me going and I'm going to look at a house tomorrow with Rosie and one of our friends, Ryan. His friend has a house that I can stay in rent free so if it's nice then that's where I'll stay. The last month has been……" I search for a word that I can say in front of my parents – not easy. "It's been tough, and it's made me think, you never know what's around the corner and sometimes you have to take a leap of faith. I need to do this, and hey, San Francisco isn't too dissimilar from Yorkshire, lots of greenery!" I try to make a joke but it falls flat. My poor parents are clearly in shock.

"Well, you know where we are if you need us. I think I speak for both of us when I say we're obviously disappointed that you're not going to be back in the UK in time for your birthday, especially such a milestone, but by the same token, you will be 30. You're a grown woman and you have your own life to lead. If you need anything, and I mean anything, you'll call us right? Day or night?"

"I promise dad. Mum, are you okay?" She's disappeared from my screen and I can hear soft sobs. I never even imagined they'd be upset, angry maybe, but not upset. I've been away from home for so long now that I just thought they'd be accustomed to it by now.

As she pops her head back into view her eyes are rimmed red.

"I'll be fine darling," she snivels unconvincingly. "It's just a shock that's all. Are you sure the house will be safe? Are you sure your friends are okay?"

"You can meet one of them now if you

like? He's here." Both parents nod eagerly and grin back at me. Rolling my eyes, I step back inside from the balcony and walk over to Ryan. Hmmm, where is James, my stomach is starting to growl. Holding the iPad out to my side at arm's length, away from earshot, I wave him over. "Would you mind saying a quick hi to my mum and dad, just so they know you're not an axe murderer?"

His eyebrows shoot that far up they practically meet his hairline. "Meet your parents?"

"No, well yes, look can you just say hi? It's not like I'm asking you to meet them as my boyfriend or anything," I hiss back at him. "I need them to know I'll be okay here on my own."

Reluctantly, he admits defeat and I bring the iPad back in front of us with Rosie hopping around in the background clapping her hands.

"Mum, dad, this is Ryan." He waves awkwardly and gives them a million dollar smile.

"Hi Mr and Mrs Jones."

"Oh Brian and Elaine, please!" My mum gushes with a schoolgirl giggle, her cheeks turning pink. My jaw drops at her shocking behaviour.

"Nice to meet you Ryan." My dad nods gruffly, shooting my mum the death stare. Oops.

"So, as you can see, Ryan is a nice, normal

young man. He's lived here for five years too so knows the city like the back of his hand. I'm in safe hands with him, I promise." I beam at Ryan and he gives me a glorious, butterfly inducing smile in return. My mum's gasp makes my head snap back to the screen. "What?" I question, confused.

"I'll leave you to it," Ryan whispers. "Lovely to…..see you? Hopefully we'll speak again soon." And with that he retreats to the other side of the kitchen counter. Talk about a rat abandoning a sinking ship.

"Hi Elaine!! Hi Brian!!" Rosie leaps in next to me and waves at my parents. I frown at her as she starts talking animatedly and takes the iPad from my hands. Thankful for the break, I take a seat in front of Ryan in the kitchen.

"I think my mum fancies you," I say in disgust.

"Of course she does, she's human."

Shaking my head, I can't help but grin at him again. I've been doing a lot of that lately and I have no idea where this sudden tooth flashing habit has come from but at this rate I'll be needing to whiten the suckers if I'm going to be constantly flashing them at everyone. Or maybe it's just Ryan that makes me want to grin. He leans forward on the counter, resting his beautifully tanned forearms out before him and spins the cup of coffee around slowly, suddenly lost in thought. I'm about to ask what's wrong when James bounds through the door with a stack of pizza boxes and a carrier bag with what I can only hope is chips and not salad.

I see Rosie's head spin around as the smell fills the room and I know that she'll be handing my parents back to me.

"Oh, I'm so sorry, James has just come back with the food. Yeah sure, say hi James." She spins the iPad around onto a startled James who has no idea who he's saying hi to, let alone why, but he plays along and even throws in a small wave himself. "Okay, well, bye!"

Thrusting my parents back into my hands, I decide it's time to wrap this call up before she eats my share of the food.

"So, that's Ryan and James." I don't really know what else to say as I look back at their shell-shocked faces.

"They look nice. Ryan is madly in love with you though." My mum smiles back at me smugly, like she's just answered the winning question on a gameshow.

"I'm sure he isn't mum. But they are both nice, very nice, and I know they'll look after me."

"Well, if you'll be staying anywhere half as nice as that place then I'm sure we've nothing to worry about. Rosie took us for a quick tour. That is some view."

"I know, this is Ryan's apartment, James lives here too. They're brothers!" I add quickly as I see my dad's eyes widen. I don't want him thinking that I'm about to become a third member of a gay relationship. I've never been into 'open relationships', I like to know where my man has been and I'm just too selfish to share.

"Oh, well, that's okay then. Stick with them kid and I think you'll be fine," he winks.

"Thank you dad. I'd better go, you know what Rosie is like when there's food about. Speak to you soon though, when it's a bit less chaotic. I just wanted to let you know the situation so you didn't expect me back on English soil Tuesday."

"Well, as long as you keep in touch then we'll be okay, won't we Elaine?"

"We will. Look after yourself my darling, I love you." As she blows a kiss at me I feel a lump start to rise in my throat. I have been so lucky to have such loving, caring, supportive parents all these years.

"I love you too mum. Love you dad."

"Love you too Lexi. Stay safe," my dad smiles back at me and has to be the one to end the call. He knows what my mum and I are like when we don't want to be the first to hang up. It really could go on forever. As the screen goes black, I sniff back some tears and focus on the food. One step at a time, and right now, there is a slice of pepperoni and mushroom with my name on it.

CHAPTER SEVENTEEN

The first thing I notice as I begin to stir is the aroma of coffee filling the air, then I realise that I'm a little bit warmer than usual. Sticking my toes out from under the cover to assess the temperature outside of my cosy haven, I feel a wall. A wall that I haven't felt before. Opening my eyes I remember that Rosie and I agreed to spend the night at the apartment, a combination of laziness and, well just laziness to be honest, took over and knowing how cold the previous nights had been walking the streets of San Francisco, we took them up on their very kind offer of a spare room. Each. I don't know what Rosie's room is like but I'm tempted to ask if I can just move in here now, I'm fairly sure I could have this as a little granny flat and not have to ever disturb anyone.

As I pad across the bedroom, my feet sinking into the delicious thick pile of cream carpet, I wonder which one of the men are up already. Ryan strikes me as more of an early bird than James. I know that I'm usually the early bird out of Rosie and I, although she has put me to shame on this trip.

Picking up yesterday's clothes from the grey suede chair in the corner, I run my fingers through my hair in an attempt to make myself look a bit more human. I'm not entirely sure it will make up for my panda eyes and morning breath but it's worth a shot.

I hear the dulcet tones of his voice before I see him and it gives me a warm fuzzy feeling inside. So Ryan is a Sinatra fan? Another thing to add to his list of qualities.

"Morning," I smile sheepishly, really wishing that I at least had some facewipes with me. I don't fare well with other people's facewash, ridiculously sensitive skin you see, so panda eyes won. The shame.

"Morning. Coffee?" I nod as he pours me a steaming cup full of brown heaven, not even needing to ask how I take it. He just knows. "Did you sleep well?"

"Yeah, really well thanks. I don't think I've ever slept in a bed as comfortable in my life, and those pillows....wow." I get gooey eyed just thinking about them. I hope the new house has the same ones because nothing will ever live up to the ones here. I've been spoilt.

Ryan chuckles as I take a seat at the breakfast counter, last night's pizza boxes sit before me and turn my stomach. The smell of stale garlic bread is pungent. Reading my mind, and probably my face, Ryan moves the boxes and places them on top of the bin. I'd rather have them in the bin but as long as they're out from underneath my nose then I'm happy.

"So, what time do you want to hit the

house today? I'm guessing you want to go back to the motel and get yourselves sorted first?"

"What, you mean the panda look isn't one you think will catch on?" I laugh so he knows that I'm teasing. "I think I definitely need to address my face and change my clothes, but around lunchtime would be good if you're not too busy?" I take a tentative sip of the coffee and sigh contently.

"Sounds good. I don't know what James is doing today, he mentioned a meeting with someone so he might not be around but Rosie will still be coming I assume?"

"Yup, she wants to make sure there's enough room for her to stay if she comes over in the next couple of months. How long has your friend had the house then? I can't imagine owning somewhere here and not living in it, where else is as amazing as San Francisco?" It really does baffle me. I have a sneaky feeling that the day I have to go back to England I will be heartbroken and security will have to force me through the gates at the airport kicking and screaming.

"Only a year or so. When he bought it he was thinking ahead, that it would be a lovely family home one day but sometimes the best laid plans don't work out. He still has the same dreams for it though, to one day settle down with the right person there, maybe raise a family, or a pet. I really hope you like it; I'm excited to show you around the place."

Raise a pet, how sweet! He sounds like a catch to me, but I don't voice that opinion, we all know how sensitive men can be.

"I'm sure I will." Our eyes meet across the rims of our cups, his soft green eyes sparkling with excitement that I can't help mirroring, and even though we both know I must have the worst morning/coffee breath, he leans in and gives me a knee trembling kiss. A girl could seriously get used to this.

As the car pulls up against the kerb, I gaze at the houses that line the street. They all look so similar yet so different, it's hard to get my head around. The old, faint grey Victorian style houses sit neatly side by side, lining a quiet suburban street that is opposite what looks to be some type of park, and by park I don't mean two sets of swings, a slide and a rickety roundabout.....or a glorified garden. I'm talking a place to go for a run, walk your dog and possibly get lost for a month kind of park. The trees blow in the mild breeze as the amber leaves hit the windscreen gently. I feel like I've stepped onto the set of a film, or at the very least a soap opera.

"Welcome to Buena Vista," Ryan holds his arms open as I slowly shut the car door and Rosie bounds out to stand beside me.

"Holy crap this place is gorgeous! What's that?" She nods to the park as two young women jog past us, iPods attached to their waists, earphones firmly lodged in their ears. Bouncing up and down on her tiptoes Rosie is like a puppy waiting for a treat, I wish I had a cookie or two just to shut her up. My stomach feels like the North Sea as lick my lips, all of a sudden I feel quite sick.

"It's a park?" He looks at Rosie frowning in confusion. "Come on, have a look at your new home." Ryan gives me a dazzling smile and takes my hand, pulling me up the stairs to the dark wooden door.

Shit just got real folks.

Stepping through the front door and into the foyer feels like when you walk into a hotel for the first time on holiday. Rosie's heels clack behind me and I wince, the laminate floor surely can't take her five inch heels. Luckily, she must realise and slips them off quietly as I take in my new surroundings. A stairway to my left, a doorway to a closet to my right, and as I take a tentative step forward, I peep through another door leading to a small den looking out onto the street. What looks like an old Indian rug spans the whole of the room, covering the laminate giving it a more homey feel, and a soft grey material sofa sits facing out of the bay window. A dark wood floor to ceiling bookcase covers the far wall and I instantly begin to imagine myself sat here getting lost in an old Dickens classic or the latest New York Times best seller. I'm lost in my own imagination and I haven't even passed through the entrance hall yet.

As Rosie tugs gently on my hand, we follow Ryan down the hall, past a large dark wood mirror that sits above a bureau with an open notebook and pen placed carefully atop. My curiosity is piqued instantly but I don't get the chance to stop and have a flick through. Hmmm, that's certainly going to be something I have a look at when I move in. I really am quite nosey, but then again, you don't leave something lying open for strangers to read if it's personal.....even if it is in your own house.

"This is obviously the main living space on this floor." Ryan gives us a small twirl as my jaw drops. The open plan living area is enormous. You could hold a dinner party for 30 guests and still not feel like you were a sardine. It is incredible. The neutral shades are thankfully a constant theme which means that Ryan's friend obviously has good taste. I scoff a little as I imagine anyone buying a house like this without taste, it just wouldn't happen. This is a very classy establishment. Walker can stick his London detached, San Francisco is where all the good stuff lives.

I count three more windows, all with street views, and you'd think this would be a problem but the street is just as picturesque as everywhere else I've seen in this city. I mean, I'm facing a park for God's sake, how bad can that be?

I walk towards the kitchen door just off of the dining space and smile. A splash of colour has managed to work its way into this room. Small red tiles line the cream walls and sit above the sleek black kitchen work surfaces; I really couldn't have designed it better myself. If someone had taken what I thought was my ideal home from my head and stood me in front of it, the kitchen would be identical. The rest, well, even my imagination isn't good enough to come up with something as good as this.

"This is all.....Ryan it's amazing. Are you sure your friend wouldn't mind me living here? I mean, why is he not living here now? Is he nuts?" Rosie has been silent for the full duration and I know she's thinking the same thing that I am. How the hell have I landed myself this place? What's the catch?

"He travels a lot, and I told you, he would love you to live here and make it feel like your home for as long as you want or need it. And you haven't even seen the best bits yet." His eyes twinkle like a child's at Christmas and as he puts his hands on both of my arms, he spins me around and I gasp. This house has an elevator. A true to life, Charlie and the Chocolate Factory ain't got nothing on this, glass elevator.

"Whoa. Where does it go, where does it

go?!" Rosie can barely contain her excitement now as she jabs at the button without an invite. I feel like my head is stuck in the middle of a cloud, that's the only way I can describe the daze that I'm walking around in. They say tea with a lot of sugar is good for shock, maybe I should ask Ryan to make me one before I go any -

"Ouch, stop shoving!" I snap. Looks like I don't have a choice in the matter now, further through the looking glass I go.

"Oh stop being a baby. So, how many floors are we talking then Ryan? It didn't look this big from outside." Slowly we move up to the next level.

"It has four. A lower level and three main floors. Okay, so this floor," he points ahead. "Over there you have a bedroom but it doesn't have a bed in at the moment, it's the only bedroom that doesn't but he wasn't sure whether to convert it into a proper library so it's an empty room. Through here," he pushes open a door to our left, "is another bedroom with a connecting bathroom."

"Connecting? Connecting where?" Rosie's scampers through and laughs. "Oh my God, another bedroom, this house is like freakin' Narnia! I don't know about you Lex but maybe I'll just accidentally on purpose miss my flight home tomorrow." I laugh as she opens up the cupboards in the bathroom, the third bedroom long forgotten. She always has had a fascination with what people keep in their bathroom cabinets. Mine houses boring things like Veet, Bodyform and my shower cap. All the essentials, obviously.

"You haven't even seen the master suite yet." A mischievous smile crosses his face as he takes my hand and crosses the landing. "Prepare to be amazed."

As he opens the door I have to grab on to the doorframe. My knees go weak and I have to take a few deep cleansing breaths. I hear Rosie begin to giggle hysterically beside me and it catches. Before I know what's happening we're both laughing like escaped lunatics at the world's largest walk in wardrobe. I run in and have my Carrie moment. Is Ryan my Mr Big? It sure feels like it. Just the fact I can actually run the length of the wardrobe tells you how big is it. The cream carpet feels like heaven beneath my bare feet. I kneel on the floor and start to open the empty drawers, imagining everything that I can fill them with and what I'd put where.

"You like?" Ryan asks, his tone a little more than amused at the two desperate women pulling at doors and checking drawers before him. I look up and somehow manage to gracefully jump up from my spot on the floor and throw myself around his neck, kissing him on every visible piece of skin. I may linger a little longer around the neck area, he smells like expensive aftershave and a very lovely soap powder. Is there any better smell? It's just so.......clean. I wonder if this is what insanity feels like? Should I be worried?

Placing me back on my feet, he nudges me forward through a door towards the end of the wardrobe - sigh - and I walk into the master suite. Master suite, who calls their main bedroom a master suite? Although one look and I fully appreciate why calling it a bedroom doesn't do it justice, hell, the hotel rooms I've stayed in would fit inside this room three times over. The walls are painted a soft taupe, and as I take a closer look at some of the artwork on the wall, I realise that they are all paintings of old San Francisco. All except one. I take a step closer and cock my head to the side as I try to work out why it looks so familiar. There's something haunting about the woman who sits in a doorway looking out at the world, her face looks tired, as though she longs to be out in the world that she can see from her step.

I run my finger delicately along the bottom of the frame. I wonder what she can see, what she wants to be a part of, what her life is like behind that closed door.

Rosie comes and rests her head on my shoulder, she doesn't say anything, she just stands with me looking at the woman in the picture. Finally Ryan breaks the silence.

"Andrew Wyeth is one of my favourite artists. I know a lot think he's quite depressing but I think his work just pulls you in and makes you think about stuff, makes you appreciate the life you have."

I think for a minute and the penny finally drops.

"Christina's World!! That's who this is isn't it?! I knew it looked familiar, I have a print of that back home......or had, did you pack it Rosie?"

"Um, no I didn't think. I was too busy packing his Rolex and suits. Sorry babe." She looks down at her feet, not meeting my eyes. She knows how much I loved that print. I mean ok so I could always order another, but still.

Shaking my head I decide it doesn't really matter now anyway, it's not like I'd have brought it out here with me.

"Don't worry about it."

"I can't believe you've heard of Andrew Wyeth. That's really surprised me I must admit. Well, this is actually Christina Olson, the inspiration behind Christina's World. She lost the use of her legs at a young age but instead of using a wheelchair, dragged herself around the land where she lived in a farmhouse with her brother. Apparently the torso and head in Christina's World belong to Wyeth's wife though, Christina was in her 50s at the time of that particular painting. I guess this picture gives a better impression of how she must have felt a lot of the time. Just sat looking out at the world she couldn't take an active part in anymore."

The more he talks, the more this picture upsets me. I swipe away a tear in the hope that neither of them has noticed. This poor woman has such strength to fight through the shitty deck of cards that she had been dealt, and instead of accepting a wheelchair, she fought to carry herself around, and here I am worried about my pathetic breakup and how much I'll miss my friend when she goes home tomorrow. This woman lost her legs and carried on. Come on Lexi, time to man up and get a hold of yourself.

"It's beautiful, and haunting, and thought provoking. I'm sure I'll spend hours staring at it when I move in." I smile, hopefully convincingly at Ryan. One glance at Rosie and I know she hasn't fallen for it, her eyes are narrowed and her mouth pursed. I silently plead with her not to say anything. And she doesn't. She leaves me be to get my thoughts back together as Ryan guides us back to the elevator and up to the top floor. The one where the gym lives. The one that I can't see me travelling up to a lot.

I'll be honest, I switch off for a lot of the top floor. The terrace is lovely and has amazing views of the city, but the rest of the floor is taken up by a gym, another mini kitchen and an office/living area. I'm fairly certain this floor will collect a lot of dust.

We take the stairs back down, just

because I feel like I should do them, and regret it when we finally reach the floor that we came in at. That staircase goes on forever.

"Keep going," Ryan encourages. "I'll show you the lower level really quickly because I'm fairly certain you'll like this a lot more than you did the gym."

He caught that then? Must remember to try and hide my feelings more from my face. My mum always said I had a terrible habit of letting my emotions show, especially when I was bored or pissed off.

As my bare feet hit a concrete floor, I immediately jump back onto the stairs and yelp. It's so cold.

"You big girl, are you staying on there or do you actually want to see the wine cellar?"

Rosie and I immediately snap our heads around to face one another. I feel mine snap in a way I didn't intend for it to but soldier through the pain like the martyr that I am. It's all for the greater good. All for the wine cellar. Eeek.

As we tiptoe around the corner I see it. A wine cellar that would rival a Frenchman's. Rosie is of course the first one to pounce on a bottle, cold feet forgotten. I'm a bit more tentative but spot what can only be described as a large material Lego piece sat in the corner, so make a run for it.

"I think that's meant to be used as a step Lex but go ahead, take a seat," Rosie teases playfully. I stick my tongue out and survey the 100s of bottles around me, curling my toes up in the hope that they don't drop off with frostbite. Okay, slight exaggeration but I'm worried that I can't feel anything on show. My nose, my toes....look at me being a poet.

"Pretty impressive collection here Ryan, what does your friend actually do? If I lived here I would never actually leave this place. And by this place, I literally mean this place. You could easily fit a bed here..." She trails off thoughtfully, sizing the place up.

"Well I'm sold on the house anyway, thank you so much Ryan, and please thank your friend too." I get to my feet, still stood on the giant Lego piece mind you.

"You like it? You're going to move in here?" He looks like a cat that's got the cream.

"Ryan, you had me at elevator." And with one last look around, I make a quick bolt for the stairs and hopefully, some heat.

CHAPTER EIGHTEEN

So, what have you boys got planned for us tonight? Something good i hope or prepare to suffer the wrath of roise xxx

Have we let you down yet? R x

I think about the last week or so and realise that every minute we've spent here has been spent doing something exciting, or at the very least it's been entertaining.

Well no that's true. But this is rosie's last night, i hope you're prepared xxx

Prepared? That sounds ominous. R x

It depends what she drinks or how much fun she has. She's a livewire is my rosie haha xxx

I'm sure we'll manage to keep her entertained. What about you, are you ok? Xxx

Hmmm, am I ok? So far I am, but I haven't waved her off yet at the airport. That is going to be a sobfest, I wonder if my mascara is waterproof, I never bother to check things like that.

I'm fine and as long as the house has good wifi i'll be fine. Thank you xxx

I'll make sure it does. And i'll be around every day to make sure you're ok, you can count on that. Pick you up at 8? Xxx

Sounds great xxx

I stare at his messages for a little while longer

than I probably should and smile. Having Ryan around every day is definitely something I could cope with.

"I can't believe you're leaving me tomorrow!" I pout in that way that only happens when a person is drunk. Or five years old. I'm not convinced it's my most attractive look but Ryan is smirking at me so I can't look that bad.

"I don't want to leave you! Why don't I stay? Oh, oh Jason could fly out with Mr Beefy and we'll all just stay here forever."

I nod vigorously in agreement. Why hadn't we thought of that sooner, we could totally do that. I lean forward to retrieve my cocktail from the table and miss by a good three feet. Trying again I close one eye, which always works when you're dizzy. Or drunk. It's possible that I'm very, very drunk.

"Whoa there, sit back, let me get it for you before you knock the whole lot off." Ryan pulls me back gently and into his strong arms. I sigh, leaning my head back onto his chest as I take another sip of my strawberry daiquiri, these things are really quite good.

"So what time do you fly tomorrow?" James settles into his seat as he watches us, bemused at how comfortable we are with each other all of a sudden. Apparently he gave Ryan the big brother talk last night which is sweet, if not slightly offensive. Warning him to take things slowly so I don't hurt him. Maybe I should talk to James later.

"It's a night flight, just after eight so at least I can recover from tonight's antics before I suffer 11 hours on a plane. I can't believe I'll miss your big birthday next week, we've never been apart on our birthdays," Rosie sniffles. I meet her eyes and feel that pesky lump stabbing at my throat again. How am I going to manage without my best friend and rock to talk me down from a cliff when I get stressed, or our take me out for 'Walkers an arse let's get hammered' nights. I leave the warmth of Ryan's body and lean across the table in a very undignified fashion to pull her into a hug. All I can say is it's a good job I didn't opt for a skirt tonight.

"We'll talk every day I promise. I mean, what else am I going to have to do with my time?" Ryan coughs behind me and I poke my tongue out at him in response. "You'll be working won't you, I'll be the loser playing Dora the Explorer daily until you finish."

"Dora the Explorer?" He looks at me puzzled.

Okay so maybe that made a lot more sense in my head. I realise that Dora is about six years old, and Spanish, and has a monkey friend, but she travels alone without human companionship. I feel a tear threaten to stray from the safety of my eye and gently try to encourage it back in but only succeed in poking my finger further in therefore not only releasing a single tear, but causing significant pain and more tears.

"I'll miss you so much!" I shout across at her.

"Me too!" She shrieks back.

The men sit uncomfortably, no longer amused at our drunkenness but quite embarrassed at the volume were talking at. I can't say I blame them, we are attracting a fair amount of attention.

I open my mouth again to impart some more words of wisdom on the group but am broken off by the intro to our number one 'stripper song'.

Now, I firmly believe that every woman has that one song that turns them into, let's face it, a bit of a wannabe stripper. Inhibitions go out of the window as we do a bit of gyrating and swing our hips sexily thinking that we're the hottest thing out there. For Rosie and I, this song is Dirrty.

No words are spoken, just a simple look is exchanged, and before Ryan or James know what's happening, we are out of our seats and onto the dance floor, gyrating like we're 18 again.

Now a lot happens in the next few seconds, and it's amazing how quickly you can sober up. By the time I can process everything

Ryan and James are by my side saving the day.

Rosie has always had a tendency to get a little too into her stripper songs, and my sobering moment was the moment she stepped onto a young couples table and flashed her very expensive - or so I'm informed - silky thongs at the whole club. Her twerking is pretty admirable for someone her age but the high kicks pushed it too far. Glasses flew, alcohol was spilled, voices were raised, screams were heard and a punch was thrown. She's a very mean drunk is Rosie.

It wasn't a pretty sight seeing her being manhandled by James as he carried her away, his arm gripping her tightly around her waist, which was currently where her black glittery skirt was resting, but there really was no other option.

"Put me down. That little poison dwarf is going to get what's coming to her! James! Down. Now."

"I'm not releasing you until were a safe distance from the club, the last thing you want is a night in the slammer." Credit where it's due, James is strong and Rosie can't wriggle free for the life in her. I stifle a giggle and concentrate on walking in a straight line next to Ryan as we shuffle our way down the busy street trying to hail a taxi.

"I don't want to go home," I whisper in what I think is a quiet voice to Ryan.

"Me neither!" Rosie shouts animatedly.

"Take us to a bar boys, this is our last night together and we want to celebrate. Wait, that isn't right, we want to commiserate. Yes, commiserate. I want to go back to Castro."

I spin around giving Ryan my most hopeful Bambi eyes, that's my aim anyway, it could just make me look possessed but I'm hoping I'm cute.

"Okay, okay. If I take you to a karaoke bar do you promise not to start a fight with a poor unsuspecting couple while attempting your finest stripper dances?"

"Or with a drag queen," I add earning myself a glare.

"Or a drag queen," he sighs.

We both nod like eager dogs accepting a treat. I don't clap my hands though, and not just because I'm not convinced they'd hit each other. Honest.

As we step into the bar it's like a sensory overload. It's a different bar to the one they brought us to on the night of Fiddler, maybe because they didn't trust us not to upset those drag queens again, but part of me is glad they saved this little delight for our last night together. I don't know where to look or smell first. I really do have a thing about smells. My mother always used to shake her head in despair when I was younger, every time I had something to eat, without fail, I would have to smell it first. Thankfully I grew out of smelling my food a long time ago, that could have made for some interesting chats on dates.

I feel like I've stepped into what the Barry Manilow song Copacabana would be like if it were a bar. The walls, from what I can tell, are a strong shade of yellow, with palm trees painted sporadically around the room. Multicoloured flashing lights bounce from every surface as I spy yet another drag queen, not too dissimilar from Lily Savage, belting out a song that I've never heard before and from somewhere in the room, coconut is being pumped out into the air. I'm one step away from spinning around with my arms out Julie Andrews style when I spot them.

Dancing flamingos.

Dancing frickin' flamingos.

I'd heard about these mythical creatures from a girl I worked with *sob* and from what I remember, they're inflatable flamingos that move around the dance floor with the heat. My feet are itching to scamper across and grab one by the neck, but I'm trying to act ladylike after that godawful scene in the club. Rosie however remains unfazed.

"Flamingos!" She screams. And before you can say hot pink bird, Rosie has grabbed one of the many floating birds of fun and is riding it back to me like a hobbyhorse.

"Can you handle her while we go to the bar?" James looks doubtful but this is nothing. I've handled Rosie as a teenager after her first Jaegarbomb experience and let me tell you, it was not pretty. This Rosie here in front of me is about as threatening as a penguin in a Santa hat in comparison.

"Oh we'll be fine. See if you can get a virgin Piña Colada though, what she doesn't know won't hurt her. Or anyone else for that matter." I survey the room and come to the conclusion that none of them would be a match for Rosie, they all look far too nice to fight with a woman….and they'd probably be terrified of losing their wigs, something we don't have to worry about.

Ryan gives me a quick peck on the cheek and I beam.

"Come on Lexi, come choose a song with me," grabbing my hand in a crushing death grip she drags me across the dance floor towards the DJ in the Hawaiian shirt.

An hour later Rosie is sat snoring in the corner, using a flamingo as a pillow and she looks so cute, like butter wouldn't melt. We all decided to let her sleep a bit of the alcohol off, it was for the best.

"So, are you moving in to the house tomorrow?" James asks as he nudges Rosie back into position.

"Yeah, are you still okay to help with my cases? I mean, I think I only have one full size suitcase but I brought a hefty hand luggage one too and I've bought far too much stuff while I've been out here. I need to figure out a way to pack Rosie's Betty too."

"Betty?" James looks confused as Ryan smiles back at me.

On the way back from our date in Castro, the guilt started gnawing away at me, so I had a brilliant idea that I hoped Rosie would love. On our first day at Pier 39 she fell in love with the Betty Boop statue and to be honest, I got pretty sick of hearing about it. I told Ryan about it and decided to buy it for her. I know it's a gift that will take pride of place in the house when she gets home, and I know that it's something she will love forever, and it will always remind her of me and our time here. So, we swung by the chaotic pier and I am now the proud owner of Betty in a champagne glass. Joy. Well, I say I'm the proud owner, she's currently living with James and Ryan in one of their spare bedrooms which I'm sure they're chuffed to bits with God love them. The trouble that I have now is how and what to pack it in so that she'll be able to get it through customs in an acceptable sized hand luggage bag, without telling her until the very last minute. I think that might be a bit of a fail.

"It's no surprise really that she's a Betty

Boop fan, you just have to look at her and it all makes sense." Ryan drains his glass dry and offers another round. I decline but ask him for a Coke for Rosie, I should probably wake her before she pops the poor flamingo.

"Ah I see," James nods in acknowledgement. "How big a Betty fan are we talking then?"

"Oh God, HUGE." I shake my head. "For years she wouldn't answer me if I called her Rosie, she would only answer to Betty. Looking back I can laugh but she was a very intense teenager."

The fog caused by the alcohol has started to clear now, although you never can tell until you hit the fresh air can you? I try not to blame the drink, drink has always been a good friend to me so I tend to blame the fresh air. That's the killer. Given that I'm starting to sober up already, I'm hoping that tomorrow will be kind to me and I'll be hangover free.

As Ryan puts the glass in front of Rosie's softly snoring face I gently start to nudge her.

"Rosie, come on you need to wake up." I use a bit more force when she shrugs me off, moaning. "Come on lazyass you're letting the side down, wake up."

"Piss off," she groans sleepily.

Rolling my eyes I pull the flamingo abruptly from under her. Piss of indeed. Her face slaps against the sticky wooden table and she yelps. As she lifts her head she glowers at me, a raffle ticket stuck to her cheek and her eyes looking very much like a panda. It's not a pretty sight.

"I think we should call a taxi," I say to no one in particular.

"Nooo, I haven't had chance to sing the Spice Girls song yet!" Rosie protests.

Frowning, I shake my head. "Rosie, not only have you been up there to sing two Spice Girls songs, you also sang a delightful Dolly Parton number. No one else has had a look in." I have the footage to prove it but I think I'll save those beauties for when she's in a better mood. They will be the perfect blackmail material. Insert evil laugh here.

"Oh. Okay then, well yes a taxi would be great." She downs the full pint of Coke with as much class as a man on a building site, proceeds to burp, giggle, then give me the sloppiest kiss on the cheek that I have ever had. And Mr Beefy has been known to give some fairly sloppy ones out.

"Okay, up you get." I pull her to her feet, wiping my cheek with a rogue napkin from the table as James comes back in to join us.

"I've called a taxi, they should be here in five. You ready to go?"

I grab our bags and with my newfound sober head, manage to guide Rosie through the tables as she shimmies away to some 70s nonsense blaring out of the speakers, waving her arms around and generally making a nuisance of herself. I really hope she comes round before we get back to the motel.

"Have I told you how much I love you Lexi-poo? Because it's a lot you know. You're like my big sister only we're the same age. Isn't that funny. We could maybe be like twins and you're like three minutes older than me. Although no one would believe us, it would have to be a secret."

Dear Lord, if you could please sober her up I promise to go to church every Sunday and find my Catholic roots again.

"Why would we even want to tell people were twins Rose?" I bend down so that I'm on a level with the card slot on our door. I don't think I'm 100% sobered up yet but I know I'm a damn sight better than Rosie is. Twins. Ha.

"Because you're my big sister that's why silly. I'm hungry, are you hungry? I hope you have some Cheetos left because I am really hungry. Did you buy any Cheetos today? Hey are you okay there, do you need me to open the door? Have you lost a contact lens again, you can be so clumsy sometimes." She laughs as she bends over the railings outside our room door, dangling her head down as far as she can.

"For God's sake Rosie get your arse away from there before you kill yourself. And yes, of course I have Cheetos, and no, I haven't lost a lens. It's just really dark out here." And it is, I'm really struggling for light, I think maybe a bulb has gone or something because I really don't remember it being so dark every other night. I give myself a little whoop and air punch as the card is finally accepted and the little green light flashes to let me know we can go in. I push open the door, kick off my shoes and grab Rosie by the waistband of her skirt and pull her inside.

I'll miss this little room. It's started to feel so much like home, it's always a welcoming sight after a long day, with its dark wood furniture and floral bed sheets. It's like being back at my grandparent's house. Grabbing a bag of Cheetos from in front of the mirror I throw them at her as I crack open a pack of cookies. Drunken munchies have always been a problem but I regret nothing.

CHAPTER NINETEEN

My head is pounding as I wake up to Rosie snoring. This is not going to be a good day, I can feel it already. I really do not want to open my eyes. Ever.

I give her a sharp nudge in the back to shut her up, thankful that the beds are big enough to prevent me from being subject to her kicking fits. You do not want to be sharing a bed with a drunk Rosie if you're partial to wearing shorts. Or breathing.

One Christmas, Walker got stuck in Boston. He'd only gone on what was supposed to be a business weekend for meetings but the snow storm was so bad he was stranded there a week. Rosie came to stay with me so that we could both feel sorry for ourselves and just drink away the Christmas period. Jason had rushed back to Yorkshire to be with his parents when his uncle was told he only had days to live – an uncle who hated Rosie so she thought it best to stay in London – so we celebrated the best way we could think of. Festive films and mulled wine. You never actually realise how many times 'Lonely this Christmas' is played either until you are. I'm fairly certain we kept Kleenex in business that year. Anyway, one particularly drunken night I failed to dodge the legs of doom and suffered a knee right in the rib cage. She's lucky I didn't suffocate her in her sleep.

"Come on Rosie, cut it out." I nudge her even harder this time and she stops. Silence is indeed golden.

I start to shuffle myself back into a comfortable position, safe in the knowledge that we booked a late check out for the room. This is going to be a bitchin' hangover and I'll need most of the day to recover.

Rosie moans and turns to face me, last night's Cheeto binge evident on her still made up face. I say made up, she looks like a badly made up clown, but I'm sure I look just as bad.

"You look like shit." She coughs as I get a face full of morning breath.

"And you smell like shit. Oh and you have a little Cheeto," I tap my cheek.

"Ugh." She rubs her face, groaning. "I never want to see another alcoholic drink as long as I live."

"Not even Pina Colada?" I laugh as I remember her declaring her 'forever love' for the drink.

"Nah that's different. That's got two of my five a day in so that's a healthy drink." She pauses thoughtfully. "Are you all packed?"

"Yeah. Are you?"

"Yup. Just got to collect the shoot clothes from James but he said he'd pack them so I'm leaving him to it. I can't even try to care about whether he remembers everything right now. I feel like hell. Remind me again why we drink so much?"

"Because we are idiots who think it's funny and always forget about the aftermath. Although I don't think Ryan and James will forget last night's escapades in a hurry." I sit up and take a long drink of the water on my bedside table. It's warm but I'd drink toilet water if I thought it would help.

"What did I do?"

"Just the usual, got up on a table, twerked your arse off, kicked a few glasses off of said table, one that a poor unsuspecting couple were sat at and had to be dragged out of the bar before you managed to punch the woman. You did take an impressive swing for the man though."

"Fuck." She buries her face under the covers so I shuffle down to join her, quite enjoying her embarrassment. It makes a refreshing change from me making a royal tit of myself.

"Oh and then there was the karaoke bar…"

"No more." She puts her Cheeto stained hand up against my mouth.

"Get that filthy thing away from me," I joke. Kind of. It really is a bit gross.

She looks at her fingers and wrinkles her

nose in agreement.

"So what's the plan today? Apart from taking plenty of pain killers?"

"Well we can't have a full English so how about the next best thing? Dennys?"

"Deal." She nods and shakes my hand as best she can. "So, another hour in bed then we drag our sorry selves down there?"

"Deal."

As I stick my fork into my omelette I catch Rosie's eye.

"Oh what? Have I got something around my face still?" She groans pulling her handbag closer to get her mirror out.

"No you idiot. I was just thinking about how much I am going to miss you. I hope I don't end up getting brutally murdered in a back alley, that would suck."

"Why would you even say that you absolute dick?" She throws a mushroom at me and shakes her head. "Like I'm not going to worry about you enough, you have to put that image into my head. You're an idiot." She points her fork rudely at me and carries on eating.

"Hey, I'm just saying. I've never been the most streetwise of people have I? Not in a new country anyway, London was scary enough and I had you there to teach me how to throw a punch."

"Exactly, and I know I taught you well so just make sure you keep eating like you have been doing and if a punch doesn't work you could just sit on them." She laughs as I stick my fingers up at her. Okay so I may have put on a few pounds since we arrived here, but seriously, everything just sounds so good that it would be rude not to have a sample or six.

"Well I won't be eating out as much will I when I have an actual house you cow……..seriously has my arse grown that much?"

"No Lexi, your arse is still tiny. Your boobs are getting bigger though, Ryan is gonna have a field day with those puppies when he finally gets to motorboat you." Cackling loudly I feel my face burn. I hear the men at the table to our left laugh and the young couple to our right just stare.

"I really won't miss you embarrassing me like that."

"Oh please, I'm just saying what you're secretly dreaming about. When you finally do the dirty with him, I want every single detail because he is one fine looking man, I bet he knows how to handle a woman if you know what I mean." Winking she takes a sip of her juice and grins.

Shaking my head, I feel a small smirk creep across my face. She isn't wrong to be fair to her, it's all I can think about lately when I'm near him. He makes my heart beat faster and my throat turn to jelly. I have no idea what the throat quiver is all about but I become a bit of a wreck around him. He just makes me feel so sexy and alive that I don't know what to do with myself half of the time. It must be the adrenaline. Either that or I'm turning into a first class loser. I'd much rather blame the adrenaline.

"So, humping Ryan aside, what are you gonna do when I'm gone?"

This is something I keep thinking about too. With Ryan at work through the week, I'm going to have a lot of spare time on my hands.

"I've been thinking about maybe hiring a car at some point and exploring Napa maybe? I don't know, I might even try my hand at writing a book while I'm here. It's not like I won't have the time anymore."

"Well that sounds perfect. I hope you'll send me your stuff when you do write it, and I want the first autographed copy, obviously."

"Obviously. Hey, maybe I'll give Walker a starring role. Chief villain?" I'm secretly excited about starting to write. It's something that I've wanted to do for a long time and something that Rosie always encouraged me to do growing up. That's the thing about Rosie, she may take the piss and embarrass me for her own giggles, but she is fiercely loyal and supportive and would always champion me when others doubted my abilities. This is how I know that the distance between us from today won't make any difference to our friendship. We are like sisters and nothing, and no one, will ever change that.

"Now that my dear girl, sounds like a bloody marvellous plan."

I hate airports when I'm not going on holiday. Frankly I think they're depressing.

Ryan and James agreed to drive us to SFO International, for which I am eternally grateful. I've been a wreck most of the day, every time Rosie put an item into her hand luggage case I had to bite the inside of my cheek so that I didn't break down like a big girls blouse. After all, nobody likes a crybaby. Although my eyes are still puffy from when I gave her Betty – I couldn't get away with not telling her in the end. First, she hit me for spending so much money on her, then she hugged me. It was an emotional roller coaster let me tell you.

The stark lights of the departure hall don't do anything for my tear stained, blotchy face either. Someone should really tell them to consider a more flattering lighting system, or at least get a dimmer fixed up, how lovely would that be?

I sneak a quick peek at a family next to us. The mother is crying softly into her handkerchief as the dad stands with his arm around her. The son is going to Europe for a year to travel but has promised to email every day and Skype at weekends. I know all of this because I am a truly nosey cow. Fact. Take for example the young couple that passed us earlier, her parents had come to visit them and she must have stopped three times on the way out just to keep hugging them. It was a very sweet sight. Or the old couple that I got chatting to that are visiting London, England for the first time ever - I do love how Americans say London, England. They told me that they'll be there to celebrate their 40th wedding anniversary and intend to spend it at Buckingham Palace. Of course I tried to explain that the likeliness of them actually meeting the Queen or even one of the corgis was quite slim, but they just wouldn't have it.

Turning back to my little group I feel my stomach begin to churn. I'm a wreck.

"Hey chin up, you're the one not going home remember?" This is clearly Rosie trying to make light of the situation. Talk about a fail. My lip starts to quiver as I throw my arms around her neck, knocking her off balance and into her case trolley that luckily James manages to stop in its tracks as it starts to move.

"I'll miss you so much!" I wail. Anyone would think I was sending her off to war not back to London. Although she does work in fashion, it is a bit of a battlefield.

"I'll miss you too babe, but we have Skype remember? And I promise not to kick your sorry little butt for staying here if you promise to keep sending me Cheetos. Deal?" She smiles through watery eyes.

I nod back at her, my breathing shaky.

As she checks her bags in, I contemplate the next two months without her in my life. They'll be quiet that's guaranteed.

"Well, that's those sorted. How freaking expensive is extra baggage here?! Totally claiming that expense back." We walk towards the direction of security as she rummages through her handbag and finally pulls out a small photoframe. "I got you this, not quite Betty but pretty special I hope."

I take the small frame from her and laugh. It's so tacky and it must have killed Rosie paying for it, but I love it. It's a silver frame with San Francisco stuck to the top in glittery multicoloured enamel lettering and it will take pride of place in my new temporary home because inside sits a photograph of the pair of us from the first night we went to James and Ryan's apartment. I don't even remember it being taken. I really should start taking more notice of who's got a camera and what they're doing with it. Or stop drinking, but let's not get too dramatic here.

"Thank you, I love it."

"Yeah, I knew you would," she shrugs. "As soon as I saw it I thought, that is just the type of crap Lex would treasure." I give her another hug and sigh.

"This is it then."

"Yeah, I'd best get myself through security, I always get pulled for something and I don't really want to end up running in these bad boys across the airport if I end up late." She flashes her foot proudly at me as I shake my head at her black stiletto ankle boots, beautifully adorned with small spikes. Lots and lots of small spikes. I hate them.

"Let me know the second you land, I mean it. And give Mr Beefy some sloppy kisses from me and tell him I miss him so much."

Rolling her eyes she nods and squeezes me tight.

"You look after my best girl you hear? And make sure she has an epic birthday next week, don't make me have to come back here to hurt you if you hurt her." She looks directly at Ryan and I feel my face flush.

"Behave," I hit her playfully and give her one last hug. I notice that she's had a sneaky spray of my perfume and try not to overthink the sentiment. She probably only used it because she'd packed her own and not because she wants to take a piece of me back with her on the flight.

"Always do," she flashes her pearly white teeth at me. "Right, I'm off. Love you loads Lexi-Loo, be safe."

"Love you too."

She gives Ryan and James a quick kiss

and heads off down the corridor, only looking back once to blow us a kiss. As soon as her skinny, impeccably dressed body is out of sight I break down. James looks to Ryan as he looks back helplessly. Men are so useless.

"Can we go please?" I ask them between heaves.

"Yeah, come on, let's get you home."

Nobody says a word on the drive back to the house. I keep sneaking a glance at Ryan who wanted to drive and keep an eye on me in the front. Did I look suicidal? Probably. I chew on my thumb nail as I think about my first night in a new house all alone. Apprehension washes over me as the nerves swim around in my stomach and I have to keep remembering that I'm a big girl now, I'll be fine as long as there's some good food in the fridge and something trashy on the television.

The roads are busy as we weave our way through the traffic, the tea time commuters wanting to get home from work to greet their families after a long, hard day, parents wanting to see their children and hear all about what they've been doing with their days. And then there's the singles, going home to an empty house not having to answer to anybody but themselves. I give a small sigh as the streets start to look familiar. We've made record time when I think about how long that trip would have taken in London.

"So, have you got much unpacking to do?" Ryan signals to turn down the road where my new beautiful house lives.

"Mainly clothes to be honest, and a few photographs. Other than that my night will probably consist of getting used to the new noises of the house and eating. And maybe abusing the wine cellar. And watching some crappy television, obviously."

I see a small smirk creep across his face as he pulls up outside the house.

"Doesn't sound like a bad night to be fair, I might do the same," James interjects, popping his head in between our seats.

I look at the house and realise how lucky I am to have these new friends in my life. Rosie's left me in capable hands.

"Let's get you in then. I'll show you where the alarm is too and how to set it, safety first." Ryan says popping open the boot.

"Okay," I nod, getting out of the car.

As he heaves out one of my cases, wobbling slightly with the weight of it, I'm forced to giggle. Wait until he lifts the one at the bottom with all the shoes in that Rosie kindly left me. I hope he doesn't have a bad back.

"Shit. What the hell kind of clothes weigh this much?!!" Case number two lands with a thud as James gets out to help.

"Yeah, that case has a lot of shoes in it." I grab my small holdall and laugh as they drag them up the stairs to the front door, keeping a safe distance just in case they wobble backwards. I have no desire to be their soft landing.

Following their lead I walk through the door and take a deep breath.

Welcome home.

CHAPTER TWENTY

Sitting alone in my new living room, I begin to take stock. Here I am, alone, surrounded by furniture that isn't mine, as lovely as it is, and in a city where I have no roots. What the hell have I done? I wonder whether it's too late to book myself on the next flight out of here.

Getting up I start to pace across the wooden floor that runs throughout the open plan space. It feels wrong to have shoes on in here, even though they're not heels. The surface is so shiny that I could probably do my make up in it. Or I could do a killer skid in a pair of sloppy socks. Hmmm, maybe later on when my boredom peaks.

I miss Mr Beefy more than I ever thought I could, he was always my little companion and it hurts when I think of being without him for much longer. I miss him a lot more than the cheating scumbag that brought him into my life. I guess he is the one genuinely good thing Walker has ever done for me. I had been so fed up after a car accident that had left me with a broken leg, whiplash and two weeks off of work that Walker thought I needed a little buddy while he had to go to the office every day. I remember it like it was yesterday, one cold winters night, just when I was about to start calling the nearest hospitals to check for a Walker Harrison, in he walked, cat basket in one hand and a bag full of kitty essentials in the other. Closing my eyes I try to fight against the threatening tears that the memories bring back. That was the old Walker. The new Walker would rather have Lauren than you, I chastise myself.

"This is ridiculous," I mutter to myself. "You are 29 years old Alexandra, go out and find something to do instead of moping." Grabbing my handbag, I decide that the best solution to this kind of attitude is going to be food and wine. I'm sure I can handle this.

Hmmmm. I don't actually need to buy wine anymore do I. Ryan told me to help myself, so just food it is. Honestly, is this what it feels like to be a kept woman? If I don't find myself a hobby soon I'm going to go stir crazy and this is only night one.

Muttering to myself, I grab my jacket from yet another closet that I discovered in the foyer and pull open the front door with such gusto that it flies out of my hand and smacks against wall. Shit. I inspect for damage, all clear thankfully, and look up to see a startled Ryan stood before me.

Double shit.

"What are you doing here?" I squeak at him.

"I thought you might be lonely on your

first night so brought us a take out?" He holds up a white carrier bag and I take a small step towards him, inhaling the spicy aroma that drifts out of the top. My stomach grumbles in anticipation and I give it a pat.

"Then please do come in. I was just heading out to get some food but you've saved me a trip. Thank you." I say gratefully. I didn't realise just how hungry I was until I smelt whatever was in that bag.....I hope he doesn't have extreme taste in Chinese take outs. At least, I assume it's Chinese, the bag indicates that it is with the little Chinese man on the side but I've been bamboozled before by many a curry shop back in London that just give you this type of bag for kicks.

"How do you feel about Chinese?"

Bingo.

"Love it." As we walk through to the dining area, Ryan wanders through to the kitchen and makes himself at home, hunting out plates and cutlery, glasses and placemats. How he managed to lay his hands on them so fast I have no idea, but if it means I get fed faster then colour me happy.

"Okay so, I wasn't sure what you liked so I thought I'd take a gamble on the standards. We have Mushroom Chow Mein, Curried Beef, Chicken in Black Bean sauce and Mushroom Foo Yung. Then I thought vegetable spring rolls, chips, boiled rice and fried rice should cover us for sides?" As he takes each plastic container out and places it on the board, my jaw drops. Firstly, holy crap how has everything fit into that carrier bag. Secondly, how much did all of that cost? And thirdly, would I seem greedy if I had some of everything? I really am very hungry.

As Ryan dishes everything up, I sit on the arm of one of the chairs and have a look through the dozens of CDs. As I trace my finger down the alphabetised collection, I finally settle on some Van Morrison and pop it into the retro machine hidden away inside an old cabinet.

"Ah, I like your style. Here, sit. Dinner is served m'lady." He bows like a dutiful servant making me chuckle.

"Silly. Sit down yourself and pour us some wine. It's been a long day."

He nods sagely, obviously not wanting to bring up Rosie and my floods of tears at the airport earlier on. Looking back I am a little bit embarrassed but these things happen, ugly crying is not something one likes to do, certainly not in front of a sexy man that you're trying to impress. But it happens to the best of us I'm sure. No point worrying about it now.

I take a sip and feel the warm crimson liquid slip smoothly down my throat. I've never been one to match specific wine with my food when I'm at home, and I'm happy to see that Ryan doesn't take his wine too seriously either. I likes what I likes, and I likes me some red tonight. And I have no idea why I'm thinking in a Cornish accent either. Shaking my head I dig into some curried beef and the conversation begins to flow freely.

After my third helping of mains and fourth spring roll, I have to sit back in my seat just to give my stomach that extra bit of room to spread. I also may slyly pop the button on my jeans open. I'm not proud.

"So, I get the feeling that underneath that charming exterior are some very interesting thoughts and opinions." Ryan stands to clear the table and I don't even attempt to help. I'm nursing what feels like an eight month food baby here, mamma needs her rest.

"Depends what you call interesting I guess," I reply watching him walk into the kitchen, the dark jeans hugging his perfectly peachy bum in all the right places. I smack my lips together and sigh. What a catch.

"Let's play a game."

"Oh no, I've seen Saw buster, if you're going to kill me just do it quickly. I don't care, you'll get no fight from me after all that food." I groan in pain as I try to sit upright. Damn, my eyes always have been bigger than my belly.

"Don't be sick, I hate those films." He takes the last of the plates as I make a mental note of that small piece of information. Ryan doesn't do horror. Or the Saw series at least. Just another positive to add to his ever growing list.

"Well what did you mean then?" I laugh, finally standing up and moving our glasses across to the sofas by the window. The streets are quiet now, the hustle and bustle of park goers has long since subsided and now there's nothing but leaves and street lights as far as the eye can see. I pull on the curtains so that I don't have to look at the haunting trees lining the opposite side of the street at the entrance to the park.

"I was thinking more of a 'which would you rather' type game. You know, like 'daddy or chips'? I want to get to know you better." He turns off the lights behind him so that only our area stays lit. Great, he's one of those energy saving freaks. Finally his negative list has an item in it.

"Okay, I'm up for that. But FYI, it would be daddy on that count, definitely, I mean there's only so many chips a person can face."

"Fair point."

"Great, so it's my turn then?"

"That wasn't my question Lexi." He tops up my glass as he thinks carefully. "Yorkshire or London?"

His question catches me off guard. I expected pizza or curry, he's started off well.

"That's a hard one. I know they say home is where the heart is but, my family is split into two back in England. Rosie and Jason, and I guess Luke to a certain degree, are like my extended family, but Yorkshire has my parents. I love going back home to Leeds because it makes me thankful for everything my parents have given me and there really is nowhere quite like where you grew up." I pause to take a drink and realise he probably only meant for scenery. Ha, what a loser Lex. "Okay, so if I could take everyone with me, it would be Yorkshire for sure."

"Interesting start. Okay, hit me with your best shot." As he crosses his ankle onto his knee I catch a glimpse of yellow sock and stifle a giggle. He's so cute it's ridiculous.

"Right, music or television?"

"Oh that's easy. Music, definitely. It was my first love and something I never tire of. I work with it day in and day out and I genuinely believe I need music as much as I need food or the air I breathe. It's such an important part of my life."

"You have a real passion for it don't you?"

"I do. I think it's important to feel passionate about things in life, don't you?" His question is simple but his eyes burn with so much more meaning. I'm fairly certain we're not talking music at this point.

"It is, I agree." My throat is dry as I swallow hard. More wine.

"Okay, easy one here. Dogs or cats?"

"Cats, obviously," I scoff. "Mr Beefy would kick my arse if I said anything else."

"Who?"

"Wait, I haven't told you about my Beefster? Oh my God, wait there." I scamper across to my phone and rush back to his side to show him the plethora of images I have of my Calico kitty, thrusting them under his nose. "There he is on his first Christmas. That's his first trip to the vets. This was his last birthday, he's just gone eight so he's still a baby really. Oh, and this was his idea of bonding with Jason." I laugh as I remember Jason getting pounced on from behind one winter, Mr Beefy firmly latched on to Jason's ridiculous furry cardigan collar and Rosie trying to pry him off. I was sat on the opposite sofa struggling to breathe with tears streaming down my face as I took a photo. Funnily enough Jason never wore that cardigan again, much to both mine and Rosie's delight.

"Well he certainly seems an interesting character," he chuckles as he carries on scrolling through my 'Beefys finest moments' album. "Is that Walker?" My stomach flips as I look at Walker sat with Mr Beefy dangling from his legs in a deep sleep. My smile slips from my face as I nod slowly.

"I should probably try crop his head out of that, I can't bear to delete the photo. He's my baby."

With a quick swipe of Ryan's finger and a click of a button, Walker's head has gone. Grinning triumphantly at his handy work, I can't help but smile back at him.

"Thank you," I whisper hoarsely. I rest my hand on top of his and stare at them as they rest on the screen of my trusty mobile. "Night or day?"

"Night, because I think it's the most romantic time in a day."

"It's also when trouble usually starts," I challenge back at him.

"True, but it's also when all the fun happens. Nightie or pyjamas?"

I laugh at his audacity. "Depends on my mood, sometimes I like to do a Marilyn. Truth or dare?"

"When did you change the game?"

"Just now. Woman's prerogative."

"Truth?"

"Do you believe in the third date rule?" I'm obviously emboldened by the two glasses of red I've had with dinner and can feel my heart racing as I wait for his answer, his eyes widening.

"With certain people I do, yes. Do you?" I nod slowly and bite my lip. "Now you Lexi, truth or dare?"

"Dare." I say with absolute confidence, not caring what he asks me to do because right now, in this moment, I would do anything he asked me, even if it meant making a fool of myself in the street. I'm lost in his eyes and completely under his spell. I just can't seem break the connection between us and a large part of me doesn't even want to.

"Kiss me."

Well, that's easy enough then.

Leaning forward, I touch the side of his face, tracing a finger slowly down his jaw and neck, never once breaking eye contact as he lets out a small groan. As soon as our lips touch I'm lost. It feels like all the pent up frustration and sexual tension is released into that one moment.

Finally breaking away for a breath I give a small chuckle, eyes looking anywhere but at him. That was intense. I daren't look up now because I know the second I do, the chances are that I may leap into his lap and demand that he take me right here, right now, on the sofa.....and on the rug.....and maybe the dining table....and maybe, just maybe, we could work our way upstairs.

I risk a peek through my lashes and catch his eyes burning into me, pure lust radiating from him.

"Oh screw it," and without giving my brain chance to second guess it, I kiss him again. This time though it's different. Ryan takes complete control and I happily let him.

As he gently leans me back onto the pile of cushions behind me, he pulls away and almost searches my eyes for the answer to a question he hasn't asked.

"You are so beautiful, you know that

right?" He dots kisses gently down my neck as I let out a soft moan and feel him smile against the curve where my throat meets my collar bone. He carefully traces a finger down towards the top button of the shirt I have on and I take a second to thank Rosie for forcing me to buy some new, sexier underwear and finally convincing me to cast aside my granny pants as she so fondly referred to them. As he pops the first two buttons, he groans in appreciation as my breasts are nudged up in my soft pink lace balcony bra.

Ladies and gentleman, tonight's viewing pleasure is brought to you by La Perla.

"Amazing." He whispers as he makes quick work of the other buttons and slips my shirt down over my shoulders. The pace is both mind blowing and torturous. My heart is enjoying every second of the romance and intimacy, my groin however is begging for the pace to be stepped up so that she can have her way with Ryan Junior. No, that sounds wrong. What should I call it, I feel that it deserves some recognition. Lower Ryan? That just sounds like a road that runs under a bridge. Mini Ryan? Probably wouldn't appreciate that one either.

"Oh God, that's, wow." I'm that busy deciding what I should be referring to Ryan's team mate as, he takes me by surprise as he pulls down the lace and takes me in his mouth, kissing, sucking, softly biting. The pleasure coursing through my veins is exhilarating. As he pulls away I whimper, earning myself a satisfied smirk. Oh he knows just what he's doing to me.

I reach for the hem of his t-shirt in a feeble attempt to remove it, but he's so tall. Nobody ever portrays the first time like this in the movies. They never say, yes the experience can be mind blowing but the getting undressed part can be a bit faffy. Luckily, Ryan steps in and is baring his delicious chest within seconds. Oh how I want to run my tongue down every single bump of his abs. He's quite obviously a man that looks after himself and works out.

"I....want......off....please," I pant like mad woman, my breath quickening.

"Your wish," he grins as he pops the button of his jeans open. "My command."

I let my eyes roam every inch of him, slowly moving down his happy trail and that perfectly pronounced V shape when I gasp. Sweet. Baby. Jesus. Mini Ryan most definitely will not suffice as a nickname.

I fumble quickly with my jeans, almost losing my balance and falling off of the edge of the sofa. Frustrated, I get to my feet, pull them off, and stand before him, all delicate lace and bare skin. I push him down onto the sofa and climb onto his lap, running my fingers through his hair, conscious that by doing so I'm pushing my breasts forward towards his face, right where I want them.

"Oh Lexi," and before I have time to

respond, I am back on my back with Ryan surrounding me, showering me in kisses, from my neck, all the way down my chest. He continues across my stomach, slowly trailing them lower. The pleasure is so intense that I ache everywhere, my body is begging for something, some kind of release, some kind of friction, anything.

"Oh God no, stop," he looks up at me like I've just hit him in the face with a shovel. "No, no, I don't mean stop stop, I just, oh please Ryan," I beg as I bow my body upwards towards him. Thankfully he understands my babble and begins to purposefully remove my underwear, taking in every inch of my body until I finally lay there completely naked before him.

"Beautiful." He whispers stroking my face before finally removing his boxers.

Thank you Lord.

CHAPTER TWENTY ONE

"Wow," I gasp, unable to peel my heavy limbs away from Ryan. We made it to the bedroom, eventually, but not before we made use of some surfaces downstairs. And maybe the elevator. Maybe.

I'm struggling to keep my eyes open and yawn against his chest as he strokes my hair.

"Yeah. Wow. You're going to ruin me you know that don't you," he laughs quietly. "I'm really glad I came over tonight. You're amazing, you know that right?"

"Psshhht," I wave away his compliment with a flutter of my fingers. They're the only thing that will agree to work for me. Arms and legs refuse to do anything until I promise no more strenuous activities. Who needs a gym?

"Hey," he shifts so that he can look me directly in the eye. "I've never met anybody like you, you both mesmerize and challenge me more than anybody else I've ever met and I can't get enough. You're like my own personal drug." He trails his finger down my nose and I catch it between my teeth, biting down playfully.

"Likewise. You really intrigue me, and right now you've exhausted me. You can still go like a 20 year old can't you?!" I joke to lift the weighty air beginning to cloak us. We've just had amazing sex, I'm fairly sure we should both be snoring, not having a deep discussion about our feelings. Wow, now I sound like a man.

"I can with you," he laughs, kissing the top of my head as I nuzzle it into the crook of his shoulder. "So, you're not much of a talker then after sex?"

"Nuh-uh." I shake my head, my eyelids feeling heavier by the second.

"Okay then, you win. Goodnight Lexi."

"Night Ryan."

And I'm out like a light, safely wrapped in Ryan's arms where I happily stay all night long.

"I really should get up, I have to go to work at some point today." Ryan gently moves a piece of stray hair from across my sleepy face.

"Do you have to?" I grumble, struggling to open one eye let alone two. Oh his hair is all messed up and dishevelled, he looks so sweet and innocent. Talk about looks being deceiving, the things he did to me last night…

"What are you thinking? You have a very…..wicked smile on your face Miss Jones." He leans in and gives me a chaste kiss as I laugh back at him.

"What can I say, my thoughts are always quite wicked when you're around." I push myself up on to my elbows, suddenly aware of the aches in places I didn't know existed. Ouch.

"When I first laid eyes on you, I had no idea how incorrigible you were."

"Ah well you see, looks can be deceiving, I like to keep people on their toes. And remember you still owe me that IHOP meal, don't think you're getting out of it Mr." I stretch across the mammoth sized bed and grab my phone to check the time. 7.41am. Ugh.

"Fine, fine, how about I take you there tonight? You need to eat and it'll get it over and done with sooner rather than later for me," he jokes as he slides out of bed. "Oh."

"S'up?" I try to care, I really do, but when you're faced with a perfectly sculpted back and an arse you could crack walnuts with staring back at you, it's hard to really focus on, or care about, anything.

"My clothes are all downstairs." Frowning he throws a silly pout at me, earning himself a pillow thrown at him in return.

"Don't pout, if the wind changes you'll stay like that. And you'll just have to find something to wrap around yourself won't you to go hunt them out. They really could be anywhere and I don't want you scaring my new neighbours. I'm fairly sure your friend would appreciate us keeping the peace with them too. Last night might have disturbed them enough." I blush as the delicious memories come flooding back. I dread to think what the neighbours thought of all the moans and screams coming from this house. I hope they're not old.

Fixing the pout firmly back on his face, he crawls back across the bed starts to tickle me.

"What if I like disturbing the peace with you?" The silly pout drops and a million dollar smile replaces it as he continues the torture, my body writhing and wriggling underneath him as I struggle to push him off and catch my breath. Finally, I see a gap below his arm and slide out quickly, catching him off guard long enough to push him down so that I can take my place firmly above him.

"I win," I say breathlessly. God maybe I should consider using that gym, I can't believe how being tickled has taken it out of me.

"Really? Is that what you believe?" He looks so smug that I wonder what I've missed. I cock my head to one side in question. As he settles his hands on my waist he shakes his head. "I have you exactly where I like you, giving me the best view in the house."

And a happy hump day to me.

When Ryan finally leaves, I treat myself to the most luxurious bath in the history of ever. The bath tub is so deep that I only just manage not to drown in the water, the bubbles meeting my chin leaving me with a Santa-esque beard. Now this is really living. The aroma of Japanese

Cherry Blossom fills the room as the steam covers the full wall mirror, and the candles flicker gently over by the double sink. And as I was going over the top with everything anyway, I figured why not make use of the music system in here?

Resting my head on the back of the bath, feeling the water slowly soak up the base of my hair, I close my eyes and relax. Truly relax. Not the kind of relaxing that I used to think I did with a 20 minute shower, Walker knocking on the door wanting to know what was taking so long. Not the kind of relaxing where I would run a bath and the landline would ring and I'd have to answer it because what if it was an emergency. It never was. This was pure indulgence. The sinful kind where I should feel nothing but guilt for using nearly half a bottle of what looked like very expensive bubble bath. But I don't. I feel genuinely happy. And a little bit smug even.

An hour later when I'm sure I'm wrinkly enough and my bubbles have all disappeared, I pull the plug out with my toe and wait for the water to drain enough for me not to cause a tidal wave when I stand up.

Wrapping a white fluffy towel around my head, and an even fluffier towel around my body, I wander back through to the bedroom, thankful for the underfloor heating and thick carpets. Switching the music to play in the bedroom, I throw myself down on to the bed. If the covers don't dry in time I'll just sleep in another room. I start to giggle at the madness my life has become. Good madness don't get me wrong, but still, who usually has the option of just swapping rooms if one set of bedding is a bit damp? Oh, come to think of it, I should probably wash it really after last night, we got a bit excited with the whipped cream and such. Hmmmm, I hope it's an easy washing machine, I never was very good at that sort of thing.

As I'm worrying about the cleaning aspect of the house, my phone rings. I stare at it over in the corner for long enough, contemplating who it could be. Well if it's a sales person they deserve the high charges they'll get.

Luke?

"Hey Luke? You know I'm still in America right?" I pace along the carpet, relishing every step. It's amazing how the simple things in life can bring you happiness.

"I didn't know your Skype name," he says quietly. Oh, I bet Jason's told him now that I'm staying for a while longer.

"Give me five minutes Luke and I'll Skype you." I hang up quickly and hit the ever faithful little blue button. He responds quite quickly and I'm shocked at just how exhausted he looks. When I last saw him he looked like the old Luke, a smile on his face and a twinkle in his eye. Now, his sapphire blue eyes look dull, dark circles sitting heavily beneath them. He looks like he's aged overnight.

"Hi Lex, you look good," he says sadly. I chew the inside of my cheek hoping he can't tell why. I'm sure I'm positively glowing after last night.....and this morning.

"You look terrible! What's happened? Is everyone okay? Hey, what time is it over there?"

"Only about half eleven. I had to see you, speak to you. You're staying out there and you didn't even think to let me know? How could you?" His eyes flash with hurt and anger.

I half choke half laugh when he says this. Shock. Just, shock.

"Are you serious?" I try to stay calm but he has really got my back up now. "You disappear for 13 years, not thinking about a single one of us, about me - your girlfriend, and you have the audacity to say that to me? And then, then you finally reappear, accidentally I know, but you reappear and don't even think to tell me you've been with 'Alice' for six months!" I used air quotes, and I mock said her name, I think he may know how I feel about her now.

"What so I still have to answer to you? I didn't see how it mattered that I was with someone, you had Walker."

"Who you knew about! I would never have hidden him from you. And you didn't think it mattered, really, you didn't feel the same spark there when we were together? You didn't feel how easy it was, how it could have been? You didn't think just once, what if? Well then silly me." I'm so angry I feel a tear start to fall as my throat constricts.

"Okay, okay, I'm sorry." He holds his hands up in defeat. "I want you back though, I miss you. Come home where you belong."

My heart stops. He wants me back?

"Wh-what about Alice?" I blink back the tears that are still working their way out.

"What about her? Once you get to know her you'll get on great and I know you'll love her like I do. Honestly."

"Oh. Oh silly me, of course you want it all your way. Of course Luke Garrett wants us both around so he doesn't have to sacrifice any of his happiness." I laugh bitterly, picking up the iPad and pacing frantically. "You want your cake and to eat it, well I've got news for you Luke, I'm not coming back. If you missed me that much then you would have thought to get in touch all those years ago at some point, you know my parents address. You don't have the right to say that you miss me and want me back anymore, you've made your choice and I've made mine. I'm staying, and I don't know if I'll ever be coming back. Ever."

That may be a little white lie but I want to upset and hurt him like he has me. I know I'll probably regret it, but venting like this feels good, especially when it's aimed at him.

"You're what?" He bellows down the screen. "No, no Lexi you can't stay there, please, come back, I need to see you. Properly. Not just over a screen. Please."

The anger is still coursing through my veins as I stare into his eyes. I'm shaking I'm so annoyed. And even though I see the sadness there in the same eyes that I used to stare into for hours, the same eyes that he is rubbing roughly to stop them from watering, I just can't back down. I can't let him do this to me again. There was me thinking he was finally saying what I waited all these years for him to say. But he wasn't. He's with Alice. And a part of me feels a little bit sick that I wanted him to declare his undying love after my night with Ryan.

"I have to go Luke. And even though it's new, I think you should know that I've started seeing someone and feel that he is important enough for you to know he exists. Now go to bed and rest. Please." I start to thaw my voice a little bit, my heart rate slowing down gradually. "It would kill me if anything happened to you." I say softly, knowing that one wrong move at work for him could be fatal. It happened to his dad and that would destroy me.

"Okay. We'll talk soon though yeah?"

I simply nod and blow him a kiss. I hope his crap keyring cheers him up when Rosie gives him it. I must remember to tell Jason to keep an eye on him.

I pick up my phone and send Rosie a quick text, hopefully tomorrow we'll find a good time to Skype, but right now, I'm drained. I have a couple of hours before Ryan picks me up and because my bed looks so inviting, I decide to just crawl under the cloud like covers and have a quick nap. A power nap as Luke calls them. Oh Luke. Why couldn't you just be happy for me?

THE STORY OF US

CHAPTER TWENTY TWO

I've survived my first three days alone in San Francisco. I use the term loosely of course, but I haven't seen Ryan since Wednesday night and to be honest, after Luke's little outburst I wasn't the best company so IHOP round two was a bust too. Poor Ryan. We decided to go out for a meal tonight, like a real fancy date night to celebrate my stay and us, whatever us is at the moment. He's been working that many hours the last few days that we've only managed the odd text. I felt awful when he said it was because he'd had so much time off when Rosie was over. I bet his boss has been busting his ass about it. Honestly, one day I'll be my own boss and I'll be very lovely to myself.

This is the first day that I've been truly bored too, I'm at a loss. James is away until mid-afternoon photographing some rich family and Ryan said he had a meeting that could last until after lunch. Hmmm, I wonder how it's going. If I send him a quick text he'll answer when he's done then so at least I'll know what's happening.

I'm not turning into a bunny boiler, honest. The time difference is killing me at the moment, not being able to speak to Rosie when I want. Hold on while I get the world's smallest violin out for you.

Hey hot stuff. How's the meeting going? X

Almost instantly I get a reply.

Should be wrapped up in about half an hour tops. Thank god.
Missing you. R x

Oki doki. Call when you're done? X

Will do. X

It's unusually warm outside today, I even managed to take my breakfast out onto the roof terrace this morning and do some photography. The heat on my skin felt so soothing after the last few days of ice cold wind and rain. This crazy ass weather is not what I signed up for Mother Nature, just in case you're listening. I wonder if I met Ryan after his meeting we could get away with a picnic in the park.

I run down to the kitchen and assess the food situation. Damn. Looks like I'll have to bite the bullet and do some shopping soon. I wonder what the little delis down the road are like, maybe I could buy our little picnic pack ready made, kind of a 'part assembly required' type of thing.

Quite pleased with myself, I pull on my cropped denim jacket and even decide not to raid the wine cellar for a bottle, I think I'll see what we get for lunch and get the correct pairing for a change. Rebel to the end.

Three quarters of an hour, achy feet and a far too big wicker picnic basket later, I trundle through the main door to Ryan's apartment in the hope that he's finished his meeting because I really can't carry this back home. As I waddle into the lift, I catch my reflection. My hair is falling out of my plait, my face is bright red and my eyeliner has melted down my eyes. I look like Alice Cooper. Brilliant. I'd run for the hills if I knocked on my door. Another reason to hope and pray his meeting has definitely finished.

As the lift dings for Ryan's floor, I hear voices. Charlie's Angel style, I stand with my back against the wall and carefully peep around the corner. My arms falter underneath the weight of the basket as I see a stunning blonde - why are they always blonde - leaving Ryan's apartment. Okay, I tell myself, she could be the meeting, it could be completely innocent and she is a very important person. Taking a deep breath, I have another peep and instantly wish I hadn't. The sight brings back the day I found Walker and I begin to feel lightheaded as I see her lean in and give him a kiss. It might only be on the cheek but she lingers there too long. I can't move away from the wall, it's my support at the moment and without it I think my legs would give way.

"Next time Rachel, give me more notice,

you're lucky I didn't have many plans this morning." Ryan's gruff voice echoes off of the stark white walls. So that's Rachel. His Walker.

"Yeah, whatever. See you later handsome." She replies in a light American lilt as she swishes past me in a cloud of expensive perfume, not even looking the side I'm on, and I'm not easy to miss today.

As she steps into the lift, completely oblivious, I weigh up my options. Do I wait and call the lift back when I know she's gone, or do I smack the hell out of Ryan's door and demand to know what the hell that was. I also weigh up whether it's worth the blood, sweat and definite tears carrying this back to the house. And whether Ryan is worth me staying for.

Taking a deep breath, I push my back away from the wall and struggle down the short corridor towards his door. Placing the basket down carefully, no need to hurt the wine, I bang on the door like a lunatic.

"What the hell!" Ryan's face is like thunder when his face appears, and shocked when he sees it's me. "What are you doing here?"

"I wanted to surprise you but looks like it's happened the other way around. Rachel seems very nice, did you have a good old catch up?"

Grabbing my arm he pulls me into the apartment and drags the basket in after me, clearly smelling the food.

"It's not what it looked like." He glares at me as he runs his hand through his hair, his whole body tensing.

"Oh please do fill me in. I'd love to know why she was kissing you too, I love a good story." I glare back at him, my nostrils flaring in anger. This explosion is not going to be pretty.

"She kissed me on the cheek for a start, she was nowhere near my mouth. Secondly, she rang me earlier saying she was in trouble and really needed my help -"

"And what you just had to be her knight in shining armour?" I snort sarcastically.

"She needed my help because her landlord is threatening to throw her out and we still haven't been able to sell the house we lived in. She wanted to know whether I could buy her out so that her and loverboy could move to San Diego together."

"And you couldn't just be honest? After everything we've both been through with lying, cheating arseholes, you couldn't just be honest with me and tell me that your meeting this morning was her?"

"I'm sorry." He hangs his head shamefully. Rightly so too. I huff, not giving him a response and bolt for the door. "Lexi? Where are you going? You're just going to storm out, not sit and talk, or argue, this out like an adult?"

"I need to clear my head and decide whether I can trust you, okay asshole?!" I slam the door behind me, my body shaking with adrenaline, and remember I haven't eaten since breakfast time. As everything starts to go dark I hear the door open behind me and feel his arms around my waist just before I hit the floor.

I wake up in a room I don't recognise. The walls are a soft cream and dozens of photographs hang on the walls. I can't focus properly to make them out but from here they look like people, family maybe? Friends? My head feels groggy as I reach for the glass of what I hope is apple juice on the table next to me. It's ice cold so must be fresh.

Waves of nausea hit me as I try to get out of the bed, my hands still shaking, so I give it up as a bad job and lay back down. I'm sure Ryan will appear soon enough.

"As long as you're sure she'll be okay Rosie, I don't want her to need medical attention and me not take her........I don't know.......probably.....okay. Of course I will, thank you, you're a lifesaver. Goodnight."

I frown at the limited conversation I could hear as the door quietly opens.

"I'm awake, it's fine," I croak. More juice.

"Rosie said I need to force feed you bananas and tell you that if you don't make sure you're eating properly, she'll fly back over and kick your sorry backside back to Yorkshire and leave you with your mum. Exact words."

I roll my eyes at her threats, what's the worst she can do thousands of miles away.

"Do you even have any bananas?" I raise an eyebrow challengingly.

"As it happens, yes." He produces a nice small one from behind his back and I curse. "I make a lot of smoothies so suck it up."

He drops the banana on my lap and sits next to me.

"I'm not eating that in front of you, I know how filthy your mind is." I try for a joke to lighten the mood.

"I'll go and chop it up if I have to but I'm not going anywhere until you've eaten it. Then I'm going to bring in that picnic you brought us. But you're on the apple juice."

"For heaven's sake, I only fainted, I'm not dying Ryan."

"That's not very funny. Eat."

Muttering a few obscenities, I reluctantly peel the banana and take a large bite as Ryan's eyes nearly pop out of his sockets. See how he likes that.

"Happy?" I splutter, trying to keep as much banana in as possible. God the texture still makes me gag.

"Very. So, do you make a habit of fainting then? I mean, for Rosie to know what works?"

"It's only happened once before, just once. I can assure you that the only reason she thinks banana works is because it's high in sugar and she heard it was good for sunstroke. Seriously, that's where her expertise end." I throw the empty skin onto his jeans as I swallow the last mouthful. "And it was only because I'd been so busy at work in and out of meetings all day that I'd forgotten to eat, so when I met Rosie in a ridiculously overheated restaurant for dinner, I fainted. She just likes to play the wise one." Huffing, I kick the bottom of the covers to allow some air to circulate. I can't believe what an idiot I was, fainting. Right after an argument too. How am I supposed to stay pissed at him when he's looking after me?

"Okay, I won't mention it again. White flag." He waves a pretend flag but I continue to scowl.

"Look, I should go home. Thanks for the banana and everything but I'm still upset over Rachel earlier."

His face softens as he shuffles closer, pulling me into an awkward side hug.

"Rachel is nothing to me anymore, as soon as the house is sold we're out of each other's lives. There's nothing else to it, that was all she wanted and I am truly sorry I didn't tell you."

"You're only sorry because you were caught. Walker was only sorry because he got caught." I know I shouldn't compare him to Walker, it was a low blow, but it just came out.

"And Rachel was only sorry when she

was caught. Remember how I'm like you here, I was on the receiving end of a cheater. I tell you what, let's look at this another way. Would you ever take Walker back or even just meet him for sex after what he did?"

His directness throws me. To be honest, after sex with Ryan I don't want to have sex with anyone else ever again, it wouldn't be fair. To me.

"No," I frown.

"Well then why would I?"

I shrug for the want of anything else to do.

"She's very pretty." Now I've lowered myself to comparing our looks. Just brilliant.

"She is," he nods slowly, never taking his eyes off of me. "But you Alexandra, you are spellbinding. I've never met anyone as perfect in every way. And pretty is nice, but it's too plain a word to use for you. You have a feisty nature that she could only dream of. You are the whole package for me."

I feel myself go red from head to toe as he takes my hand and kisses it tenderly. I don't even mind the way my full name rolls off of his tongue, it doesn't feel like I'm being chastised like it did with Walker.

"Thank you?" What else do you say to something like that? He makes me feel amazing, like I'm the only girl in the world. But given recent circumstances I'm particularly wary, and I shouldn't be when someone is as genuine as Ryan, I should be open to giving him a chance, which I was until I saw HER. Ugh. Stupid green eyed monster. Okay, now is the time to be rational and think carefully about whether you want to risk what you could have with Ryan by letting jealousy spoil things. I've seen it happen so many times before with friends and it never ends well. A good relationship needs 100% trust.

The silence in the room is suffocating. I want to trust him. I need to trust him. Sighing I rest my head on his shoulder. "Don't ever lie to me again."

I feel his whole body relax next to me, I didn't even realise how tense he was.

"I won't. And I promise I'll make it up to you. I don't want my past ruining my future with you, you know that right? I'll look into buying her out, that way she's out of my life forever." He kisses the top of my head and I close my eyes. Just five minutes and then we can eat. Just five minutes.

CHAPTER TWENTY THREE

Five minutes turned into five hours and by the time I open my eyes dusk has fallen outside. And I am really hungry.

Pushing back the covers that are stifling me, I go in search of Ryan when I hear shouting. Pushing my ear against the door, I strain to hear the conversation. I'm nosey, I know. I also know that no good ever comes from listening in on other people's conversations but it's just too hard to resist. I'm weak.

"I don't care what your excuse is, I'm through. Stop turning up at the apartment when you feel like it, I have nothing more to say to you. I'm going to have a look into my finances next week and I'll call you when I know more okay? When the house is gone, I don't want to ever see or hear from you again........what? Our relationship went wrong when I found you wrapped around your yoga instructor!"

I jolt back from the door. Wow, he's not holding back. I start to feel sorry for what I'm assuming to be Rachel when I think of Walker. Then I want to get my pompoms out and go cheer him on. I slowly crack the door open and peep out. Where is he?

"Well I don't miss you........No it really hasn't done you any favours has it, where's

everything he promised you? We could have
had it all but you threw it away. You made your
bed Rachel, it's time for you to lay in it while I
get on with my life…..yes I am with somebody
else, and I'm very, VERY happy. I'll be in touch."

My stomach flips when I hear him
mention me. At least I hope it's me.

As I round the corner into the main living
area I gasp, holding my hand to my mouth.

There before me is a table set for two.
Candle are lit, wine sits in an ice bucket and the
San Francisco skyline begins to shimmer as the
city prepares for night time. The picnic basket
that I struggled over with earlier sits in the
kitchen, emptied, and I can't help but hope he
hasn't had a binge while I've been asleep. The
thought makes me smile a little. I know he
wouldn't do that, but the image of him with a
napkin tucked into his t shirt as he feasts on an
array of picnic food makes me laugh.

"Something funny?" He slips his hand
around my waist and pulls me back against his
chest as he kisses me lightly behind my ear
sending a tingle up my spine. I breathe out
contentedly and look up at him.

"No, just silly thoughts. This is beautiful."
I turn around and put my arms around his neck
as he smiles shyly back at me, his hair damp
from the shower.

"I thought I should check that there was
nothing to refrigerate when you fell asleep, I

didn't realise it would be everything. I thought a night in might be better than going out, seems a shame to waste all the food you bought and I didn't know when you'd wake up. James isn't coming home tonight so we have the place to ourselves," he wiggles his eyebrows at me.

"Thank you. Sounds perfect."

He lets go of me as we make our way to the fridge, he gets the food out and I start to plate up on the table. It all smells so good that I just want to face plant it. Death by meat suffocation, wouldn't that be a funny coroner's report. Ha, I always have had a sick sense of humour.

"So, I couldn't help but hear you on the phone earlier," I start cautiously as I pop an olive into my mouth. These are some good olives.

"Sorry, it wasn't me that woke you up was it?"

"No, no I was awake anyway. Are you okay?"

"I'm fine. Or I will be once I know what I can do with the house. She thought that she would walk away with 1000s of dollars from the sale of the house but it doesn't work like that. The house hasn't been on the market that long but then again, she never has been the most patient woman on the planet. Stanley is welcome to her."

I start to choke on a mouthful of juice as the image of an old greying man that stands no taller than my shoulder flashes into my head. Thinking of him in a compromising yoga position is enough to put me off of my parma ham.

"Breathe Lexi, breathe. Are you okay?!" He shoots around the table and pats me on the back as my eyes finally stop streaming. Don't you hate it when that happens, and then your nose starts to run. Not a pretty sight.

"I'm fine, I'm fine." I hold up my hand. "I just, Stanley? I always picture an older man when I hear that name."

"Well, he was really. Too old for her anyway. She's only 25, he's 47. She thought that she could become his trophy wife, that he had already made his money so she would marry me, get a nice tidy divorce settlement and then they would live happily ever after. Turns out, Stanley is comfortable but not rich and wants to move to the beach, San Diego more specifically, so that he can be somewhere warmer in his older years. Somewhere relaxing."

"Sounds like she made some pretty poor decisions to me." I can't help but imagine how hard it must have been to be faced with that scenario. I mean, to be traded in for a younger, bigger breasted model was hard for me, but to be traded in for a man 16 years older than you. Brutal.

"I don't think she did now. I think she did me the biggest favour of my life, if I had never found out about her and Stanley, I would have married a gold digger and never met you. Never had this."

I can't help but grin back at him from ear to ear. He's right of course, without Walker and Lauren I would have never come to San Francisco.

"Well I propose a toast." I raise my glass and he follows my lead, looking at me quizzically. "To exes. Without them, we would never have met."

"To exes." There's a toast you don't hear every day, but for the first time, I am thankful for Walker and Lauren. Who'da thunk?

As soft music fills the room, we've taken our night to the comfort of the sofa. Ryan suggested the balcony but as soon as I stuck my head out I refused. It is a cold, bitter night and I would much rather cuddle up in front of the fire with a film and wine. Or just some wine. I'm easy. Ahem.

"Have you spoken to anyone back home lately then?" As he pours me some wine, finally, I get the feeling he's fishing.

"I spoke to Rosie yesterday, Mr Beefy is giving them hell meowing in the early hours. I think he misses me."

"Can't you bring him over here?"

"I did think about it. I suppose I need to look into it properly, and get Rosie to do the same over there. He doesn't have a kitty passport yet."

Shaking his head he chuckles. "I really can't wait to meet this cat. He sounds like he needs an ASBO."

I gasp in mock offence. "I'll have you know that my little Beefster is no ASBO cat. And anyway, Antisocial Behaviour Orders don't exist anymore, you've been out of the UK for too long clearly."

"ASBO cat." He says defiantly with a twinkle in his eye. "I like it." He chuckles a low hearty chuckle that does something funny to my insides.

"No ASBO cat," I shove him playfully as he tries to save the wine. "Jason has just had a promotion at work too so he was thrilled when I spoke to him. He can now say he is the head of the commercial property department at the law firm he works for. They were going out to celebrate this weekend."

"Good for him, it's always gratifying when your hard work pays off."

We sit nodding at each other like those nodding dog toys that sit in the back of a car. John had one on his desk at the office that I used to flick all the time when he annoyed me. Poor little thing, I'm surprised the spring didn't snap.

I know what he's waiting for though, and it's not to hear about anyone other than Luke.

"I had an argument with Luke on Wednesday via Skype too." I sip my wine steadily and study his face for any indication of what he's thinking. It doesn't slip.

"Really?" He gives me his full attention.

"Yeah, cheeky sod had the audacity to demand to know why I hadn't told him that I was staying out here. Can you believe it?"

"Why didn't you tell him?"

"I don't know. I didn't think I suppose, I was more bothered about my parents and missing Rosie. I've been that used to not thinking about him I guess I just....forgot?" I begin to feel guilty as the words leave my mouth. I did forget him.

"And he was upset?"

"Livid. He said he wanted me back there where I belong. I don't think I helped matters by telling him that I might not ever go back but I just wanted to upset him really. How much of a bitch am I?"

"He still loves you." Ryan says so quietly that I only just catch it, his face drops, like he has been defeated.

"No, no Ryan he doesn't. He thinks I'll get on brilliantly with his girlfriend. Hey, what wrong?" I lift his chin up so he has to meet my eyes. "I'm here with you, and I'm the happiest I've been in a long time. Honestly. He has his life over in London, and I have mine. Here. With you."

I put down my wine and climb onto his knees, facing him with what I hope is a seductive smile.

"But he's your first love?"

"I guess, but that was when I was a teenager, I'm now a grown woman who knows herself a lot better than she did back then. Speaking of which, how about we have dessert in bed?"

I don't need to ask twice as he stands with me wrapped around his waist and carries me into the bedroom. Who needs fancy restaurants when you have the man of your dreams?

As he flicks a light switch on in the bedroom I woke up in earlier, it dawns on me that this must be his room. I mean, I knew that he wouldn't put me in James' room but I thought it might have been yet another guest room.

He drops me gently on the bed and stands before me, his eyes full of hunger and want. As I kneel up to meet him, I pull on his shirt collar so he is forced closer to me.

"I think you a far too overdressed Mr Furrows, don't you?"

"Well then, let's do something about it." He holds out his arms and gives me a wicked grin. I feel my breathing change as I unbutton his shirt, the heat radiating off of him, enhancing the aftershave he's wearing. Every single sense is on edge as I glide my fingers down his chest, then lift my hands to nudge off his shirt. As it pools on to the floor behind him, I move off of the bed so that I'm stood before him.

"I think you need to have a lie down." I stalk around him so that the back of his knees are resting against the foot of the bed, give him a tender kiss, and nudge him onto his back as he laughs.

Lifting my vest above my head, I make sure that I watch him as I slowly undress, hoping it's having the desired effect because I know that I'm dying not leaping straight onto him, but secretly enjoying giving him a show.

"Lex." His voice is strained as his breathing gets faster, his eyes darkening as I stand in nothing but black lace, my hair now draped over my shoulders in loose curls. I lean over him, reaching for the buttons of his jeans when he grabs my hand and presses it against him. My eyes widen as I feel how hard he is in the palm of my hand and the need inside me builds. I make quick work of his jeans after that and pull them down, off of the edge of the bed and throw them to one side.

I slowly climb up the bed and lean over him, trailing kisses up every inch of his body. Oh I am going to enjoy this.

"Oh Lexi, I'm all for delayed gratification but not tonight. I need you." And before I have time to react he reaches his arm around me as he sits up and flips me back onto the bed making me squeal. "Now to make short work of these." Within seconds he has me naked and wanting. He's right, screw delayed gratification, I need him as much as he needs me, especially after the day we've had.

"Do you have any idea how happy you make me?" I whisper into his ear as he leans over me, my heart racing.

"Not as happy as you make me," he kisses me softly as his hand trails down my body, my lips parting as my breathing becomes heavy. It's in this moment that I realise just how quickly we have fallen for each other, and this time, I'm playing for keeps.

CHAPTER TWENTY FOUR

Pulling on my old black leggings and baby pink vest, I pull my hair into a high ponytail and grab my iPod. Today, for the first time in my whole life, I am going to go for a run. I have no idea how well equipped my body is for this, the shock of actual exercise might just kill it off. I mean, I ache like a biatch after sex with Ryan. He is a machine.

I bite my lip as I think about his hot and sweaty naked body above me. Hmmmm, I wonder how he'd take a booty call.

Catching sight of myself in the mirror I wrinkle my nose. Maybe I'll save the booty call for after my run when I'm freshly showered, then he can get me dirty again. Or maybe we could just take things into the shower, we haven't christened my bathroom yet and the shower is certainly big enough for two.

I slip my jacket on and pull out my phone.

You and me, my shower, 11am. Don't be late ;)

I wait a minute or two, knowing that he'll answer that message pretty quickly.

Your wish is my command. Be ready. I've missed you xx

I smile at my screen and pop it back into my pocket, pick up my water, secure my iPod and head for the park. I have two hours to get lost and explore and I cannot wait.

I still have to pinch myself every time I leave the house. I can't believe I live here, the location is everything and more than I ever could have wished for, and to be so close to a park has spurred me on to start my keep fit regime that I promised myself I would start on New Years Day. Better late than never so they say.

Standing at my front door, a strange feeling washes over me. I've never felt uncomfortable like this, not even in London, but my skin prickles as I scan the street. I feel like I'm being watched, but there is no one about other than an old lady next door sat in her garden pulling up some weeds – she must be at least 80 and she certainly looks fitter than me. That's a little bit embarrassing.

I cross the road and walk up the few stone steps into the park, giving myself a quick pep talk. Of course no one is watching me, silly girl. The early morning surge of joggers has died down and it's now mainly dog walkers so far entering with me. As I step out of an old man's way, I switch on my iPod and find my motivational playlist to get me in the mood.

The cold breeze blows the ends of my hair around my face as the golden brown leaves swirl around my ankles. It's so pretty here. I can't wait to see what it looks like when we hit autumn properly. As I get in to a steady rhythm, I think about how good a permanent move here could be for me. I still miss Rosie and Jason, and Mr Beefy of course but I could get Mr Beefy out to live with me. He would love Ryan, I can just imagine the fun he'd have winding him up with that furry little face. That's my next task after Ryan in my shower, find out how to get my beloved over here with me.....oh and maybe look for a job and sponsor.

After an hour and a half of what feels like pure abuse of my body, I decide to head back home to get a quick pre shower before Ryan arrives. I'm sweaty and smelly and just plain gross.

I tried to make an effort and remember what I'd passed as I ran so that I could find my way back out of here but other than leaving a trail of breadcrumbs that I thought may be frowned upon, my memory was my only hope. Bit silly really given that one tree looks pretty similar to the next one. Crap. Shrugging, I decide to just follow the path I'm on back down the hill in the hope that I make it to the edge of the park and can figure out where I am. Or that I pass someone that looks like they know what they're doing.

As I pick my way down through the

leaves and rocks - note to self, shortcuts are stupid - I hear someone swear behind me. I turn around and see a blonde woman picking her water bottle up that she's dropped. I can't be that far off the beaten track if there are other joggers still around. I notice a young boy walking towards us too so that helps my panic. He smiles as he passes me by and I'm still amazed that people are so friendly.

"Excuse me, does this path eventually lead to Buena Vista Avenue please?" I wait for the blonde to acknowledge me and as she lifts her head my heart stops. I don't know whether to be worried or just plain freaked out that I'm face to face with Rachel. Of all the people to see looking like shit after a long run, it had to be the real life Barbie didn't it?

"It does, yeah." She stares at me for what feels like an eternity, her eyes assessing me carefully, looking me up and down.

"Great, well, thanks." I turn away from her, hoping that she doesn't recognise me. After all, I'm pretty sure she didn't see me at Ryan's, she was too bothered about how she looked and checking herself out in the lift mirror to notice little old me stood there gawping and seething.

"Lexi, right?"

I stop walking and sigh, rolling my eyes. Not going to get away that easily then.

"To my friends, yes." I match her icy tone as I meet her hard grey eyes. She really is a fine specimen of a woman, definite girl crush territory if she hadn't been engaged to Ryan. And possibly a little bit of a stalker?

"Okay," she says steadily. "Now I get it. He's right, you are stunning, and that accent.....wow. I'm not surprised you're his current crush." She nods like she understands something I don't.

"I'm sorry?" I take a step closer and am suddenly hit by the smell of expensive perfume. Who wears perfume for a run?!

"I said I'm not surprised you're his current crush." She emphasises the word 'current'. "He does go through phases you see, he spent a while obsessing over my best friend who's Australian, then I found him with a young Latina. Like I said, phases."

"Oh I see, you think I'm just a little fling?" I step closer to her to show that I'm not intimidated. In reality my insides are shaking like a leaf and my mouth has dried out so I take a quick drink of my water. "You see, that's where we have a difference of opinion. Both Ryan and I know that this is something more than a fling, and that I'm here to stay. How's Stanley these days? Any creaky joints yet?" I raise my eyebrow as her face drops. She quickly recovers herself and laughs.

"Oh you Brits, always looking for the best in people. I'm here to do you a favour. Ryan will be back with me again soon, he always came back with his tail between his legs after each indiscretion. The thing about our relationship is that we always come back to each other, the attraction will never die. We're much stronger than our little betrayals and he will forgive me."

"No, he really won't Rachel." I shake my head and laugh at her audacity.

"Is that what you really think? Deep down do you believe that this thing you have will last when you go back to London? You think he'll give up his life here to move back to the UK?"

I falter as she hits a nerve. She has a valid point. What will happen when my visa is up here? What if I don't manage to find a job and a sponsor? Sensing my doubt she carries on, her eyes dancing with joy.

"And did he tell you that we had sex when I met up with him the other day? Long, passionate sex where he kept telling me how much he missed me? That he read your text out to me? That you only just missed us when you turned up with your pathetic picnic basket, and then passed out? He told me all about how he couldn't get rid of you after that to come and see me as we'd arranged."

"You're lying." I state simply, my voice shaking.

"Really? How would I know any of this if he hadn't told me? How would I know where you're living so that I could wait for you and get you alone? That you came here with your best friend who went back home last week?"

"You're a psychotic stalker?"

Throwing her head back and flashing her perfect white teeth she lets out a loud laugh and shrugs.

"Okay, if that's what you want to believe. Well we'll see won't we? You forget that we still own a house together, and until that sells I will make sure that I am a constant presence and a thorn in your side. I will make your life hell until you run back to England and leave me and Ryan alone. He's mine, I deserve him and I will win him back. Not that it will take much."

"And what about Stanley?"

"Oh he's just a bit of fun. He promised me the world and hasn't come through. We won't last long, he can't provide for me like Ryan can."

"I'm done listening to this crap." I turn my back on her, my legs trembling as I try to get some distance between us. I feel physically sick at the thought of them having sex. I can't believe it. I won't believe it.

Oh God what if it is true.

I'm that busy having a conversation with myself in my head that I'm not prepared for the impact of Rachel's full body slamming into mine as she jogs past me, laughing. My legs give way and I stumble head first into a mound of rocks, my arms not cushioning the blow as my head hits the ground, the thud sickening me as everything goes dark.

As I begin to stir the pain in my head shoots through me and I wince.

"Fuck." I hiss through gritted teeth as the hot tears start to fall down my cheeks. I slowly open my eyes and realise I'm still in the park, I can't have been out for that long. The cold makes me shiver though as I lay next to a large eucalyptus tree. Slowly, I try to push myself onto my feet, my wrist throbs and struggles to support my full weight as I haul myself up against the tree trunk. I really need to get home.

Lifting my hand cautiously to my head, I check for blood. Thankfully I'm all clear, but I'm pretty sure I should seek some kind of medical attention. Ugh, how much is that going to rob me? Maybe I'll just pop a painkiller instead.

"Excuse me ma'am, are you okay?" A young woman, probably no older than me, appears at my side.

"I'm fine. Well, I mean obviously I'm not fine fine, but I will be. I just need to get home."

"I saw you get up, I'd say you need a hospital more than you need to get home."

"Seriously, I just need to get home." I say through clenched teeth as she stays beside me.

"Well then at least let me make sure you get home okay? How far are you?"

"Buena Vista Ave." I carry on hobbling as

she offers me her shoulder for support.

"Nice. Well the good news is that you're not far at all. The bad news is there's a really steep slope coming up with no steps." She puts her arm around my waist and lets me rest most of my weight on her. I'd be quite ready to believe that she was my guardian angel if she'd have turned up a bit sooner. Still, I'm thankful for her kindness. I doubt anyone would have looked the side I was on had I been Hyde Park.

God bless America.

"Jesus Lexi!" Ryan runs across the road without even looking as we finally exit the park. My new friend, who I now know as Tamera, laughs at him.

"That your boyfriend?"

"Yeah, kind of," I smile.

"He's hot." I notice her cheeks go red as he gets closer to us.

"What the hell happened to you?!" He looks like I feel. Battered and devastated.

"I'll leave you to it. Make sure you go to a hospital." Tamera gives me a stern look that earns her a glare in return.

"I'm fine."

"Oh you're seeing a doctor lady. She'll get to a hospital, even if I have to carry her there myself."

"I like you. He's a keeper." She laughs and

gives me a pat on the shoulder. "Stay safe."

I nod as she gives us a wave and jogs away down the street.

"Come on, let's get you inside and cleaned up. I tried calling you, why didn't you answer your phone? I've been sat outside ages."

Shit. I put my hand in my pocket and let out a small sob as I see my smashed phone. I must have landed against it when I fell. I can't believe my iPod survived and my phone didn't. Gutted.

"That's why." I hand him my smashed phone and sigh as I whimper at the steps up to my door with despair.

Reading my mind like my knight in shining armour, Ryan lifts me up gently and carries me up them, placing me down once we're safely at the top.

"I have an old iPhone you can have, don't worry."

"Did you have sex with Rachel that day I saw her there?"

"What?!" He lets the door swing open as he turns to stare at me dumbstruck. The sharpness of his voice making me jerk back.

"You heard me. Am I a little fling like the Australian or the Latina girl?" I gulp back the tears as he pushes me abruptly through the door and guides me into the den where I flop onto the soft grey sofa, making some of the cushions fall to the floor.

"Where the hell has this come from? Did you bang your head?"

"As a matter of fact yes, I did. I smacked it against a pile of rocks that your ex fucking fiancée pushed me into after she'd told me how you would run back to her soon enough. That you were supposed to go see her that night I passed out with the picnic basket, that during long passionate sex you kept saying how much you missed her. She knew about Rosie going back to England and said she'd be a thorn in my side until I went back home.......She wants you back Ryan."

I notice his jaw clench tightly as he lets out a bitter laugh.

"And of course you we're quick to believe that bullshit? You believe so easily that I would cheat on you with.....THAT?! After all we said the other night? I thought we'd sorted all of this out?"

"No, I didn't believe her, I told her I thought she was a psychopathic stalker but how would she know all that stuff if you haven't told her?"

We stare at each other for what feels like an eternity. Neither one backing down.

"I don't know," he says eventually. "I really don't. I mean, I know that one of her old friends was a model on that shoot? Rachel has always been very quick at reading people's weaknesses and their reactions too. No offence, but she'll have read your face like an open book and landed pretty lucky with her attacks. And she could have just followed me here, I wouldn't have noticed her. I'm sorry if that's how she found you."

"Maybe. But she didn't see me that day at your apartment though." I pick at my nail varnish, not daring to meet his eyes.

"How do you know?"

"Because I watched her get into the elevator, she was more bothered about her own reflection that anything else."

"Her reflection?"

"Yes." I frown up at him. "That's what I said."

"Yes, she was looking in a mirror Lex. How do you know she didn't see you in it? Please Lexi, when will you trust me one hundred percent?"

He cups my face and kisses me passionately, like he is almost pleading with me to believe him. I close my eyes and get lost in his arms. Today was not supposed to turn out like this.

"How about I get you checked out at a hospital then stay here again tonight? I don't want you left alone, for more than one reason, and I need to sort Rachel out once and for all. You could press charges you know? I can't believe the lengths she would go to. I never thought the Rachel I knew was like this, you know?" He sits back in the seat next to me, resting his head back as he stares into space. "When we first met all those years ago, I never thought I would end up like this. I never imagined I would be so desperate for a way to get her out of my life, but I am. I'm going to make a few calls and see what I can do to keep her away from us. From you. I'll use the house as leverage if I have to, threaten to leave her with nothing, I just want her out of our lives."

"Thank you. For everything. Except the hospital, I hate those damn places. How much will they charge?" I screw my face up in disgust.

"Don't worry about that, just get your head checked.....and everything else, you could have broken bones or anything."

"Fine, fine." I admit defeat. My head hurts too much to fight him on this one, and if I'm honest, I do feel a bit sick.

I really hope he makes Rachel pay.

CHAPTER TWENTY FIVE

I didn't sleep a wink last night knowing Ryan could be seeing Rachel today. He wouldn't tell me much yesterday after the hospital visit, instead he insisted on playing nurse all night and taking perfect care of me. The good news is nothing is damaged or broken, just a sprained wrist and a few cuts and bruises but I promised to take it easy today. There will be no jogging in the park again for a while, that's for sure. Not that I needed an excuse to be lazy.

I pull the covers further over my head to drown out the stream of light coming through the curtains and feel a twinge of longing for the morning companionship of my grumpy little kitty. Mr Beefy would always have a tale to tell me in the morning, and then he would demand his food. Same routine every day and I feel lost without him.

My new phone buzzes softly on the now cold pillow that Ryan left this morning. I admit it has been nice having him around on a night and the days go faster when he's about.

Given that I've been ordered to rest – by Ryan - today is absolutely going to be the day I sit around eating chocolate, drinking chocolate, thinking of chocolate, and watching Choccywoccydoodah on the television, possibly followed by Honey Boo Boo. It's officially a write off anyway because this mood is not going to go away until I know Rachel is on her way to San Diego with Mr Flexible.

Finally relenting and peeping out from under the warmth of my fluffy duvet, I swipe my phone and pout when I realise it's only a Candy Crush request, then give myself a small slap across the face, not enough to leave a mark but hard enough so that my mood knows I mean business.

"Snap out of it you cranky cow," I snarl, throwing my phone back onto the pillow. "Time to get this show on the road." It's probably a good job Mr Beefy isn't here right now, if there was a kitty equivalent to Child Services, I'm fairly certain he'd be dialling it today with my crazy chitchat.

Two hours later I'm bathed, dressed, eating an enormous bar of Dove, or Galaxy as I insist on calling it and drinking a mug of hot chocolate. This is how Mondays should be spent. Chocolate and channel surfing. I decided that today would be spent slobbing around then tomorrow I would continue with my San Francisco adventure again. I might even hire a bicycle and cycle across the Golden Gate Bridge now I don't have to worry about losing Rosie somewhere along the way. This also helps me justify wasting a day in front of the television, something I usually loathe.

"Okay America, hit me with your worst." I flick through around 30 channels, all of them either have an ad break or are shopping channels selling something that nobody would ever want or need, although the adverts are thoroughly entertaining in themselves. Eventually I settle on a pageant show and admire all the gorgeous little girls, marvelling at how ahead of their years they are.

I remember Rosie and I raiding my mum's wardrobe when we were around seven, we forced Luke and Jason to keep watch in case she came home early. When she did come home and found us wearing her makeup, drowning in her clothes and saturated in her expensive perfume, she went ballistic. Mostly with my dad because he was supposed to be keeping an eye on us - a responsible adult he was not. The memories make me smile. Not the getting told off side obviously, hated that part.

I'm just about to set the TiVo box to record the whole series when I hear a tap on the door. Totally not answering that today either. This is the good thing about having more televisions and kitchen spaces than is necessary, I can hide away on a different floor and not have to answer to anybody. I do still mute the television though, just to be safe.

The unwanted guest carries on with their

incessant tapping and I groan in frustration. Sorry Tootsie, I'll have to pause you, you little beauty.

Stomping down the stairs, just to get my point across to whomever is outside, I grab the keys from the table in the hall, muttering to myself, and pull open the door.

Aw hell. Not again.

Can you talk lex?

Little bit busy at the moment! Something you'd like to tell me rosie?

Ah, so he's been in touch then? Just do not see him until you've spoken to me. I repeat do not!

Been in touch? Bit late for that, he's already landed on my doorstep. Thanks for giving him my address by the way you traitor. I'm so confused now.

Bollocks. Just don't do anything stupid, i really need to speak to you.

What classifies as stupid?

Fuck. Why?

I'm about to text her back when my doorbell goes. Given the circumstances, I think I'll ignore it. Staring into my wine glass I realise that I have no idea what to say to Luke, he's flown all this way and I just have nothing for him as he sits across from me, just watching me. He's already declared his undying love for me, told me he's ended it with Alice and has come here to prove how much he's prepared to do to win me back.

Pretty romantic really.

The doorbell goes again.

God dammit. Sighing in exasperation, I leave Luke sat at the dining table to go and answer the door. So much for my peaceful day of rest! I am in no mood for small talk with strangers on my doorstep, even if they are pleasant Americans. I wonder whether they have door canvassers in America? Hmmm.

Answer me lexi!

**Alexandra louann jones do not make
Me Skype your ass!!!!!!!!**

Tap tap tap

"Hang on already!" I shout. Jeez somebody's eager to sell me something.

Pulling open the door I smile, part relief that it's not a salesman, part goofy love. It sounds silly but I really have fallen head over heels for this gorgeous man stood before me, I just really need to sort my shit out with Luke and clear up just what we are. Friends. Nothing more, nothing less.

"Hey Ryan. What's up? I thought you were sorting out the house with Rachel today? Is everything okay?" I slide through the door and shut it behind me.

"Nothing's wrong Lex, in fact everything's great now. I just wondered if you wanted some company, it's a lovely day and I thought we could go out somewhere, Sausalito maybe? I can explain everything over a bite to eat." He cranes his neck to try and look through the door. "What you hiding in there Jingle, because no offence but I don't really fancy coming to visit you in prison. And I don't think orange is your colour," he jokes, but I can't laugh. I have a sinking feeling in the pit of my stomach. He is not going to react well to this.

"Not hiding anything. Um, Luke arrived about an hour ago, bit of a surprise for my birthday I think." I bite my lip and try to gauge his reaction, hoping he can't tell that I'm bending the truth a little. Okay, a lot. I just don't want him to freak out just yet. His face doesn't change though. The same smile sticks to his face like he's been frozen, I want the ground to open up and swallow me.

"Oh. Luke's come all the way out here? For you? Okay. Of course. Right, so I guess I'll catch up with you tomorrow, or sometime. Have a good day Jingle."

My heart breaks as he walks quickly down the steps. I close my eyes and debate which direction to go in.

"Shit. Ryan, wait!" I call after him and start to follow him but trip on a stupid plant pot and fall head first onto the concrete pavement, cursing my bad luck. He doesn't even turn around. He didn't even acknowledge my shouting him, or my yelping as I fell unceremoniously to the ground. This is not the same Ryan that carried me up the stairs yesterday, or the same Ryan that insisted on waiting on me hand and foot all night just in case something hurt me.

Picking myself up cautiously and assessing the damage I wince. When the hell did I get so clumsy? My hands are grazed, my knee is bleeding and my chest hurts. It hits me that the thought of losing Ryan kills me, I need to go after him and explain to him what's actually going on, but given my current state I realise that I can barely walk, again, let alone go on a man hunt. I hobble back up the steps and feel a hot tear trickle down my cheek. I hear Luke talking to someone as I make my way through to the lounge.

"Here she is. Bloody hell what's wrong? Here sit down." As Luke puts his arm around me I sigh.

"Hey! Lukio! Hand her over! Lexi?!" As Rosie's voice booms out of nowhere I notice my new iPad on the coffee table. Picking her up, I smile wearily.

"Hey Rosie."

"Good God Lex, I've barely been gone a week and already you look like crap. What's happened?" Sensing my hesitation she narrows her eyes at me. Doesn't have the same effect thousands of miles away though. "Luke? Beat it, I need to talk to her."

"Get lost Rosie, I've only just got here and she's a mess, you should see all of the blood pouring down her leg."

As the two continue to bicker, I rest my head back on the sofa and close my eyes again but all I can see is the hurt look on Ryan's face. Sure he was a bit of a dick for not looking back or helping me up, but would I have done the same? Probably. Hell, if Walker had fallen down the stairs the day I caught him and Lauren, chances are I'd have kicked him in the balls for good measure when he was down. When someone has hurt you, the last thing you want to do is help them.

"Fine, if you want to hear all about my periods Lukio then so be it."

That one word makes him blanch and me giggle. Smiling nervously, he hands me the iPad and walks away heading back to the kitchen.

"Okay so firstly, don't ever ignore my texts again! Have you any idea how stressful the last 15 minutes have been? Secondly, listen and listen carefully, and do not interrupt before I've got everything out."

I give her a silent salute and turn the volume down, conscious that Luke could be within earshot. We were clearly dealing with mean Rosie today, and although she may be halfway across the world, I still didn't want to piss her off. I have Choos coming my way one day remember.

"Right." As she takes a deep breath I notice Betty in the background and I smile. I knew it would go up in their bedroom, I wonder what Jason said about it.

Crap, must pay attention.

"So, about an hour ago Jason and I had a visitor…..Alice. Now, I don't want to freak you out but, well, you haven't done anything yet have you?"

"What do you mean, 'done anything?'" I snap.

"Don't play coy with me, you know exactly what I mean Missy. Have you bumped nasties?" I laugh at Rosie's way with words, and the fact that she looks so furious with me but can't do anything about it.

"You're a cheeky bitch you do know that don't you? No Rosie, Luke and I haven't 'bumped nasties', what do you take me for? I'm with Ryan and he's only been here an hour anyway."

"You never used to need that long so don't give me that crap. But that's good. Don't. Ever. Alice is pregnant."

My whole world stops as her words hit me like a bucket of ice cold water. Luke has travelled all the way over here and left his pregnant girlfriend. Surely not?

"P-pregnant? Does he know?"

"She's says not, she came here looking for him because they aren't together anymore apparently, broke up the other day. She didn't know he was heading your way though. Kind of puts a spanner in his big romantic plan doesn't it?"

It's a funny feeling finding out your first love has come all the way out here to declare his undying love for you, not knowing he's going to be a dad. Talk about a game changer. This day is turning out to be a bit of a mess really. I never imagined my life would become such a soap opera, I mean seriously, you couldn't make this stuff up.

"Right. Well then, best let him know huh?" I can feel the back of my eyes start to burn. This is so screwed up. I am in love with Ryan and know that I don't want to be with Luke like that anymore, but this news really chokes me up. I must be hormonal.

"Okay doll, let me know how it goes will you? I'm exhausted so really need to hit the sack but, are you going to be okay?"

"I will do and yes. Thank you. Love you loads Rosie." I sniffle down the camera.

"Love you too Lex." She blows a kiss my way and waves as she disconnects our call.

Throwing myself back into the cushions again I squeeze the bridge of my nose, wondering whether it would be wrong to just crawl back into bed. Then I remember the blood tricking down my knee that needs addressing. I'm pretty sure blood stains and a pale sofa would upset Ryan's friend. It would upset me.

"Luke?!" I hobble through to the kitchen, hoping that there's a first aid kit in here somewhere. Luke has disappeared, true to form, what man is ever around when you need them. Ryan is, my subconscious reminds me, like a little devil tapping on my shoulder, forgetting about the times Luke has been my rock. She is right of course, Ryan would be here if it was a normal day. It takes me a second to remember that Ryan walked away from me as I was calling his name so technically I guess this is his God damn fault for overreacting. I wince as I dab my knee with some antiseptic - or at least I hope it's antiseptic, it smells like it anyway - and start to bandage the poor thing up. My hands sting but a quick rinse under the tap and they're fine, just a bit ugly looking. Picking up my glass of wine from where I left it, I take a tentative sip and begin to relax. Hot chocolate is not strong enough for what I'm dealing with today.

"Luke, where are you, we need to carry on our little talk. I have some news." As I walk back through the living room and into the den I see him sat staring out of the window, looking onto the street towards the park.

"Hey you," I say softly as I take a seat next to him. This is one of my favourite rooms to sit in and people watch, it makes sense that Luke has taken to it too.

"I've just switched my mobile on, Alice

has been trying to get in touch. I don't even know what to say to her, I told her I needed time." He looks in pain as he talks, the inner fight clear on his face. Time to bite the bullet, but first another slug of wine.

"Yeah," I swallow. "I kind of know why."

He turns and looks at me confused.

"She's pregnant Luke." I take a second to let the news sink in. I thought about building up to it but really, how do you build up to something like this? All the colour has drained from his face as his breathing starts to shake. "She really needs you right now." I look at my hands, not knowing where else to look. I consider offering him my wine but decide that I need it more. He wants some, he knows where the kitchen is. I'm nice like that.

"No," he whispers, his eyes slowly beginning to fill. I rest my hand on his back and give him a couple of supportive strokes. Then I carry on trying to find the answer to my problems in the bottom of my glass. If in doubt, numb the pain, even if it is only early in the day - its six o'clock somewhere in the world, right?

"Yeah." God I wish Rosie was here, she is great in awkward moments, even if she has to crack a joke she manages to break the tension.

"But, I love you Lexi. I want you. I need you. I've flown all this way to beg you to come home and give me a second chance. That day you answered your front door to me my world tipped on its head, how could it not, you were my everything when we were young. I still think about you every second of the day now, what it would be like to just lean across and kiss you, to do the simple things like hold your hand. It was fate, Lexi. It was fate." He says the last part so softly that it takes everything I have not to break down in tears with him.

"I know Luke, but you left. We grew up and things change. I still love you but...."

"Lexi don't do this. Please!" The desperation in his voice hits me like shards of glass, it's so painful and I can't bear to know that I'm the one that's caused it.

"You'll always be my one of my best friends Luke. I'll always be here for you, and I'll try to be the coolest aunt ever. Obviously I'll be way cooler than Rosie." I joke feebly. "But don't you see how it just won't work? It would break my heart every time you had to go be with Alice for something to do with your child. When it's born. It's first injections. It's first illness. It's first day at nursery. At school. It will be a forever thing and when she rings you, you'll have to drop everything and go, but that's okay, because that's the right thing to do. It's what you should do. But I can't deal with that with our past, and I feel like a piece of me is dying inside saying this to you, but I honestly think that this is it for us. End of the line."

"I don't want to be with her though, I can't

love her the way I love you. Every inch of my body feels so alive when I'm near you." He touches me face and I have to pull away. I can't take anymore, he's almost begging me and I feel like the biggest bitch walking shoe leather.

"Nobody is saying you have to be with her Luke, just support her. And you will find someone that will make you feel like this and more, trust me. You need to talk it out with her. And I need to see my time out here. I like it here Luke, I like the new life I'm building." I give him a small kiss on the cheek and leave the den. I need some space, I can't breathe. And I really need to find Ryan. So much drama in one day.

I grab my phone and bag, texting Rosie to let her know that I'd told him and would call her tomorrow and head for the door.

"I'm nipping to the shop Luke, give you a bit of space, do you want anything?" I think I need to give him some time to think things through properly without me in the vicinity.

"No, I think I'm just going to unpack and borrow your iPad to speak to Alice if you don't mind? I know it's going to be kind of late but you're right, I need to speak to her." He smiles sadly and I just nod when an envelope on the welcome mat catches my eye.

"Did you hear the letterbox go?" I pick it up, eyeing it suspiciously. It's probably a poison pen letter from Rachel, just to top my day off.

"No, why what is it." He always has been

bloody nosey. He comes and stands over my shoulder as I rip it open and gasp. Inside is a small handwritten card and a printout of a booking for Cavallo Point.

My Dear Lexi,

When I saw you today, I knew I had lost. If Luke is your happy ever after then you have to go for it. I wish you all the luck and love I can. I booked for us a stay at Cavallo Point for your birthday, you should still use it.

All my love

Ryan xxx

The tears are streaming down my face as I read and reread his letter. This isn't supposed to be how it ends. Why are men always jumping to the wrong conclusion and now I'm a crying wreck again, ugly crying at that. Shaking, I hand over the card to Luke and slowly sink to the floor, resting my back against the cool, wooden door.

"Wow." Slowly sitting down next to me he pulls me into one of his famous hugs as I saturate his t shirt with my tears.

"I feel like all I've done since you've been back in my life is cry on your shoulder." We sit in silence as he strokes my hair, his heartbeat slowly relaxing me as it steadily hums against my cheek.

"Go find him. Don't let me be the reason that you lose the happy ending you deserve. I made that mistake 13 years ago and have regret it every single day since. If you think he's the one, then go for it." He's beaten; I can hear it in his voice.

I look into his eyes and know that he means it. I can't believe that I've been given another chance with my first love, and yet, I don't want it. I feel like I need Ryan as much as the air I breathe. Luke is always going to my rock, as I will his, we know each other inside out and back to front and I love him dearly, but not in the same way I love Ryan. Not anymore.

Today really has been cathartic if nothing else. We have finally let each other go, but we will never be gone from each other's lives again. I realise how truly lucky I am to have three lifelong friends that I know I can always turn to when I need them.

We both stand together and as he gives me a quick kiss, I pull him into my own bear hug.

He still smells amazing.

CHAPTER TWENTY SIX

"Is Ryan here?" I huff and puff standing in front of James as he eventually opens the apartment door. These hills should come with a health warning.

"Nice to see you too. And no, he's not, he's supposed to be with you." He wrinkles his brow at me suspiciously. Isn't he even going to invite me in? I realise I look like some kind of crazy person with my curls scooped up into a loose ponytail and rushed together outfit of jogging trousers with Ugg boots and big fluffy jumper that I'm really regretting wearing now. It's like a sweat box.

"I just really need to find him and speak to him. He called by earlier but when he found out Luke was there he just walked away. When he left me he looked so upset. He must have come back though because he pushed a note through my door." I rub my forehead, this really is getting too much. Maybe I should just give up on men altogether, just settle down with Mr Beefy and become a spinster.

"Come in, I'll try his mobile, see if he'll tell me where he is." Thankfully James doesn't question me any further.

As I walk through the door I'm hit with the view again and there's something that's quite soothing about it. I notice the computer in the corner has photographs from the shoot up on the screen and wander across to have a look. Rosie must be thrilled with now they've come out, they look like they're straight off of the pages of Vogue and I can't help but feel a huge sense of pride for my best friend. Probably best she isn't here though, she'd probably slap me senseless for potentially ruining the relationship I have with Ryan over Luke. Of course she loves Luke like a brother, but she can probably see something we can't. I wouldn't ever want to lose Luke if our relationship didn't work out, the thought of ever hating him is sickening.

I turn around as James comes back in, phone up to his ear, his brows knit together again. I consider making a smart remark about him needing Botox if he carries on but it's probably best that I keep my mouth shut.

"Nah that's fine man, just wondered but I'll get on with some more editing if you're at the office for the rest of the day. See you later."

"Okay, right, so where does he work? I've never noticed any music sh- hang on did you say office?" I'm confused - not that it's for the first time today.

"Yeah, he works downtown, I'll take you if you want? I could do with a break anyway. Although I really feel I owe it to Rosie to tell you that you look like shit. Do you want to get changed first?"

"But, I thought he worked in a music shop?" I ignore his comment about my clothes. I was already fully aware that I looked a mess, I didn't need him to rub it in.

Now it's James' turn to look confused as he cocks his head to one side.

"What on earth gave you that idea?" As he pulls his leather jacket on and picks up his keys he comes to a standstill in front of me.

"When we first met he said he was in music and I......." Oh my. See this is what happens when you assume. How embarrassing. I can feel my face starting to burn.

"You thought working in a music store could pay for this apartment, the house you live in and a place in Sausalito?" He looks at me like I've just asked whether the Pope really is a Catholic.

Whoa, rewind, did he just say....

"What do you mean the house I live in?!" I screech as he guides me towards the apartment door. So much for my heartfelt plea for him to listen to me, looks like he has some explaining of his own to do.

"I thought you knew? Well that's me probably finding a new place to live now when he finds out I've blabbed so I guess I may as well tell you now. Yes, they're all his but he gets a bit funny about money, doesn't like to bring it up."

The colour must drain out of my face because I certainly feel it get colder, I never want to go through the menopause if this is what it's like all the time. Hot, cold, hot, cold.

Taking a deep breath I ask the million dollar question.

"Why does he get funny about money James? How well off is he?"

Stopping at the lifts he turns and grins.

"Absolutely stinking rich."

Sweet. Baby. Jesus.

James knocks on Ryan's office door then scampers off. Wimp.

"Yeah?" I hear Ryan's gruff voice come from behind the large wooden door before me. His name etched into a small silver plate makes the humiliation so much worse. This isn't some small time office where you sit in a 6ft by 8ft cubicle, a bit like Mooneys. Oh no, this is big boy territory nestled deep in the heart of downtown San Francisco, all glass walls and shiny elevators. It's certainly an imposing building that makes its presence known. I can't believe I assumed that he worked in a music store, not that there's anything wrong with that, but he's hardly going to get a visa through that now is he. The pieces all fall into place now as I think back over the conversations we've had. Rachel being a gold digger, him paying for her yoga lessons, him having an accountant! And then there's the stay at Cavallo Point for my birthday.

Cautiously I bend the handle and pop my head through, giving him a small smile.

"Hey you." I shut the door behind me and wander across the spacious room, the smell of sandalwood filling the air. He's sat at an oversized desk in front of a view of the city that almost rivals his apartments. Floor to ceiling windows are the things dreams are made of. I think I'm gawping a little.

"What's up?" His voice is cold, his arms crossed tightly. I feel like he's on lockdown. Taking a deep breath I decide to take a seat at his desk, may as well, I think I'll be here a while.

"Look," I sigh, "we clearly need to talk. You have some serious explaining to do mister; I can't even begin to explain how hurt and angry I was on the drive over here. Did you not think to tell me that you were stinking rich? You owe James your life for calming me down." I smirk at him gesturing I'm the direction of a very heavy looking paperweight where I notice a large wooden photoframe containing a picture of us from our day in Castro. I can't believe he has that on his desk at work. We look perfect together, so happy and carefree, the look of love crystal clear on both of our faces. What I wouldn't give to turn back the clock a few days.

"So I didn't tell you I was rich. So what? You're the one hiding Luke," he grumbles petulantly.

Oh he's a sulker. Should have guessed.

"Hey, I came here so that we could clear the air. I was not hiding Luke, Luke and I will never be more than good friends. At least he's been honest with me though unlike you! You lied to me Ryan, and not just a small one or even a little lie of omission, I'm living in your goddamn house! You didn't think it would be nice to tell me? I want to pay you rent, in fact I insist. How much does a house like that cost a month?" My pitch is definitely higher than I would like but I'm so pissed at him and he isn't even breaking out into a sweat for God's sake.

He sits back causally in his chair, his face never slipping. He is infuriating.

"I don't want your money Lexi."

"How much Ryan? I'm giving you something, why can't you get that through your thick skull?"

"$21,000 a month."

Well fuck.

"Oh. Okay so I don't actually have enough to live there, little bit soul destroying. Why didn't you tell me? Don't you trust me? Because it works both ways remember. You know that I'm nothing like Rachel. Hell, the woman has crazy stalked me, knocked me unconscious and tried to convince me that you cheated on me that afternoon I caught her coming out of your apartment." I silently pray to whichever God is awake and listening to me that he won't say no. Or at least if he's thinking it that he's too polite to say it.

He gets up and walks around the desk, sitting in the seat next to me and taking my hand.

"Lexi I trust you with everything I own. It's just a lot of people, well they get weird about money. I mean really, can you blame me? Just look at what I've been through. I wanted you to get to know me for me first, before any of the bells and whistles that come with me. That's why I wanted us to do normal things, a walk around Castro, the drive to Sausalito -"

"A night at Cavello Point?" I raise my eyebrow and he shrugs.

"It's your birthday. If you can't treat someone on their birthday then when can you?"

He has a point, I'd do it for him if I could.

"I just wish you hadn't lied about the house too. I should have known it was too good to be true."

"I don't understand? You're not moving out are you?" He shoots up from his seat, towering above me.

"What else can I do?!" I stand up and throw my arms up in exasperation. Am I stupid for feeling this way, is it an overreaction? Should I just say, hey it's okay that you lied about the house to me, fresh start? Again.

Maybe I am overreacting. Even though it feels like longer, the fact of the matter is I've only known him three weeks, he doesn't owe me anything. In the time that I've known him he's been nothing but generous and kind since we cleared the air that day. He's even letting me live in an amazing house rent free. A house that quite frankly, Rosie, Jason and I put together couldn't afford to rent.

"Money causes so many problems Lex, I didn't want to risk losing you over it. Just look at how you're acting now, if you move out what's to say you won't just forget about me? I can't imagine not having you in my life anymore. The thought terrifies me more than I'd care to admit, you bring out the better man in me. I need you Lexi." My heart swells with his words as I watch him pace around his desk running his hands through his hair.

"You know that I'm not going anywhere, I love it here in San Francisco, I love my life now, I love you and I'm not going to be leaving that house. Okay?" I snap, slumping back down in to my chair. I am exhausted.

My flesh turns stone cold as I realise what I've just said. It's like time stands still and I hold my breath, praying that he didn't pick up on it, because let's face it, men aren't always that observant. They hear what they want to and hopefully he just heard 'not leaving the house' and 'I love my life now'.

"What did you just say?" His eyes heat as he takes a step closer to me. My heart slams against my chest, pounding hard and fast as he gets dangerously close. Pulling me up and wrapping his arm around my waist he draws me flush against his chest. I can feel his heart racing against my own.

"I love my life?" I squeak, staring into his eyes.

"After that."

"I'm not leaving the house?" I try. I'm grasping at straws and am met by a heart melting smile.

"Before that." He whispers.

Gulping I try to steady my breathing before I answer again. He doesn't seem mad though, in fact he seems very, whoa-

He doesn't wait for long and as his lips meet mine, my legs turn to jelly. I'm completely lost in him. My wits, well they're scattered across his office floor and I can't help but wish my clothes were there with them.

"I love you." I say quietly, raking my fingers through his soft waves. There. I've said it. It's out there. I've never fallen for someone as fast as I have Ryan, it took Walker and I four months just to say it to one another, and I don't think Luke and I ever did say it. We were teenagers, we just assumed we loved each other when it was probably lust. I don't know. I suppose I'll always class him as my first love, but this right here, right now, this is 100% head over heels, walk over hot coals, want to marry you and have your babies love. Best not say that bit out loud though.

"And I love you too Lexi, more than you could ever imagine. Please don't ever scare me like this again. You are everything to me."

I don't remember much after those words, all I know is that when he kissed me again, I saw stars.

ELLEN FAITH

FLYNN DYSON SOLICITORS
25 Barker Road
London
E14 2LR

Miss A Jones
C/O A Little Piece of Yorkshire
The Grove
West Wickham
BR4
Our ref: TB/HLP/Harrison

23 September 2013

Dear Miss Jones

Separation Matters

We have been instructed in relation to the above matter by Mr Walker Harrison.

Our client informs us that following the unfortunate breakdown of your relationship, you decided to leave the property that you jointly owned and are now residing in San Francisco for an unknown duration.

Our client does have concerns about your intentions for the property as he is now in a new relationship and would like to draw a line under all financial matters so that you can both move on with your lives. We would like to propose a more than generous offer of £30,000 as payment for your name to be removed from the mortgage and the property be transferred into Mr Harrison's sole name. I think you will appreciate that given the current climate, and the fact that our client has advised us that he is more than happy to arrange to get the payment £30,000 to you before Christmas, this is an offer than should be carefully considered.

We would also ask that you provide us with an up to date postal address and/or email address to save time so that we may write to you directly and not through a third party. Our client believes that this will only exacerbate matters should they inappropriately get involved.

Finally, our client has asked us to raise the matter of some 15 suits that he believes to have gone missing since your separation and wondered whether you could perhaps shed any light on this.

We look forward to hearing from you or your appointed solicitor as soon as possible.

Yours sincerely

Terence Bland
FLYNN DYSON

From: Alexandra Jones (lexilou12@hotmail.co.uk)
To: T.Bland@flynndyson.co.uk
Date: 7 October 2013 14:21
Subject: Your letter of 23 September 2013

Dear Mr Bland,

I read your letter with some interest and have to kindly decline your offer of £30,000.

I do appreciate that the current market is slow, but I also know that things are steadily picking up and that our £800,000 house won't have lost that much value. Our mortgage was for £500,000, therefore I would happily accept an offer in the region of £130,000 which should be something near my 50% share of the current equity, and that is allowing for a slight loss with the market.

My email address at the moment is the best, and most efficient way to contact me. When the transfer for the property does need signing, I am happy to receive a scanned copy to sign and return to you. I would prefer not to give you my postal address.

Finally, in relation to Mr Harrison's suits, I'm afraid after I caught him with his secretary in our shower, I asked a friend to pack up my belongings. In the rush, some of his suits may have accidentally slipped in. Should he wish to try and track his suits down though, he should try contact North London Action for the Homeless. I can assure you that it is a very good cause and I'm sure their charity greatly accepted his donation.

I look forward to hearing from you in relation to the property.

Kind regards

Alexandra Jones

EPILOGUE

Stretching my legs out towards the bottom of the bed, I wriggle my toes and sigh happily. I've been in San Francisco now for eight months and things are going remarkably well. I have a job that I love that has allowed me to both stay in San Francisco and write for a living. I now work for the company that Ryan owns, and I realise that that sounds a bit weird but things have worked out well. We don't work side by side but it's nice knowing that he's around for me when I need him, and also when I need a ride home. Or lunch.

Home. Our home. Ryan moved into the Buena Vista house and let James have the apartment. Oh, and Mr Beefy arrived safe and sound to join us. I'm not sure that they're going to bond anytime soon to be honest which is disappointing, but just having both loves of my life with me under one roof does something funny to my stomach. I go all warm and fuzzy. Hold on while I get you a bucket.

I hear a loud purr in my ear and smile. Looks like somebody is ready for breakfast. Waiting for him to walk across me so that I don't send him sailing across the bedroom, I push the covers back and give him a quick kiss. I'm just happy that he's settled so well, and he never even got jetlag. Do animals get jetlag? Must remember to Google that.

I can hear Ryan pottering in the kitchen and decide that I should probably go help him. I do love our Sunday mornings together. We spend our nights and weekends going out places and talking until the early hours, a contrast to my life with Walker.

Hmmm, Walker. Well, let's just say that I would have given my right kidney to be a fly on the wall when he told precious mummy that he had managed to impregnate Lauren and that she was going to be a grandma to a child that would probably have less class than a monkey. Oh how I laughed. I did end up paying Walker £1000 as a gesture for his suits though, not that that covered more than one but his solicitor obviously advised him to take it. I didn't really mind considering the same solicitor finally accepted that I was owed more than a poxy £30,000 for my share of the house. Damn straight considering it was valued at £800,000! So now my bank account looks extremely healthy and Walker must be extremely unhealthy. Walker a dad, ha, I wonder how long he'll last. Always had a weak stomach you see.

Opening up Facebook on my phone, I have a quick check in on everybody back home. Luke and Alice will be ready for having their baby soon, a little boy apparently, and he is so excited about it. They eventually managed to work through their problems and although a baby wasn't something either of them wanted just yet, they have embraced it and dare I say it, Alice is even starting to be pleasant to me. Rosie still hates her though which means that she'll never be Aunty Alice. Smug, me? Yes. Rosie announced her amazing news via Skype and I cried. A lot. Rosie said if she could have, she would have slapped me. Hard. Thankfully though there was a lot of water between us. I'm still upset that I might not be as much of a presence to her baby as I might have been had things played out differently, but truly, I wouldn't change my life now for the world. Ryan agreed to come back to England for a few weeks around her due date so that I could see her and hopefully meet the little bundle of joy. He also thought it would be a great chance to meet each other's parents properly. Yikes.

"Okay, okay stop trying to kill me Beefster, remember I'm the only one that will feed you around here. You can't expect to keep biting Ryan's feet on a night and him to give you your pongy food now can you?" As he weaves between my legs he meows in acknowledgement.

Throwing on my dressing gown, I scoop him up and head to the kitchen, following the smell of bacon as Mr Beefy wriggles and writhes trying to get there before me. Not a chance. He used to try climb the cupboards at Walkers and on occasion managed to bag himself a prime piece of meat from the kitchen worksurface, the little terror. Oh I do love him. Tightening my grip on him, I shuffle down the stairs but come to a grinding halt when I hit the bottom. Of course sensing this apprehension Mr Beefy seizes the moment to stick his claws in and leap down, flicking his tail smugly in my direction. Just touching my toes on the floor, is the beginning of a trail of white rose petals. I hold on to the bannister for support as I try to get my thoughts together, reminding myself to breathe.

Taking a cautious step forward, I slowly follow the petals through to the dining area where they carry on from the table and into the kitchen. I hear a sizzle in the kitchen and Ryan curse which makes me giggle, he really is going to a lot of effort, and my jealous little kitty is clearly doing his best to hinder the process. He must sense me loitering in the doorway of the dining room and turns around.

"Hi." He whispers sheepishly, a faint pink coming to his cheeks.

"Hi," I respond with a grin on my face. "What's all this?" I look down at the petals that Mr Beefy is now happily skidding through, sending them in every direction imaginable. Every direction other than the one they're meant to be in.

"A surprise?" He shrugs. He really couldn't look any cuter if he tried. He has my pink pinny tied around his waist and flour on the end of his nose making him look like a little boy attempting to bake for his first time.

"And it is. Is that my breakfast that's smoking?" I laugh as he spins around in horror, quickly turning the hob off and throwing the pan in the sink. Poor bacon.

"Shit. Okay so looks like it's just pancakes and fruit for breakfast, no bacon for us."

"Or you Mr B." Flicking his tail at me again he struts back through the kitchen and back to his petals. "So, are you going to dish up?" I wink playfully and make a move to help him.

"Don't come in!" He practically slams the door in my face and I swear I hear Mr Beefy do a little kitty giggle. With my nose pressed up to the door, I try in vain to see what's going on but give in and take a place at the table. Twiddling my thumbs I watch a bird flutter from branch to branch on the tree just outside the window that I'm next to. Poor thing's probably frozen out there. I'm tempted to let it in from the cold April shower but hear the kitchen door open as Ryan slowly makes his way towards me with an enormous tray of food. I don't offer to help, mainly because it looks too heavy for him let alone me, but also because I don't want him to panic again and lose his grip.

He smiles as he lifts a plate straight from the tray and holds it close to his chest. Butterflies start to swim around in my stomach and my heart picks up speed as he gets closer. Is he about to do what I think he's going to do?

"Lexi, from the second you walked into IHOP with that lunatic friend of yours, you were under my skin. You were all I thought about from the second I woke up to the second I went to bed, and even then there were times I dreamt about you." He laughs nervously. "The day that you came into my office when Luke had landed on your doorstep, I thought I was going to lose you. I've never felt as sick in my whole life. Well, maybe today beats that, but all I wanted to do was keep you near me. I love you Lexi, and I want to keep loving you until we're old, grey and senile. I want us to live a long and happy life together, see the world, maybe have a family, but I definitely want to spend the rest of my days with you by side as Mrs Furrows. So, Lexi….." Placing down the plate before me, I feel my eyes start to well. On the plate are four very large chocolate chip pancakes with 'Will You Marry Me' written on them in chocolate sauce. By the time I look back to Ryan, the tears are streaming down my face and he is on one knee holding open a ring box.

"Are you sure?!" I manage to choke out.

"Are you serious?" He asks incredulously. "I love you more than anything in this world. Please put me out of my misery, I think my knees are about to crumble!" He laughs as he says it but I know he means it, his knees are quite dicky, especially in the cold weather. Oops.

Pulling him to his feet I kiss him with everything I have, wrapping my arms around his neck and burying my hands in his messy hair. This man has changed my entire outlook on life, on love and has restored my faith in men. I know I'll never love another man as much as I love him. Without any hesitation I take the ring from the box and place it on my finger. The teardrop diamond sits on a slim platinum band and fits my finger perfectly. As I hold it up to the light I feel Ryan smile against my cheek.

Perfect.

THE END

ACKNOWLEDGEMENTS

First and foremost I want to give a shout out to my family, without their support I would have probably lost the plot a long time ago. They have put up with the crazies that come out of my mouth for longer than necessary, they deserve some kind of medal.

I want to thank the people that have encouraged me along the way, you all rock in your own special way.

Kirsty – Where would I be without our daily chats? It's hard to imagine not having you in my life now, if people could hear some of our conversations we'd probably get that padded cell a lot sooner than we anticipated. I know for a fact that nobody else would share my love of lolcats and all things sweet like you do and I feel lucky to have you as one of my best friends. Kitty and cake buddies for life xxxx

Becca – I feel like I've known you forever, we're so alike in so many ways it's mind boggling. You make me giggle on a daily basis and to have you there championing me along really does mean the world! Soul Sistas baby ;) xxxx

To the new friends I have made through Facebook and Twitter, Nikki, Malinda, Olivia, Gary, you all make me smile and have helped me tremendously.

THANK YOU X

ABOUT THE AUTHOR

Ellen Faith lives in the wonderful county of Yorkshire, England where she spends most of her time baking, eating, baking, and eating. Occasionally she does leave the house to go to the cinema or do some food shopping though.

After spending years with an overactive imagination, she decided to put all the magic in her head to some good use and put finger to laptop where The Story of Us was born and became her debut novel.

She loves to travel, her favourite destinations so far have all been in America, hence the love of all things, and all people, American. The food rocks pretty hard too, she ate until her jeans begged her to stop while she was there. True fact.

Aside from day dreaming and eating, Ellen is a sucker for a lolcat, penguins and monkeys – she has never claimed to be normal.

If you haven't had enough of her already, come and be a part of the crazy over on Facebook at www.Facebook.com/ellen.faith.50

Made in the USA
Charleston, SC
10 March 2014